Just You Wait

Books by Jane Tesh

The Grace Street Mysteries
Stolen Hearts
Mixed Signals
Now You See It
Just You Wait

The Madeline Maclin Mysteries
A Case of Imagination
A Hard Bargain
A Little Learning
A Bad Reputation

Just You Wait

A Grace Street Mystery

Jane Tesh

Poisoned Pen Press

Library of Congress Catalog Card Number: 2014951266

ISBN: 9781464203671   Hardcover
       9781464203695   Trade Paperback

Poisoned Pen Press
6962 E. First Ave., Ste. 103
Scottsdale, AZ 85251
www.poisonedpenpress.com
info@poisonedpenpress.com

Printed in the United States of America

To my mother, Helen "Peggy" Tesh,
whose beautiful voice inspired me to sing
and to love musical theater.

Chapter titles are from *My Fair Lady* by Alan Jay Lerner and Frederick Loewe

Chapter One

"Get me to the church on time."

Although I was expecting a call from a client this Friday morning, things had been slow for the Randall Detective Agency lately, so slow I actually called Jordan Finley at the Parkland Police Department. I'd been reading about the mysterious disappearance of elderly Viola Mitchell. What interested me about Viola's case was her connection to the Parkland Little Theater. According to the newspaper, she was a regular performer and well-known for her character roles.

"We do not need your help, Randall."

Jordan's standard reply. The trouble is, I usually end up being a lot of help, and Jordan really hates that. I was pretty sure his stiff black hair was bristling. "Just answer one question. Did she disappear from the theater?"

"No, and why is that your concern?"

"Camden's going to be in their next show, and Kary's playing in the orchestra. If there's a Bermuda Triangle backstage, I want to know about it." Camden's psychic ability guarantees he'll be a lightning rod for anything remotely weird, and Kary's insistence on helping with my cases will have her burrowing into whatever dark corner she can find.

"Nothing happened at the theater. She was last seen at her home. A neighbor heard the animals and went over to see what was going on. They hadn't been fed. The neighbor said Mrs. Mitchell would never neglect her pets, and that's when we started looking for her."

"Let me in on this. Missing people are my specialty."

"No, getting in my way is your specialty, and it's not going to happen today."

On this, Jordan hung up. I was not deterred. I went back to the *Parkland Herald's* account of Viola Mitchell's disappearance and found her address. It wouldn't do any harm to wander over there and see what was going on. Jordan could complain all he liked, but the last time I looked, Parkland, North Carolina, was a free city, and I could roam about the streets as I pleased. Camden could come with me to talk to the neighbors. People always talk to him because he looks completely harmless. What they don't know is his psychic insights could be very useful in my investigations. If I could unscramble the visions.

My cell phone rang. It was my client, Mrs. Folly Harper. Her voice was light and feathery. "Sorry, Mr. Randall, but I'm running a little late. Could we make it three-thirty?"

"Let me check my schedule." I counted slowly to five. "You're in luck, Mrs. Harper. I can fit you in then."

"Thank you. Now, what was your address again?"

"It's 302 Grace Street. A large yellow house with white trim and pink azaleas."

"I'll be there at three-thirty."

"I'll see you then." This was the third time she'd changed the appointment. I was beginning to think that whatever she needed found, I could find. She sounded like the type of woman whose missing glasses are on top of her head.

Yep, whatever was missing, I could find, all right, because I was so damn good at finding everything except when it counted the most.

This time of day was usually quiet in the neighborhood. Even the busy traffic on Food Row one street over was muted, a soft murmur of white noise. Birds chirped at the feeder and rustled in the branches of the oak trees. A slight warm breeze billowed the sheer curtains at my open office window.

But the peace was shattered as I heard Ellin's voice rising in one of her classic scolds. I turned my chair around to the window. My office has a good view of the front porch and the old oak trees that keep everything cool and shady. Ellin Belton, Camden's fiancée, was on the porch talking with him. He was, no doubt, in his favorite seat, the porch swing, and she was—as everyone in the neighborhood could probably hear—engaged in her ongoing and futile effort to pry Camden from 302 Grace Street.

"If you would just consider it, Cam. We could live in my condo until I sell it. I know I can get top dollar. We could afford a new house anywhere in the city."

"Ellie, I've told you over and over, I'm not going to move."

"But this house is falling down! It needs constant repair."

"And I enjoy fixing it."

She paced by my window. "But what about this constant stream of boarders moving in and out? There's Rufus and Angie and grumpy old Fred and Randall and Kary and who knows who else you'll let in. How can we ever have any privacy?"

"I told you I'd remodel the third floor any way you wanted it."

"We need a place of our own."

"This is our place."

"But these people!" She made an exasperated growling sound not unlike a lioness who does not want to share the gazelle. Then she checked her watch and rolled her eyes. "I've got to meet with the caterer, and Mother said my sisters might pop in for a surprise visit. That's all I need. I know they're planning something stupid and disruptive. We'll continue this discussion later."

"I'm not going to change my mind."

"Neither am I!"

By rolling closer to the window, I glimpsed her blond curls bouncing indignantly as she charged out to her sleek silver Lexus. She looks really good going away. She has a dynamite figure, plus big blue eyes and a great smile. But I'm rarely on the receiving end of that smile, and Camden, gripping the edge of the porch railing, didn't look like he was smiling, either. He'd recently proposed, Ellin had accepted, and everything had been hearts and rainbows for about a week. Then reality set in. Because of Ellin's work schedule and her lifetime goal of controlling the world, she'd decided they would be married by the end of May—this month—so the past two months she'd been, as our resident redneck boarder, Rufus Jackson, would say, "Wild as a buck."

I left my office and went across the foyer and through "the island" to the kitchen. We call the main sitting area in the house "the island" because the blue armchair, green corduroy sofa, and other various chairs are parked in the middle of the room on a worn oriental carpet, as if someone had called a meeting of the living room furniture. The TV is there, as well as a coffee table covered with books, magazines, and a stack of coupons held in place by a paperweight shaped like a pear. There's always a scattering of cat toys even though Cindy, our gray housecat, usually amuses herself with an empty toilet paper roll. Kary's needlework is piled in a basket by one chair, and Camden's growing collection of UFO materials sits by another. Mismatched lamps and cushions complete the gypsy caravan look.

I got a can of Coke out of the fridge. Camden came in a few minutes later and put two Pop-Tarts in the toaster with a little more force than necessary.

"I don't know why the hell we just don't elope."

I popped open the Coke and took a sip. "It's never too late. Sling her over your shoulder and head for the border. You know she loves that cave man stuff."

"Her mother would hunt me down and kill me."

If he wants to know what Ellin's going to look like in thirty years, all he has to do is eyeball her mom. Ellin looks exactly like Jean, only Mrs. Belton is shorter, stouter, and lightly wrinkled. Lately, I had seen far more of Ellin's mother than I ever wanted to see. She isn't really sure Camden's a suitable husband for her daughter, but then, who would be? Ellin's father, a reasonable sort of man, did a lot of sighing as he handed over credit cards and checks. He'd indicated to Camden he'd be glad to see Ellin married to anyone willing to put up with her moods. Ellin's sisters were already married and living out of town, but they'd be here for the wedding in full force. Four Belton women in one place. I wasn't sure the ozone layer was ready for this.

I took another sip of Coke. "Mom still hasn't given her seal of approval?"

"I think Mom is a little afraid of me."

"Well, she should be. You are damned scary." This is a laugh. Camden's about five-foot seven and looks like somebody's sloppy little kid brother. His pale hair is always in his eyes and he dresses like a starving artist. It's the eyes that get the girls. They're large and blue and they See All, no joke. If he shakes hands with someone, or touches an object, he can get powerful impressions. This psychic ability is mighty attractive to Ellin, who has no psychic powers at all, but to Mrs. Belton, it's all about "my weird son-in-law, the fortune-teller."

The Pop-Tarts popped up, and Camden put them on a plate. "Jean thinks Ellin should marry Reg."

"Reg Haverson? Mr. Prep?"

"At least he doesn't have fits." He got the tea out of the fridge and poured some into a large plastic Carolina Panthers cup.

"Is that what she calls it?"

"And he has a proper job."

"She doesn't think being a part-time sales clerk at Tamara's Boutique is a proper job? She should be thinking about all those employee discounts she and Ellin can get."

We wandered back to the porch. On the way, Camden peered into my office. "Don't you have a client?"

"She's coming by later." I sat down in one of the rocking chairs. "You and Ellin get anything settled?"

He sat back in the porch swing and took a bite of Pop-Tart. They're the brown sugar kind, appropriate, he assures me, for any hour of the day. "Well, let's see. I wanted to be married in Victory Holiness, but I've agreed to Ellie's choice of Parkland Methodist. Ellie found her wedding gown, but she's still working on the type of flowers and the music. She keeps changing her mind about bridesmaids. I think she's finally settled on four."

"She has four friends?"

"The invitations spelled her name "E-l-l-e-n," God forbid, so they had to be redone. The church hall had to be rescheduled for the reception. And I haven't even mentioned the cake, the rehearsal dinner, or the photographer."

"Wow. I can't believe I went through all that two times. Of course, all I had to do was show up."

"And she doesn't want to live here."

"I believe I may have heard something about that."

"She said we'd never have any privacy. I said we have the whole top floor to ourselves. She said we need a place of our own. I said this is our place. Then she said, 'But these people!'" He did a fairly accurate impersonation of Ellin's exasperated tone.

I joined in. "Not these people!"

The odd collection of tenants Camden attracts is his family and he isn't going to abandon them. I think he took over the big three-story house for the express purpose of filling it with strays. That includes me. If I trace my path backwards, I can see the chain of events that led me to 302 Grace Street—the car crash that destroyed my perfect little American dream, the argument with my second wife that cast me adrift, a tenant moving out, leaving the downstairs room free for an office and an upstairs room free for a bedroom, the odd cases that kept me financially afloat. I'd come in as one of Camden's strays, and like so many before me, I'd stayed.

I often stand on the porch and think, what the hell are you doing here? Then I think, because if you can possibly keep from screwing things up, you have found a new family and a new chance for love, if you can convince Kary of that. And I'm not giving up my peaceful green second-floor bedroom, my conveniently located office, my favorite faded blue armchair, and being in the same house as Kary Ingram, especially not to please Ellin Belton.

"As far as I'm concerned, it's settled," Camden said. "Her place is too small. This house is perfect. The neighborhood's quiet, lots of big trees, she can get to work easily off of Food Row, she knows everybody here. What's the problem?"

"Did she bring up all the times I drag you into these cases to help solve them for me?"

"Once or twice."

As if she never uses his considerable psychic talent to further her goals with the slightly off-the-level Psychic Service. "You know she's much more likely to drag you."

"No kidding."

"How could the two of you afford a new house, anyway?" Fortunately, 302 Grace is paid for. When Camden first came to North Carolina, he'd stayed in the boarding house. After he saw something in the owner's future that saved him from financial ruin, the man gave Camden the house. Getting a big old house that always needs repair may not have been a bargain, but, as I said, it's paid for. "Ellin's still producing the TV show, right? But it doesn't bring in the big bucks, does it?"

"It's doing surprisingly well."

"Even without you."

"Even without me."

Ellin is always after him to be on one of the programs, but he hates to do anything that even halfway resembles flaunting his talent. "You could be raking in the dough."

"No, thanks. Things have been very calm lately, and that's the way I want them."

"So all is well with the cosmos?"

He nodded and took another bite of Pop-Tart. "Just get me to the church on time."

"Well, before all that, I want you to come to Marshall Street and talk with Viola Mitchell's neighbors. She's still missing."

He frowned in concern. "Viola's missing?"

"You haven't gotten any vibes about that? Has anyone from the theater stopped by to check on her? Is she likely to wander off?"

"A member of the cast said he thought she was visiting a cousin. She wasn't needed for every rehearsal, so she could leave town for a few days."

"Somebody filed a missing persons report. I want to see what's going on."

"I definitely want to come along. Let me check on Fred first. He hasn't been feeling well lately."

"How can you tell?" Fred, Camden's oldest tenant, gacks and wheezes like a rusty air-conditioner, has skin the color of old liver, and maybe three sprigs of hair growing from unlikely places.

"He hasn't asked me for any money today."

Camden finished his nutritious snack, went down the porch steps, and headed in the direction of the park. Fred spent most of the day with several other old fossils hunched over checkerboards and drinking out of paper bags. The only good thing about Fred is he doesn't hang around the house. I'm all for local color, but this would be laying it on too thick. The sight of moldy old Fred draped across the porch railing might discourage clients.

Camden came back and reported all was well with Fred, so we got into my white '67 Plymouth Fury, a dashing choice for an ace private investigator, and drove over to 494 Marshall Street. There was a "For Sale" sign in Viola's front yard with a big red "SOLD" sign pasted over it. The small brick houses were spaced widely apart, but the next-door neighbor knew everything that had happened. She was a thin woman with a permanently alarmed expression.

"Wednesday, I heard the awfullest racket, and it was all of Viola's pets going wild. I went over there and gave them some food and water, and I didn't see Viola anywhere. The same thing happened Thursday, so that's when I called the police."

"You didn't see anyone else at her house?" I asked.

"No, but she never did have many visitors. Kept to herself mostly. Her only friends were those theater people. She didn't drive, and I didn't see any strange cars at her place. Mostly she took a taxi if she wanted to go anywhere, or somebody from the theater would give her a ride home."

"When's the last time you saw her?"

"A couple of days ago. She came out to get her mail the same time as me, and I gave her a little wave."

"When did she put up her house for sale?"

"About a month ago. She's moving to a condo at Silver Hills."

"No family? Nobody she'd go visit?"

"I heard her mention a cousin once."

I could hear cheeping sounds from the house. "What about her pets? Can she have them at Silver Hills?"

"Yes, that was why she chose that place. She has cats and birds and some kind of lizard."

"Does Viola have any health issues? Any sort of condition that might have caused her to wander off?"

"Oh, no. She's sharp as a tack."

"Would you say she was friends with everyone here in the neighborhood?"

"Like I said, she kept to herself, but she never was mean to anyone. Nobody would have cause to harm her."

I'd heard that before. "Would you let us look around her house?"

"Well, I don't know about that."

Camden didn't have to pretend to be concerned. "Ma'am, Viola and I work together at the theater, and I'm really worried about her. I promise we won't disturb anything."

Not many women can resist the appeal in those big blue eyes. "All right. But just for a few minutes."

The neighbor took a key from a hook inside her door, and we walked across to Viola's house. As we entered, we were met by a chorus of cheeps and squawks. There were three birdcages in the living room. In one cage, two little blue budgies scooted back and forth on their perch. In another, a large green parrot cocked his head as if giving us close inspection. The third cage was occupied by two small gray birds. There was also a glass cage where a bored-looking lizard sunned himself under a light bulb. Three striped cats ran out and immediately coiled around Camden's legs, purring furiously.

The neighbor tried to shoo them away. "Oh, every time someone comes in they think they're getting more food. You've already been fed today, all of you. Let me check your water dish."

She went down the hall to the kitchen. Two of the cats trotted after her, but the third stayed a moment longer, his yellow eyes staring at Camden.

"Uh, oh," he said.

Cam tells me he can get impressions from animals when they let him. "Are they telling you something?"

"This isn't good, Randall. I need to talk to Jordan."

"Let me have a look around first."

I knew Viola was in her seventies, so to find her bedroom as frilly and pink as a teenage girl's was a surprise. Framed posters for plays decorated the walls, along with fancy wide-brimmed hats and scarves she must have used for costumes. Her dressing table was also pink with an array of perfume bottles and paperweights, all shaped like hearts. The rest of the house was devoted to her pets. All the furniture was covered with blankets or towels. I counted six different cat beds, three scratching posts, a playhouse, window seats, and enough cat toys to fill two large plastic containers. The cat food in the kitchen could've supplied a cat army, and large bags of birdseed were stacked in the pantry.

The neighbor waited by the door, arms folded. "If you don't mind, I've got errands to run."

She locked the door as we left the house. I thanked her for her help, and as soon as she was back in her own house, I called Jordan.

"Camden thinks he has something on Viola Mitchell."

I was pretty sure I heard Jordan's veins pop. "What the hell are you doing? I told you that was not your business."

"You want to hear it or not?"

"Put him on."

I handed my phone to Camden. "Jordan, you need to check the basement." Jordan must have answered, "We already did," because Camden said, "Check it again." He returned my phone for the cop's warning.

"This had better be good, Randall."

"You know it is."

"Where are you?"

"At her house."

"Damn it."

"Camden was concerned about her. They're doing a play together."

"That is the flimsiest excuse you've ever come up with. If you've contaminated a crime scene—"

"You've been in her house, right? Every inch is contaminated by some kind of animal."

"Don't touch anything else. I'm coming over."

In ten minutes, a squad car pulled up and Jordan got out. A second squad car parked behind. A charging rhino would have second thoughts about confronting Jordan when he was in one of his thunderous moods. He whipped off his sunglasses, his squinting eyes blue chips of fire.

"One of these days I'll have your license, Randall, and when I do, I'll make you eat it."

"You're just jealous because I have a clue."

"No, you have Cam, and you know how I feel about you dragging him into these situations."

"He didn't drag me," Camden said. "I wanted to come check on Viola."

Jordan's little eyes narrowed even further. "And you think she's in the basement?"

"I'm afraid so."

"What tipped you off?"

"The cats."

Jordan paused. "I'm not even going to ask."

It took twenty-five minutes for the policemen to find Viola Mitchell's body buried under the basement floor. By the time the coroner arrived and the ambulance, all the neighbors had come out to see what was going on. Their curious voices turned to gasps and little cries of "Oh, my God" and "What happened?" as the EMTs carefully lifted a body bag onto a stretcher. Camden steadied himself against the Fury. The neighbor who'd let us into Viola's house stared in horror.

"I can't believe this! You mean all that time I was in there taking care of her pets, she was lying dead underneath the house? Who would do such a thing?"

Jordan assured her that in light of this new development, the police would question everyone again. He cut his eyes at me. "The police and only the police are handling this investigation. Does everyone understand?"

"Can I have a look in the basement?" Camden asked.

"After we've finished."

Camden and I watched Jordan explain to the neighbors that it appeared Viola was the victim of a homicide, so anyone with any information should come forward. He reminded them that Viola's house was now a crime scene and to stay off the premises. From their stunned expressions none of them wanted to be anywhere near the house.

Camden looked queasy. "Are you sure you want to go down there?" I asked.

"I'm okay."

"I want in on this." I glanced over to where the neighbor woman was being questioned by an officer. "Maybe she knows how to get in touch with Viola's cousin?"

"Someone at the theater might know."

After a while, Jordan motioned us over. We went back into the house and down a flight of stairs to the basement, a large unfinished room that ran the length of the house. The space was cold and smelled of dust and stone. Part of the floor was concrete, but another section was smoothly packed gray dirt or had been until the police dug it up to discover Viola's body.

Camden slowly moved around the hole. The murderer must have planned to bury Viola here because the makeshift grave was neatly squared.

"How tall was Viola?" I asked.

"Almost as tall as you."

"So the murderer knew what size the hole had to be and had plenty of time to dig it."

"And knew Viola lived by herself and rarely had company. He or she wouldn't have been disturbed."

Jordan watched him warily. "You're not sensing anybody else in there, are you?"

Camden stooped down and felt the floor. "Something in the wine."

"Poison?"

"A present."

Jordan turned to one of his men. "Check the trashcans. The bottle might still be there."

"A present from a friend. A card. *Congratulations. You Deserve It.*"

I felt sudden chills. "That could be taken several ways."

Camden shook off whatever he'd been seeing and stood up. "She was already dead when she was brought down here."

"Any impressions about the killer?"

"He's all covered up. I can't get anything."

"Covered up? Black clothes? A mask?"

Camden rubbed his eyes. "I can't tell. Sorry."

"We'll take it from here." Jordan pointed. "You two go home."

Chapter Two

"And with a voice too eager…"

I was hoping for another look through Viola's house on the chance she had an address book or a letter from her cousin, but there was no getting past the wall that was Jordan Finley. I might have better luck at the theater. Camden had had enough murder on his mind, and I did have a client on the way, so we headed home. We stopped at the Quik-Fry to get him a milkshake, which he says calms him down, and which I believe is just a good excuse to eat more ice cream. At the house, he said he was going to check on Fred and sit in the park for a while. I sat on the porch to wait for Mrs. Folly Harper.

Mrs. Harper arrived a few minutes later in her peach-colored Cadillac. She was a well-rounded little woman with an elaborate blond hairdo and aggressively coordinated clothing. The suit, shoes, and leather handbag were all peach-colored and her large gold earrings matched the clasp on the bag and the buckles on the shoes. She had three thick gold bracelets on one plump wrist and a gold and diamond watch on the other. When she held out her hand, I noticed a gold ring on every finger. Her nails were also peach with white tips.

"Hello! You must be Mr. Randall. I'm Folly Harper. I'm so glad we could meet at last."

I wore my best dark suit, blue shirt, and blue striped tie. My hair was combed. Unlike Camden, I care about how I look. I could tell Mrs. Harper liked what she saw. Most women do. That's one of my problems. Not a pressing one.

I shook her hand. "David Randall. Pleasure to meet you, Mrs. Harper."

I escorted her into the house and to the right. I showed Mrs. Harper to the chair and took my seat behind the small polished mahogany desk. She'd applied an expert, though thick, layer of peach makeup, but I figured her to be around fifty. Her blue eyes with dark, curled lashes took in the bookcase, plants, and curtains Kary had added to give the place a reassuring atmosphere.

"It must be much more pleasant to work out of this fine old house instead of a soulless skyscraper."

Since Parkland has three buildings tall enough to be considered skyscrapers, I had to agree. "Yes, I enjoy walking down the stairs to work instead of fighting traffic into town every day."

"Oh, you live here, too? How very convenient." She leaned forward, clutching the peach-colored purse. "Let me explain my situation, Mr. Randall. I have a business associate who unfortunately skipped town with a large amount of my money. I didn't want to go to the police because, quite frankly, this whole matter is very embarrassing. I treated George like my own son, and I don't want the whole world to know how he betrayed me."

I promised her I'd be discreet. "I'll need George's full name and his last known address, and if you have a picture, that would be helpful."

"George Mark McMillan, 1925 Sable Court. I should have suspected something. Eight is not a good number for me."

I paused before typing the information into my computer. "Eight?"

"Yes, 1925 adds up to eight," she said as if this explained everything. "One plus nine is ten and two plus five is seven. If you take ten and add the one and the zero, you get one. One plus seven equals eight."

Ooo-kay. "When I locate Mr. McMillan, do you want me to confront him, or call the police in at this point?"

"Oh, no, no, don't call the police. I'll handle things from there. I'm sure I can convince him of his wrongdoings and get my money back. It's crucial for my company right now."

"What is your business?"

She searched her pocketbook again and handed me a brochure. "BeautiQueen Cosmetics."

According to the brochure, BeautiQueen was a local company, one of those home cosmetics deals where women have parties and make each other up, apparently in shades of peach.

"My late husband and I started the company. George is my partner. Everything was going so well. I can't imagine why George would leave now."

"He never said anything to you like, I'm bored, I need a change, I need a vacation?"

"No, but I would have understood any of those reasons. We were a team, Mr. Randall. We discussed everything."

Apparently not everything.

"A picture?"

She dug around again in her peach-colored pocketbook. "I think I have a picture—yes, here we are at the company picnic."

She handed me the photo. Folly Harper in all her sunlit peach glory and a serious-looking man with dark hair and a thick moustache stood squinting into the lens. George McMillan was medium height, burly and square, his posture stiff and his head tilted up as if to say, "Yeah, I work for a cosmetics company. Wanna make something out of it?"

"Do you have any idea why he took your money and ran?"

She took turns twisting her gold rings. "I'm completely perplexed. We were working together on several projects, and I knew together we could revolutionize the business."

I asked her for more details. She told me George had a large dog, drove a blue Ford Explorer, and often talked of visiting Florida.

"Would he take the dog with him?"

"Oh, yes. He's very fond of his dog."

"Any particular place in Florida?"

"I believe he mentioned Clearwater."

So he puts the dog in the SUV and hightails it to Clearwater for a little R and R. This case was as good as solved.

I was curious, though, as to why Mrs. Got Rocks here chose the Randall Detective Agency when she could easily afford one of the big corporations in town. "Were you by any chance referred to me by another client?"

"No, I chose you because you were the sixteenth listing in the phone book."

I added the numbers. "Don't tell me. One plus six gave you a lucky number seven."

She smiled. I'd scored points there. Hope they added up to something good. "I really don't want any of this to get around. My friends all think I'm too flighty and too trusting. I don't want to hear 'I told you so' everywhere I go. I told them George had gone on a business trip for me, to learn about the latest colors for spring, but I can't keep that story going for long."

"I understand," I said. "I'll work as quickly as possible."

She took out a peach-colored leather checkbook, wrote me a peach-colored check, and handed it over. "I appreciate this very much, Mr. Randall. I've worked hard to build up my clientele, and I'd hate for a scandal to ruin my plans. By the way, are there any ladies in the house? I'd love to leave a few samples of BeautiQueen products for them."

"There are two ladies."

She beamed, her financial troubles forgotten. "Excellent! Let me get some things out of my car."

I wanted to say, don't bother. Kary didn't need any enhancement, and Angie, Rufus' wife, would need a bucketful. Mrs. Harper came back to the porch and gave me a little peach-colored paper bag with tubes and sticks inside.

"My card's in there and a brochure listing the complete line of BeautiQueen products. Have them call any time. My machine's set up to take orders day or night."

"Thank you," I said. "I'll call you as soon as I have some information."

She waved good-bye and got into her car. She was pulling out of the driveway when Ellin's car drove up. Ellin had to wait until Mrs. Harper was out of the way. Then she zipped into the driveway and almost unhinged herself getting out of the car. She hurried up the porch steps.

"Was that Mrs. Harper? Mrs. Folly Harper?"

"Yes." I jiggled the bag. "She left some treats."

Ellin looked astonished. I thought it might be the little bag or the idea of me giving her something. "What was she doing here?"

"She's a client."

I thought I was going to have to scrape her jaw off the lawn. "She's a *client?*"

Maybe this would work better if I made myself perfectly clear. "This is a detective agency. I have clients. Mrs. Harper is a client. I will detect for her. She will pay me."

Ellin ignored my sarcasm. "Mrs. Folly Harper is one of the Psychic Service's most avid supporters."

"I won't hold that against her."

"Did she meet Cam?"

"He went to the park to check on Fred."

Her reaction startled me. "Damn! She'll be back, won't she? Don't you give your clients updates, progress reports, something like that?"

She was seriously worked up. Not a good sign. "I keep them informed about the case, sure. What are you babbling about?"

"She's been dying to meet Cam. Didn't she know this was his house?"

"She didn't mention him."

"She must not have known, or she'd have asked about him. When will she be back, did she say?"

"Wait a minute." I had her number now. "You know Camden doesn't want to tell anybody's fortune. Didn't we decide we wouldn't do this anymore?"

Like Camden, Ellin has big blue eyes, but hers can flame on like an acetylene torch. "There's no 'we' here, Randall. Mrs. Harper only wants to ask Cam a question, that's all. She's a very wealthy woman. He could name his price."

It's always about the money. "Good lord. You're going to marry the man, and you still don't get it. What are you doing back here, anyway? I thought you'd done enough damage for one day."

"Not that it's any of your business," she said, "but I came back to apologize. Contrary to popular belief, I don't like to argue with Cam. I'm sure we can work things out."

This was sweet and nice and lasted five seconds.

"But," she continued, as I knew she would, "if he'd talk with Mrs. Harper and accept a little money, we'd be in much better shape financially."

"You can discuss that with him. I have work to do."

She doesn't like to argue with Camden, but she's made it her life's work to argue with me. "What did Mrs. Harper have to discuss with you, anyway?"

"You know I can't tell you that."

"I don't see why not. I've been involved in all your other screwball cases. Is it a psychic matter? Why didn't she consult the Service?"

"Forget it. It's none of your business. If you want to run after Mrs. Harper and hound her, go right ahead. Better yet, tune in on her brainwaves and get the latest scoop."

Remarking on her lack of psychic ability is the best way to really rile her, and I like to use it as often as possible. Today, it didn't have full effect, for Ellin was already halfway down the steps to her car and paused only to give me a look that could have easily felled one of our big trees.

I went back into my office to start my search. I have a nifty little phone directory program with directories for every state. If you're lucky enough to have someone's driver's license or social security number, nine times out of ten, you can trace a person using one or both numbers. I'd found countless runaway spouses this way. I'd even found Camden's mother. I didn't have those numbers for George Mark Macmillan, but Mrs. Harper had mentioned a large dog. Using the phone book program, I checked the nearest vet to Sable Avenue, George's last known address, and gave him a call.

"Good morning. Doctor Andrews was recommended to me by George Macmillan. Do I have the right vet?"

Three calls later, and I had George's vet at the Happy Pet Vet. The receptionist was happy, too, and glad to share a little nonconfidential info. George's doberman is named Danger. Yes, they'd be glad to see my doberman. The vet was quite fond of big dogs. Yes, she often recommended vets in other states if you were going on vacation.

"I have to be in Florida for a week, and I'm bringing Trixie with me," I said. "If she got sick, I wouldn't want to take her to just anyone. Who would you recommend in Clearwater?"

"If you're going to be in the Clearwater area, then you should call Happy Tails Pet Hospital. I'll give you the number."

"Thank you." I called Happy Tails Pet Hospital and explained my situation to another secretary. "You were recommended to me by George MacMillan."

"Oh, yes. We board Danger for him when he comes down."

That sounded as if George made more than one trip to Florida. "We were supposed to meet for a fishing trip, but his cell phone must not be working. You wouldn't happen to know where he's staying, would you?"

I heard her speak to another woman. "Do you know where George stays when he comes down?"

The other woman must have answered, because the secretary said, "We think he stays at the Best Western, but we're not sure."

"Thanks."

"Be sure and bring Trixie in to see us if she needs any care."

"I will, thank you."

I hung up and checked the Best Westerns in the Clearwater area. There were two near Happy Tails. Neither had a George MacMillan registered, so I tried several more Best Westerns with no luck. Maybe he hadn't gotten there yet. Maybe the woman at the vet was mistaken. On the Internet I found other hotels in the area, including three that allowed animals. The Paradise Sands didn't allow large dogs, and the Parrot Lodge was closed for repairs. I tried the third and last hotel, the Green Palms.

The man who answered my call sounded friendly if a bit sleepy. "A big dog's no problem, sir. You leave a deposit, and if your pet doesn't do any damage, you get that money back."

"I have a doberman, but she's very friendly."

"No problem. We have a guy who brings his doberman every three weeks or so. Great dog. He calls it Danger, but it's a real sweetheart."

Bingo.

"You come on down, bring your dog. No problem at Green Palms. We want people to enjoy their vacations with their pets."

"No Problem" must be the hotel's slogan. "That sounds like what I'm looking for," I said. "I heard about your hotel from a friend of mine, George MacMillan. Is he staying at Green Palms?"

"Hang on a sec." I heard clicking noises as the man checked his computer. "Oh, yeah, he's the guy with the doberman. I don't see anything right now. Try us tomorrow."

"Thanks." I wanted to find George and get back to the more serious business of discovering Viola Mitchell's killer. It looked as if finding George was going to be, in the words of the Green Palms employee, no problem.

Chapter Three

"Wouldn't it be loverly?"

With George as good as found, I went back to my computer and my search for Viola Mitchell. There wasn't much to go on regarding her or her case. Most of the facts I already knew, and other than a few photos on the Parkland Little Theater's website, there was nothing about her on the Internet. Like many from her generation, she didn't have a Facebook or Twitter account. The secretary at the theater, being new, didn't know her, but offered that the director and all the actors would be there tonight if I wanted to stop by.

On the Little Theater's website, captioned pictures of Viola showed her as Aunt Eller in *Oklahoma*, one of the witches in *Macbeth*, and Mother Superior in *The Sound of Music*. A slightly younger Viola was shown as Mama Rose in *Gypsy*. In all the pictures, Viola looked pretty tough and snarly. Maybe she had made enemies in the theater. People were always competing for the best roles. Could someone seething with jealousy have wanted to play Aunt Eller?

As I'd mentioned to Jordan, Camden and Kary were both involved with the latest production, *My Fair Lady*. Kary was playing in the orchestra, and the members of the Little Theater had fallen over each other to get Camden to play Freddy. From what I remember of the story, the girl rejects this handsome young rich guy for a crusty old bastard who can't even sing. Freddy has this one big number, "On the Street Where You Live," and the theater crowd was delighted when Camden agreed to sing it. So we got to hear it for weeks.

I figured I might have the inside track, and this would be an ideal and fairly safe job for Kary, who'd taken me to task several times about leaving her out of the detecting loop. I'd learned the hard way that I'd better inform her about my cases and give her something useful to do, something that did not involve a trip to the library.

I'd have the chance to ask her. It was four-thirty, time for her to be home. Sure enough, her lime-green Ford Festiva, ironically nicknamed "Turbo" for its amazing lack of power, turned into the driveway and parked beside the Fury. Kary had finished her teaching degree in March and was substituting for another teacher on maternity leave. She swung out of her car and came up the walk, silky blond hair tied back in a ponytail, dressed in a pink tee-shirt and denim skirt. Little stick figures holding hands and the words "Teachers Make a Difference" in primary colors decorated her big canvas tote. If she'd been my teacher, there'd have been no more trips to the principal's office for me. I'd have been teacher's pet.

As is my tradition, I had a Diet Coke ready for her. She took a drink, thanked me, and sank down into one of the porch rocking chairs. Camden's porch swing is white, but the rocking chairs are dark brown wood with slatted backs and seats, well-worn and comfortable. I sat on the railing to face her. "Long day?"

"Rufus would say those second-graders were hopping like peas on a hot griddle, and he would be absolutely right. How was your day?"

I handed her the little bag. "I have a new client who works for BeautiQueen. She left some samples for you."

"Oh, great makeup, but so expensive." She took out one tube of lipstick. "'Perfect Peach.' I'll try it."

She doesn't need lipstick or eyeliner or any sort of war paint. She is a perfect peach. I watched her profile as she admired the other items, noting the graceful swirl of her ear, the fresh color on her cheek, the sweep of her long blond hair.

Her smile made my pulse jump. "Get to work and solve her case fast. Maybe she'll leave more stuff."

"It's a deal."

"What did she need you to find? Anything I can do?"

"Her business partner's run off to Florida, but I'm pretty sure I've found him. There's something much more serious for you to do. Camden helped the police find a missing woman, but unfortunately, she was dead and buried in her basement."

Kary blinked. "Her own basement? That's intriguing. Gross, but intriguing."

"Someone went to a lot of trouble to commit this crime. The hole in the basement floor was exactly her size, and the killer knew she lived alone and never had company. You've probably heard of her. Viola Mitchell. She did a lot of plays with the Parkland Little Theater."

Kary stopped rocking. "She's playing Henry Higgins' mother—or I guess I should say she *was* playing his mother. That's awful! Do you have any clues?"

"Camden couldn't get much, except to say she'd been poisoned. Not yet the official cause of death, but you and I know he's never wrong. Viola was in *My Fair Lady*? The show you're rehearsing now?" This crime was suddenly uncomfortably close.

"Yes, I've heard all sorts of stories about her. If you needed a cranky old woman for your show, Viola was the one to call."

"Was she cranky in real life? If she got all the best cranky roles, I'm thinking someone might have a grudge."

"I can find out. I'll see who replaces her in the part."

"Good idea. And can you find out the name and address of her cousin? According to Viola's neighbor, the cousin is the only family Viola has. I don't know if it's a man or a woman, but maybe someone at the theater knows. Maybe the cousin came to one of Viola's performances."

"David, this is dreadful news. That poor old woman! Do you suppose she suffocated?"

"Camden said she was dead before the killer buried her. That's not much consolation."

"She was such an imposing figure on stage. You could tell she loved being in command. Why would anyone want to kill her? How could she have been a threat?"

"I'm hoping the cousin will hire me to find out."

"Count on me for this one. Is Cam okay? Where is he?"

"He's in the park with Fred. He says he's all right."

"I'll keep an eye on him tonight at rehearsal."

"Thanks. And by the way, will you marry me?"

"Not today."

We're caught in a delicate dance of almost more than friends, and at the moment, I'm working hard to keep from stepping on her toes. The fact that she often wears the silver bracelet with little dangly stars I gave her for Christmas gives me hope. I like to think of it as an engagement bracelet. "Okay. But you know I'll keep asking."

"Ask away." She continued as if the subject hadn't been mentioned. "Just a few more days of end-of-grade tests. I know the kids are worn out."

"Don't they get to have a wild party after the tests?"

"Not too wild. Give them a cupcake and a handful of potato chips, and they're very happy." She took another drink of cola. "I've decided to enter the Miss Parkland Pageant."

This was news. In the past, Kary entered pageants for scholarship money, but she had grown tired of the drama. "You don't sound very happy about it."

"It looks like all the teaching positions are filled for next year. Unless somebody moves away or retires unexpectedly, I'll have to take an assistant's job. Not much money."

"Cheer up. You could win the pageant. That's a couple of thousand bucks, isn't it?"

"You know I really don't want to do any more pageants, but it's the only way I can think of to make extra money quickly. I only have six piano students at the moment, and Turbo needs new tires now."

I would've given anything to have enough money to help her out, but everyone's finances, except Ellin's, hovered on the edge of ruin.

She set her drink aside. "And I've thought of a way to infiltrate Baby Love."

I tried to keep an interested expression and not say anything I'd regret like, "Hell!" Baby Love was a subsidiary of a larger company called Mothers United that supposedly matched the perfect parents with birth mothers who, for whatever reason, decided not to keep their children. Because of an unfortunate unplanned teenage pregnancy, Kary lost her baby, a little girl she'd named Beth, and was unable to have children.

I understand this grief all too well.

On the second shelf of the bookcase in my office is a DVD of my daughter Lindsey's dance recital. I'm not sure which is more painful, wanting to watch it or actually watching it. I've managed to watch it twice. The image of Lindsey dancing reminds me of her radiant joy, her poise, even at eight years old, her grace. It's as if I'm in the auditorium, and in the next few minutes, she'll be running down the aisle, so full of pride, so glad I was there to see her. But then the recording ends.

I had a wonderful dream not long ago, a dream I hang onto when the days are especially tough, so I know she's forgiven me, but I can't quite forgive myself for not being able to save her. In that dream, she's smiling and getting ready to join other children in a beautiful playground, but I still have nightmares about the crash, the flames and rolls of black smoke that kept me from finding her. I've never told Kary about my nightmares, and she's never told me about hers. Our separate griefs over lost children weren't the elephant in the room. They were a whole herd of elephants, huge, dark, and immovable. Like our relationship dance, we tiptoed around the subject, afraid to make each other collapse, afraid to open old wounds. When Lindsey died, I wanted everyone I loved to die and get it over with. I never wanted to go through that unending sadness again.

Before I could descend into that particular pit of depression,

I turned my attention to Kary's new plan. I couldn't imagine being a father again, but she was determined to adopt a child, and determined to discredit shady online-adoption sites. Kary suspected Baby Love of scamming hopeful, desperate people and planned to go undercover to expose what she felt were illegal practices. Her first scheme involved Omar the Ring Master, the amateur magician she assisted for a while in March. She wanted him to perform for a Baby Love meeting, and while he had the audience's attention, she planned to snoop around the house for evidence of wrongdoing. Thankfully, Omar didn't agree to this. So what sort of idea had she come up with now? I was afraid to ask.

"How about this?" Kary said. "You and I could pose as a couple looking for a child."

"I like the couple part."

"It could work. At a meeting, one of us could be the distraction while the other looks for clues."

"Have you thought about checking up on the company via the Internet?"

"Yes, but you know how I feel about being relegated to the computer. I want to actually do something. I can't believe that any company would be so heartless! If they're cheating people out of having children, having the families they've always dreamed about, I want them stopped! If they're yanking people around, ruining—I want—" She had to stop and swallow. Her reaction was so abrupt and raw I looked at her in alarm. She held up a hand as if to keep me and the emotional elephants at bay. After a few moments and a few deep breaths, she was calm. "So, are you in?"

I wanted to say, Kary, please, share this pain with me. I've got my emotions locked down, too, but grief has a sneaky way of attacking when you least expect it. Together we can get through this. But she wasn't ready. All I could do was join in her Baby Love plans and be there if anything went wrong. "Yes, of course."

She was back in control now as if nothing had happened. "Good, oh, and Charlie wants to talk to you about something. I told him to call."

Charlie Valentine plays piano for a terrific little jazz band called J.J.'s Hot Six that performs at the Tempo, the only club in town that features traditional jazz. I knew the "something" he wanted to talk about was his girlfriend, Taffy. Their romance was almost as fiery as Camden and Ellin's. When he didn't have a gig, Charlie was the accompanist for *My Fair Lady*, which meant he and Kary spent a lot of time in the orchestra pit together. I would've been concerned about this, except I knew Charlie was insanely in love with Taffy. At least, I hoped he still was.

"Are he and Taffy still together?"

"As far as I know. He didn't go into detail."

Our housecat, Cindy, had four kittens under the porch. They were now old enough to wobble up the steps and get in the way. The black one lost its nerve halfway up and meowed pitifully for assistance. Kary scooped it in her hands.

"What a fuss!"

"We call that one Ellin."

She gave me a teacher look. "She wants a home of her own. I understand that. She'll reconsider living here."

"We have to live through the wedding first."

"We got through Rufus and Angie's, didn't we?"

"That was different." Last month, Camden's other tenants, Rufus and Angie, had gotten married on Rufus' cousins' farm in the neighboring small town of Celosia. The weather had been perfect for the outdoor ceremony, and then everyone had gathered round for what Rufus called a "shindig," which is another word for "hoedown." In any case, we all partied till the cows came home—literally.

"We'll get through this one, too," Kary said.

I found myself wondering what our wedding would be like. Kary would look like an angel, of course, and I'd be so pathetically grateful, my tongue would probably be hanging out all the way down the aisle. Her first wedding, my third. Third time's the charm? That's how the saying goes. I'd be content to sit out here with her forever. But only with her. Not with a baby. I'd have to find some way around that particular little snag.

Kary tucked her hair behind one ear. "Ellin knows Cam wouldn't be happy anywhere else. Besides, we won't always be here. Rufus and Angie are looking for a place of their own. Fred is getting very old."

"But you'll stay, won't you?" I hoped I didn't sound too desperate.

She rubbed the kitten's head. "I don't know. It depends on where I find a teaching position."

A second kitten, white with a black ear and a black nose, edged its way over the top step and stood for a while, pleased by its accomplishment. It turned and mewed encouragement to the third kitten, panting and heaving its striped belly up and over. The second immediately pounced and they rolled close to the edge. Kary snatched them before they fell.

"Silly things!" All three settled in her lap, purring like miniature outboard motors. "Where's the other one?"

"He's a mama's boy. Always hanging around Cindy."

Camden came back from the park in time to help locate the missing kitten, a rogue red one with a crooked tail.

"How's Fred?" Kary asked, as he handed her the squirming kitten.

"He's okay. He's arguing with Oscar again about the space program."

Oscar's another old coot. He is certain the entire space program was a Hollywood production. Fred, who must harbor a secret desire to be an astronaut, would argue with him for days.

"Then he must be okay. And how are you?"

"All right."

"Good. You and I have an assignment tonight to find out all we can about Viola Mitchell. I can't believe what happened to her."

"I'm up for that."

She handed him the kittens. "My turn for supper. Tuna casserole sound good?"

Camden and I did our best to look pleased. Tuna casserole was the one thing Kary can fix, and although good, it's not my idea of a great meal. "You bet. Extra crackers for me."

"Ready in thirty minutes." She went into the house.

Camden offered me a kitten. I declined. Cindy was all right, but these little furballs snagged my clothes and punctured my ankles.

He put the kittens down on the porch. "How did things go with your client?"

"You should've been here. According to Ellin, Mrs. Harper's one of your biggest fans, and you could make piles of money seeing into her future."

"Ellie came back?"

"Like a boomerang."

He pried one kitten's mouth off his bare toes. "Do I need to see into Mrs. Harper's future?"

He tries not to get involved in my cases unless it's really necessary. "No. It's pretty straightforward. Her business partner's run off. I can find him."

"Ow. Good grief, these little teeth are sharp."

All the kittens had decided his feet were tasty. I was about to suggest he roll them back down the steps when Rufus and Angie arrived in the bigfoot truck, and the two of them got out.

When you see Rufus and Angie together, you have to imagine that a ridge of the Appalachian Mountains decided to put on clothes and lumber into town. Rufus is pro wrestler size with a scraggly red beard. As usual, he was stuffed into bib overalls and wearing a cap over his bushy hair and long skinny braid he calls a rat tail. Angie's the biggest woman I've ever seen. Not only fat, but big all over. The porch steps groaned as she climbed up. Her tiny eyes twinkled at Camden.

"Cam, honey, you have made another conquest. Those people down at the theater couldn't stop talking about you."

"Yeah," Rufus said. "When do we get to see this little fairy show of yours?"

Angie smacked his arm. It sounded like twenty pounds of raw meat landing on a slab of granite. "Will you quit acting so stupid? It's *My Fair Lady*.'"

He put on a superior air. "I know all the musicals, dearest. Got season tickets to the opera, too."

"It's next weekend," Camden said. "I'll get tickets for everybody."

Rufus was still teasing Angie. "Well, hell, I don't know why you don't sing something realistic like 'Your Love Ain't Worth A Spit, But I Want You Anyway.'"

This earned him another playful smack. "Why don't you sing it for us, then, you big baboon?"

To my horror, Rufus threw back his head and warbled in true country fashion, that is, through his nose:

"Your love ain't worth a spit, but I want you anyway,
Your love's just like a toilet, flushing me away,
Down the sewers of my heart, to the ocean of my soul,
Love you so much, darling,' I would even catch your cold."

Camden laughed. "That is sheer poetry, Rufe."

He grinned. "Ain't it, though? Sing that at your next rehearsal, Cam. That'll make 'em sit up and take notice." He sniffed. "Kary cooking supper?"

"Yes," Camden said.

"Damn." He patted Angie's huge shoulder. "What say we make a pass at Chunky Chicken? Bring you guys back some?"

"No, thanks."

I didn't want to hurt Kary's feelings, so I said no thanks, too. Rufus and Angie galumphed back to their truck and heaved themselves in. As Camden went down the steps to return the kittens to Cindy, my cell phone rang.

When I answered, a familiar voice said, "Randall, it's Charlie. We're playing tonight. Did Kary tell you I wanted to talk to you?"

"Yes. See you there."

He thanked me and hung up. I hoped I could solve his problem with Taffy quickly and easily. I wanted to find Viola Mitchell's killer, and I wanted to convince Kary to trust me. Right now, I had no idea how to solve either mystery.

Chapter Four

"The rain in Spain..."

The tuna casserole had some crunchy bits that might have been green peas and a strange aftertaste that reminded me of the glue I sampled in first grade. After bravely eating two helpings, I dropped Kary and Camden off at the Little Theater and went on to the Tempo. The Tempo's a dark little place right in the middle of downtown Parkland. There's a bar with a mirror behind it that reflects the seating area, round tables with four chairs each, and a raised stage with enough room and light for small music groups to perform. When I arrived, the club was almost full of the usual customers, older couples who were big fans of traditional jazz, with a few younger folks sprinkled in, curious about the music. There was laughter and the clink of glasses as everyone gathered to their tables. On stage, J.J.'s Hot Six was setting up. J.J. was J.J. Farino, a gnarled little drummer who could be any age between forty and sixty. The other members of the band, the trumpet player, saxophone player, trombone, and clarinet, greeted me.

"We can get started now," J.J. said. "Randall's here."

Charlie Valentine looked up from the piano, holding a glass of beer in one hand and a cigarette in the other. The remains of several other cigarettes filled the ashtray at the end of the keyboard. His shirtsleeves were rolled up, his tie was askew, and his dark hair was rumpled. He and Camden must subscribe to *Sloppy Small Men's Quarterly*. Like Camden, Charlie's hair is always in his eyes and his tie's always undone. And like Camden, he has plenty of women fussing over him because they feel he's cute.

I strolled up to the stage. "I think you're trying too hard for the burned-out jazzman look."

He put the glass down, took a long pull on the cigarette, and propped it in the ashtray. "But I am a burned-out jazzman."

The clarinet player laughed. "An incredibly jealous one." He put the clarinet to his lips and played the first few bars of "Frankie and Johnny." The bouncy yet mournful blues theme foreshadowed the doomed couple of the song. "That's what we call those two."

Charlie tossed back the rest of his beer. "She's driving me crazy, Randall. I know she's seeing someone else."

"What makes you think that?" Personally, I didn't see why Taffy would run around on him. He may be a little intense, but he treats her like a queen. Still, he is a musician. Probably doesn't make enough money.

He sucked the last dregs of the cigarette and blew out the smoke. "This makes four times I've asked her out, and she always puts me off. She's giving me lame excuses, too. One night, she's washing her hair. You know something's seriously wrong when they give you that one."

I had to agree. "And the other times?"

He ground the cigarette down to a wrinkled stub. "Going to a friend's house. Too tired. Coming down with a cold. The odd thing is when she's here singing with us, she's fine. I call her up the next day, and she's giving me some excuse. I thought we had something going. There for a while, we went out every night."

"Have you talked to her? Told her how you feel?"

"She knows how I feel. I've been crazy about her ever since I met her."

"You got any old girlfriends in the closet? Maybe she's been talking to them."

He put his hand to his heart. "Swear to God, ever since I met Taffy, I haven't even said hello to another woman."

"You'll have to do better than that. I've seen how the ladies come on to you."

"And I've resisted all temptation."

Now the band members snickered. He glared. "Did I invite any of you to this conversation?"

The saxophone player, a large black man, grinned. "Please find out what's going on, Randall. He ain't no good to us like this."

"I'm fine," Charlie said.

"Oh, yeah? How many beers you had this evening?"

"Fifty-five."

"Smartass. And didn't the doctor tell you to stop smoking?"

"Didn't the doctor tell you to lose a hundred pounds?"

"Ooo, the boy is touchy now. Must be love."

Charlie's grand gesture upset the ashtray. "Yes, I admit it! I am in love! Get over it."

"Shut up. Let's play."

I sat back at one of the small tables while they ripped through "Mule Walk." The trumpet sounded like liquid gold, and the clarinet darted like lightning around the melody. Despite his romantic trials and his alcohol and nicotine abuse, Charlie ripped through the number as if riding a hurricane, merging the black and white keys into one perfect storm of sound. J.J. often remarked Charlie played better when he was drunk.

The crowd roared their approval, and the Hot Six swung into one of my favorites, "Wildman Blues." They were halfway through when Taffinia O'Brien appeared. If the sight of Taffy sauntering down to the stage didn't set your red blood cells dancing, you must be mummified. With each step of those long legs, her honey-colored hair and her graceful hips swayed in their own special rhythm. She likes to wear green to set off her exotic slanted green eyes. Tonight's outfit was a green leather skirt and jacket and a gold blouse. If somebody hadn't already invented the phrase, "She looks like a million dollars," this sight would've inspired them.

Unaware of all the approving glances from the patrons, she slung her studded green leather pocketbook onto my table. "Hi, Randall. Hi, guys."

The members of Hot Six kept playing, acknowledging her with lifted eyebrows and nods. Charlie paused to knock back the remains of his drink and continued with the refrain. Taffy readjusted her skirt and came up to the microphone. She tapped it a few times and settled onto the tall stool. Seeing her cross those magnificent legs made me glad I got up this morning.

The band finished "Wildman Blues."

"That was a little rough," J.J. said. "Who's supposed to take the chorus second time around?" The clarinet player raised his hand. "Okay, and lighten up a little more when the sax takes the lead. Charlie, you follow, and then the trombone takes it. Good evening, Ms. O'Brien. Thanks for joining us."

She spoke over her shoulder. "What do you want to start with?"

"We'll start with 'I Love My Baby,' and then 'Someday Sweetheart,' if you're ready."

"I'm always ready."

Taffy sang as if channeling a great blues singer of the twenties or thirties. Charlie played the introduction and provided a beautiful counter-melody to her singing. She didn't even glance his way. She sang in warm smoky tones that made my tie close around my throat and my heart beat like a snare drum. When she finished her set, the audience gave her another round of applause and cheers, which she acknowledged with a regal nod. Then she left without even a backward glance at Charlie. Charlie continued to smoke and drink steadily, so by ten o'clock, he was good and stewed.

Even though I knew it was useless, I tried to get through to him. "You know, this isn't going to solve anything."

"But I can't figure her out! Why wouldn't she want to be with me?"

"Because she doesn't want to be Taffy O'Brien Valentine. It sounds like too many holidays."

The other members of the band thought this was funny, but Charlie took a swing at me that would've connected if he hadn't been so drunk. I caught his arm and pushed him into a chair.

"Look. I go through this all the time with Camden. Either declare yourself or find another woman. I'm tired of all the drama."

He hiccupped. "But I have! I've told her I love her."

"What did she say?"

"She says if I really loved her, I'd love her songs."

"What does that mean?"

"Hell if I know."

J.J. said, "I'll take him home, Randall."

Years of maneuvering Camden have made me an expert at getting small disoriented men in and out of cars. I helped J.J. wad Charlie into the backseat of his Ford Escort.

J.J. shut the door. "Don't look like it's getting much better."

"What's Taffy talking about 'loving her songs'? Charlie loves the old stuff."

J.J. leaned against his car and folded his arms. "I think Ms. Taffinia's got herself another gig somewhere."

"That's all right, though, isn't it? With a voice like that, I imagine she's in demand."

"Think she's getting tired of us."

I couldn't believe this. "Quit J.J.'s?"

"Mm-hm. That's what Charlie's most afraid of. Do the boy and us a favor, Randall. Talk to Ms. Taffy and see what's going on with her. She was born to sing the blues, and I can't say that about just anybody."

"I will if you'll see what you can do about Charlie's bad habits."

"He don't listen to me. Sometimes I think the boy wants to head for an early grave. These women'll drive you mad."

"Tell me about it."

J.J. looked at his watch. "'Bout time for our next set. Let me get him situated. He's no good for the rest of the night. I'm counting on you to straighten this out, Randall."

With Viola's murder, George's disappearance, and Kary's

emotional crusade to expose Baby Love, all I needed was one more thing to straighten out.

◇◇◇

With Charlie done for the evening, it was time for me to return to the theater and pick up Camden and Kary. The Parkland Little Theater sits in the downtown arts complex, which includes a dance studio, a rehearsal hall for the city orchestra, classrooms, and a small art gallery. I parked the Fury in the adjoining lot. Double glass doors led to a foyer decorated in gray and burgundy, and another set of doors opened into the auditorium. Little groups of people sat in the plush gray seats and clustered around the stage. Strangled noises came from the orchestra pit as the violins attempted to tune.

An annoyed voice spoke from the front row. "Could we run that scene once more?"

The lead, Eliza, was learning how to speak like a lady, and everyone hopped around singing "The Rain in Spain." The scene was pretty lackluster. No rain. Maybe a sprinkle, at best. The director, a thin man with wild hair—probably from pulling on it in frustration—stopped the action halfway through. I looked around for Camden and found him sitting in the middle row, surrounded by attractive women dressed like parlor maids. He introduced me before the women were called away for wardrobe adjustments.

"The Rain in Spain" cranked up again. "Doesn't seem to be going too well," I said.

"It's still rough."

"And this show opens next week?"

The actress playing Eliza had a good strong voice and plenty of pep, but the guy playing the professor kept missing his lines.

"He'll get it," Camden said. "It's his first show, so he's a little nervous."

"It's your first show, too."

"All I'm worried about is the haircut." He brushed a hand through his hair. "The wardrobe mistress says she can't wait to get her hands on it."

"You mean Freddy doesn't look like a sheepdog?"

"Not in this production."

"Anybody broken up about Viola?"

"Most of the cast have worked with her, so they couldn't believe she was murdered. Viola was a force of nature. Someone said she would've appreciated the dramatic way she was found buried under her house."

"Anybody looking particularly pleased?"

"Not that I can tell."

"Who's the best person to talk to?"

"I'd talk to our director, and our stage manager, and Millicent Crotty. She and Viola were best friends. She was too upset to come tonight. Rehearsal should be almost over, unless they want to do 'The Rain in Spain' again."

Apparently everyone had had enough rain in Spain. The director called the cast down to the auditorium and gave them notes, answered questions, and warned them to learn their lines. After he'd dismissed them, he agreed to talk to me for a few minutes. He'd calmed down, and so had his hair, which wilted around his face.

"I worked with Viola in several shows. She was an ornery old gal, but she was always prepared. Not many people her age try out for our shows, so there's usually no competition. No competition, no jealousy, no bad feelings, so who would kill her? It must have something to do with her private life."

"Do you know anything about a cousin of hers?"

He shrugged. "You got me there. Never heard her mention any sort of family."

"When was the last time you saw her?"

"At our Wednesday night rehearsal. She was playing Henry Higgins' mother and doing her usual good job."

"Who has that role now?"

"I'm going to ask Millicent Crotty if she'll take the part."

"Do you know if Millicent wanted to be Higgins' mother from the beginning?"

"She didn't try out for it, so I'd say she didn't want it."

The stage manager, a young man with dark curly hair and glasses, didn't know about a cousin, either, and was equally puzzled why anyone would kill Viola. He scrolled through the cast list on his tablet. "I can't remember Viola quarreling with anyone. She liked to give new people advice, you know, like how to stand and how to keep in the light. She always knew what she was talking about, so even if she was abrupt, people appreciated her acting tips."

"And her relationship with Millicent Crotty?"

"Oh, they've been friends for years."

I'd still have a word with her.

◇◇◇

Kary and Camden joined me as I walked back up the aisle, and Kary had good news.

"One of the guys in the ensemble said an older woman who looked very much like Viola came to see her in a play called *Arsenic and Old Lace*. Viola introduced her as Dahlia, which is why he remembers her. He said he'd never met anyone named Dahlia before."

"That's great, Kary. That's a starting point, at least. There can't be that many Dahlias in the world."

"Everyone else said working with Viola was like working with the Grand Duchess of the Theater. The violinists and the percussionist worked with her on *Sound of Music* and *Oklahoma*. They said she was very demanding, and if the orchestra was the tiniest bit off, she'd complain."

"Didn't you work with her on this music?"

"Her character doesn't have a song, thank goodness. She only has to look shocked and appalled, and she was very good at that. I didn't have any direct contact with her. I'll have to ask Charlie. Was he at the Tempo tonight?"

"For a while. Then he got drunk and J.J. had to take him home."

"Are things that bad between him and Taffy? I'll have to call him tomorrow and see if he's okay."

Oh, I didn't want that. "No need to bother. I'm sure he'll be all right. I'll get their romance back on track."

Camden didn't say anything, but his expression was full of humor.

"Charlie's such a great guy and so talented," Kary said. "Taffy's crazy if she lets him go."

I was surprised by the spike of jealousy I felt. Sure, Charlie was charming—when sober—and also a talented musician and only three years older than Kary, not six, like me. Then I reminded myself I'd been admiring Taffy's legs and all the rest of her and having a little fantasy during her songs. It must be the same thing with Kary and Charlie, mutual admiration, that's all. Kary and I had an understanding, didn't we? Did I have anything to worry about?

Taffy's not the only one who's crazy around here, I thought. Pull yourself together. Then get Charlie and Taffy together. You've got a job do to, so do it.

◇◇◇

That night, Camden and I stayed up to watch the Psychic Service Network, Ellin's show. It's one of those late night quasi-entertainment programs. Two of the Service's more photogenic women take turns as hostess, and Reg Haverson, Mrs. Belton's choice for Ellin, is the emcee. Reg embodies the best qualities of a Ken doll and a game show host combined—plastic perfect looks, a matching wardrobe, and a fake smile with plenty of white teeth. An audience of believers oohed and ahhed in the right places and looked suitably stunned by the predictions. While I slumped into the blue armchair, Reg posed carefully and aimed his toothy smile at a young woman, urging her to spill her innermost thoughts and learn her destiny.

"Jeez, Camden, you might as well give up right now. Look at that suit."

"Oh, that reminds me." He handed me a slip of paper from the coffee table. "You'll have to go by Suit City sometime and check on your tux."

"Thanks." I put the note in my pocket. "You know the only reason I agreed to be your best man is to see you in a tuxedo."

He indicated the roomy Carolina Panthers tee-shirt and pajama pants he had on. "I begged Ellie to let me wear this, but for some reason she and her mother said no. And speaking of Mother, Jean will be by tomorrow. Something about the pictures."

"Again? How many photographers have they gone through?"

"I've lost count."

"What time can we expect the Belton invasion, and why can't they discuss this at Ellin's?"

"Sometime after noon, I believe."

"I'll close my door." I reached for the remote. "Can we watch something else?"

"There isn't too much on now."

"When did that ever stop us? Staying up late, eating junky snacks, watching mind-rotting TV. Once you're married, life will change."

"I don't think so."

"Excuse me? You're telling me when Ellin's upstairs in your bed you'd rather be down here?"

Camden thought it over. "No."

"See?"

"But I'll need an occasional restorative break."

I counted the syllables on my fingers. "'Restorative.' My Lord, and it's after midnight."

Assorted squeaks and mews came from the basket in the corner where Cindy was attempting to feed her troublesome kitties. Camden got up to retrieve the red kitten that had fallen out and was scampering toward the kitchen. He rearranged the brood so that everyone had a chance to get some dinner. As the kittens squirmed and fought for position, Cindy turned her head and gave me a look as if to say, you think you've got problems?

With this crisis averted, Camden returned to the sofa. "Things won't be that different, Randall."

"You forget I've been married before. Things will definitely be different."

I could tell he didn't believe me, and maybe things wouldn't be that different for him. But I knew Ellin saw me as another unwelcomed cat and would do her best to find me another home.

◇◇◇

Home.

As I lay in bed that night, after way too many Cheetos and most of *The Land That Time Forgot*, I thought about home, the one I'd shared with Barbara and Lindsey, the new house in a development on the north side of Parkland. For some reason, I pictured myself walking through the house. There was Barbara's best black dress on the bed, her jewelry on the bureau. We must have been going out that night. There was the formal dining room with the oak table and chairs she'd inherited from her grandmother. We hardly used it, except at Thanksgiving. There were the strange yellow glass grapes on the coffee table. I never understood why they were fashionable, but everybody had some. There was the screened-in side porch where Lindsey kept her little red bicycle, the one with a horn and multicolored streamers.

Now I was standing at the back door, looking out into the large backyard. Lindsey had lots of friends in the neighborhood, and they liked to play in our yard because I'd bought a deluxe swing set and full-sized sliding board. I watched as the children chased each other in never-ending games of tag and hide-and-seek or even the games I recalled from my childhood, Mother, May I? Red Rover. London Bridge is Falling Down.

Damn, why was I thinking about this?

You lost one home, I told myself. Maybe you're afraid of losing another.

Maybe. I punched the pillow into what I hoped would be a more comfortable shape. Maybe I ate one too many Cheetos.

Chapter Five

"I have never been so keyed up."

Saturday morning, I woke up determined to keep my mind on business. First up, find George McMillan. I called the Green Palms Hotel. George McMillan had checked in. I then called Folly Harper to tell her George was found.

"Oh, thank you so much, Mr. Randall," she said.

"You're sure that's all you need me to do? I'll go to Clearwater and talk to him if you like."

She hesitated. "I'll call the hotel. I know he'll talk to me. This has to be some kind of misunderstanding."

"All right."

"I'll send the rest of your fee today, and thanks again."

She said good-bye and hung up. I sat for a while, wondering why I didn't feel my usual sense of closure. Folly Harper had sounded as if she didn't know what to do next, and having met her, I figured she really didn't know what to do next. She'd probably dither around until George got wise and left the country. But if she didn't want me to pursue him, then I'd done all I could.

Next I called Millicent Crotty, but she was too upset to talk to me. I asked if I could call later, and she said she needed time to process the whole horrible incident. She'd call me if and when she felt like it.

Okay. Truly upset, or really guilty? I'd have to wait. Next, search for Dahlia. After finding plenty of sites for dahlia flowers and the infamous unsolved Black Dahlia murder case, my Internet search brought up three Dahlia Mitchells in North Carolina, along with convenient addresses and phone numbers. One Dahlia Mitchell was listed as age thirty, probably too young to be Viola's cousin. No ages were listed for the other two, and nobody was home when I called. Only one had an answering machine, and "Hello, I'm a private investigator trolling for work. Did you know your cousin Viola was murdered?" was not the message I wanted to leave. I hung up and decided to try again later.

Then I got a phone call from Ted O'Neal, head pharmacist at Drug World.

"Randall, I've got a problem with shoplifters. Can you come prowl the aisles for a couple of days?"

"I happen to have an empty slot in my busy calendar. What's up?"

"I've been losing several packages of vitamins."

"Your thief's a health nut?"

"Must be. I can't figure why anyone would want bottles of vitamins and mineral oil when there're all kinds of drugs to steal."

"You're in luck. I've got a special on Store Detective this week."

"Come in tomorrow if you can."

I went to the kitchen to refill my tea glass. As I looked out the back bay window, I had a moment of disconnect. There was no swing set, no sliding board. Camden was trimming the hedge that separated his yard from the house behind, clipping the wild roses and honeysuckle into shape. The old oak trees spread shade across the grass. No children's voices, no cries of "You're it!" Only the rhythmic clip of the hedge-trimmers and a slight hum of traffic from a few streets over on Food Row.

Camden paused to talk over the hedge to a neighbor. Cindy's kittens chased each other in the grass and tried to pounce on insects. I could hear the pleasant ticking of a clock in the quiet house. Pleasant and quiet. Two things that were going to change radically when Ellin moved in. I wondered again if I should find another place, but damn it, I was here first. I couldn't afford to move, and I didn't want to leave Kary. But Kary's plans and mine never seemed to mesh. And now Charlie was in the mix.

I was brooding on this when Camden came in, took a can of Coke out of the fridge, and popped the top. He was singing "On the Street Where You Live," so I told him to shut up or sing something different. He put the can on the counter that separated the kitchen from the dining room and sat down on one of the stools. He looked particularly grubby in his baseball cap, tee-shirt and frayed jeans, bits of hedge sticking everywhere.

I gave a pointed look at his attire. "Aren't you expecting Ellin and her mother soon?"

"I'll be through by the time they get here."

"Let Reg have Ellin. Everyone will be happier."

He grinned. "Dream on." He took off his cap and tossed it on the counter, where it collided with the can and knocked it off the edge.

I grabbed for the can but wasn't fast enough. Yet as the contents started to spill, the can abruptly righted itself. I stared at it, wondering if I'd lost my mind, or if I'd been staring at the computer screen too long. I turned to Camden. "Did you see that?"

He stared at the can, a look of horror in his eyes. "Oh, God."

I had to revise my question. "Did you *do* that?" I felt a bit horrified myself.

He nodded. He's usually pale, but this latest trick set him back about three shades to paper white. His voice was uneven. "I was hoping it was a fluke. Yesterday, one of the kittens fell off the steps. I couldn't reach it, but it didn't fall. It scooped back on the step, like a movie running backwards."

I was determined to stay calm. "Okay. Maybe it did one of those weird little kitten moves. You know how spastic they are."

His voice was now on the rise. "And the day before, when I needed a pen to sign some checks, one hopped out of the pencil holder." He stared at the Coke can as if he expected it to go for his throat. "What's going on, Randall? Is this stupid power never going to stop?"

"All right, hold on. This could be nothing but a few odd tricks. Try something."

He glanced at the stack of mail on the counter. As I watched, the latest edition of *UFO Monthly* magazine detached itself from the stack and slid to the floor. One by one, the remaining objects—a cat toy, one of Kary's textbooks, an apple core, and one of Rufus' pal Buddy's carved wooden ducks—hopped off to join the magazine.

My insides did the rumba. "That's pretty good. How are you at bending spoons?"

Camden put his head in his hands. "No, no, no. This is all I need."

"Take it easy." I retrieved the magazine and the other objects, giving myself time to think of a logical explanation. "Could be temporary, could be the weather." My own mind reeled. Damn! Where had this come from? Were his powers expanding?

When he lifted his head, I almost expected flames to shoot out of his eyes. Now his voice was way too calm. "I can't handle this. I don't want this. I never asked for this. What's next? I start flying? Changing shape? Walking through walls?"

"Don't flip out. So you can move a few things, so what? Nobody has to know."

I didn't think it was possible, but he got even whiter. "Ellie." He didn't have to say anything else.

I tried to lighten things up. "Well, it might come in handy. When you're redecorating the place, for instance. 'Honey, could you move this for me? A little more to the right. That's perfect.'"

Camden was far too agitated to appreciate my humor. He slid off the stool. "How can I keep it from her? You know how she is. I don't want any secrets between us, but, my Lord, she'll go crazy if she finds out." He stopped for a moment, aghast. "The children."

"Children? What children?"

"I can't handle this. I can't marry her. It's too much."

He was out the back door before I could stop him. About that time, I heard Jean Belton's voice as she and Ellin came in the front door. Mother and daughter were arguing, as usual.

"But he doesn't have a regular job, and these fits—"

"Not fits, Mother! Visions. Trances."

"Well, whatever they are, it's not natural," Mrs. Belton said. "Can't he take something for it? And are you still planning on living here with all these people?"

These people. She said it exactly the way Ellin did.

"It's only temporary. I'm sure Cam and I can work something out."

I peered around the corner. The women had stopped in the island. Jean had Ellin's hands in hers. "Dear, I know you've been seeing Camden for a long time, and he's a nice young man, really, but I'm not sure he's the husband for you. You need someone with drive and ambition. Camden reminds me of those bohemian types you hung around with in college. I'd hoped you'd outgrown those kind of people."

Ellin pulled her hands free. "Cam is not 'those kind of people.' He's a sensitive, kind, caring man. Who else would take in these hopeless deadbeats?"

Jean sat down on the green sofa. "I still say you're in love with his talent. You always went overboard for any mystical otherworldly nonsense."

If you're in love with his talent, you'll be thrilled over this new wrinkle, I thought.

Ellin sighed. "Could we take care of business, please? Cam? Are you home?" She came around to the kitchen and stopped short when she saw me. Ordinarily, I'd have gotten a lecture about eavesdropping, but with Mom there, Ellin was on her best behavior. "Where's Cam?"

"He had to step out for a minute." I came around to the island. "Hello, Jean."

"Good afternoon, David." She had a large book in her lap that looked like a collection of sample wedding photos. "How is your detective agency coming along?"

I knew she didn't really approve of my line of work either, but at least I was busy most of the time. "I recently found a missing person." I left out the part about murdered and buried in her basement.

This impressed her. "Well, don't let us keep you. We need to get Camden's input on the wedding photographer. When will he be back?"

"It may be a while. Could I take a message?"

Ellin looked around the dining area as if she expected him to be hiding under the table. "Where did he go? Didn't he remember we were coming by today?"

Like the Grinch, I thought up a lie and I thought it up quick. "Yes, but Tamara called and said she needed him at the shop for a while."

Ellin looked at her mother. "I suppose we could stop by there."

Another diversion was necessary. "I think they were going to the south-side shop to pick up some merchandise."

To my relief, Jean wasn't in the mood to tangle with the south-side traffic. "I don't want to go all the way over there, Ellin. Why don't we go see about the bridesmaids' dresses and stop by here later? Will he be home by five, David?"

If he hasn't decided to try another dimension. "I hope so."

"We'll be back at five."

"Hello! Anybody home?"

At the sound of cheery voices, we turned. Two tall dark-haired women came in, laughing and talking at the same time.

"Surprise!"

"We couldn't wait!"

"We stopped by the house and Dad said you were over here."

"Where's the lucky bride?"

"Congratulations, sis!"

Jean got up, her face alight. "We weren't expecting you girls until tomorrow."

Ellin's face wasn't quite so thrilled, but she hugged her two older sisters. "Hi, girls."

The taller of the two tugged one of Ellin's curls. "Oh, we really couldn't wait another day. We've come to help."

This, I knew, was the last thing Ellin wanted. Caroline and Sandra have bossed her around since birth. They look enough alike to be twins, but Caroline is two years older than Sandra and wears her dark hair in a short flippy style, while Sandra's hair is long with long bangs. Both have Mr. Belton's high forehead, snub nose, and serious dark eyes, but there's nothing serious about either of them.

If that isn't enough to rile Ellin, her big sisters think I'm pretty hot.

Caroline gave me a kiss. "David, I swear you get better looking every time I see you. I wish you'd marry Ellin so we could keep you in the family."

Sandra looked around. "Where's Cam? Where's the lucky man?"

"He had to go to work."

"Too bad! I wanted to lay a big wet one on him, too. Come here, David. You'll have to do."

Their mother put an end to the serious smooching. "You girls want to help us pick out a photographer? We've been through several, and we can't find the right one."

Caroline plopped down beside her on the sofa. "Why not let Uncle Nick take the pictures?"

Ellin was already twice as tense as before. "That's not a good idea."

"Just because he gets everyone's rear end? You shouldn't worry, Ellin. You've got a cute little tush."

There it was, the veiled antagonism. Caroline and Sandra had been extremely jealous of their tiny blond baby sister. Now that they were adults, their relationship was better, but I wasn't sure how long the treaty could survive wedding plans.

Sandra sat down on the other side of Jean and turned the pages of the album. "Do you have a cake yet?"

"Fulsom's is doing it."

Sandra wrinkled her nose. "You really should go with Sweet Nothings. They're much cheaper. What about the bridesmaids' dresses? You'd better not have us in puffy sleeves."

Caroline laughed. "Or empire waists."

I could tell Ellin was trying to control her temper. "As a matter of fact, Mother and I were on our way to have a look at the dresses. Why don't you come along?"

"Great! David, are you coming?"

"No, thanks." Four Belton women in the house were already making the ground quiver. "I'm working on a case."

Sandra gave me another kiss. "We'll want to hear all about it."

They went out, Jean first, followed by Caroline and Sandra. Ellin was the last to go. She gave me a look that spoke volumes. Volumes of encyclopedias.

"I was hoping for one more day of peace."

"I think they're really happy for you, Ellin."

"I guess so."

I found myself in the odd position of comforter. "They wouldn't have come if they didn't care about you."

"They're probably hoping I'll trip and fall down the aisle."

"That's not going to happen."

She refused to be comforted. "Oh, so now you're psychic, too? If you see Cam, tell him they're here, would you? At least one of us will have a warning."

The car horn beeped. Sandra called, "Come on, Ellin!"

Ellin sighed, exasperated. "Damn. Maybe we should've eloped."

Chapter Six

"Oozing charm from every pore…"

Now I'd like to say I tuned in on Camden's brainwaves or had a vision or sensed where he was, but nothing like that happened. He has to send me a message, and right now, he was probably as scrambled as that premium channel you didn't pay for. It's better and faster to use common sense. He'd headed out the back. He'd no doubt seen the Beltonmobile. There were two choices: Food Row or the park. I opted for the park.

I walked down Grace Street. The sidewalks are cracked and in some places, curved around tree trunks and buckled by roots. All the houses have flowers, magnolia trees overloaded with fat white blossoms, oak trees, and these orange flowers called day lilies that look like trumpets bursting out of the ground. I waved at one of our neighbors who was mowing his lawn in the hottest part of the day, as usual, and as Rufus would say, sweating like a big dog. Passing the two-story brick apartment house, I could hear somebody practicing piano. Somebody else's cooking smelled pretty good, mingled with the scent of flowers tangled in all the hedges and along the low stone walls separating driveways. An occasional bike or plastic toy lay on a front lawn. Everything was hot and thick and green, a far cry from the bleak windy little Minnesota town where I grew up.

At any other time, this would be a pleasant walk, but I was

wondering where I'd look next if Camden hadn't gone to the park. I waved at old Mrs. Austin, sitting on her front porch with her tiger-striped cat, Whiskers, in her lap. It's the consensus of 302 Grace that Whiskers is the father of Cindy's kittens. He certainly looked smug enough.

A winding bike path between two houses leads to the park, an expanse of green grass and oak trees between Grace and Willow streets. Besides the usual duck pond, swing sets, and flower gardens, there are benches for old geezers like Fred. I didn't see Fred, but I saw Camden hunched on one bench, his chin on his knees, his bare feet up under. A couple of joggers huffed by. A mother and her small son threw bread to the ducks. I could tell by Camden's stillness he was miles away from the scene.

He didn't say anything when I sat down beside him, but he wasn't in one of his zombie trances.

"How many children do you see?"

"Three."

"Damn." I thought this over. "Any of them psychic?"

"That's the trouble. I can't tell. You know my own future doesn't come in clearly." His eyes were a cloudy gray. "I wouldn't wish this on anyone, Randall, especially not my kids."

"But there's a big difference here. Your kids will have you and Ellin to help them handle it. You had to go through it alone. They won't have to."

"I'm still going through it." He unfolded himself and looked off toward the pond. "It scares the hell out of me. Now, on top of everything else, I'm telekinetic. I put a squirrel back in a tree a while ago. I kept an old codger from tripping over his feet. I could probably knock you off this bench without touching you."

"Try it!"

"Damn it, Randall, this is serious."

"Can you control it?"

"Yes, thank God."

"I mean, I had this picture of that guy in *Star Trek*, you know, the one in the pseudo-Roman robes, tossing everybody around because he was in a funk."

This earned me a dark look. "I can't marry Ellie. I can't risk passing this freakish talent on to our children."

"But your fortune will be made. Ellin will trot them round to all the talk shows. The Amazing Camden Kids! They tell the future, find lost treasures, walk on hot coals for your entertainment."

He gave me another look. "You're not helping."

We sat in silence for a while. "You know you're going to marry her. You love her. You'll find a way around this. If your future's unclear, then maybe none of the kids will be psychic. Your problem now is telling her about this new trick."

"I'm not going to tell her. Not yet."

"She and Jean will be back at five. I told them you and Tamara had to go across town. Oh, and Caroline and Sandra have arrived. Now the fun really begins."

"Thanks for running interference. I kind of lost it for a minute."

It made me uneasy to think that besides levitating squirrels, Camden might one day have a child in the house. "We're in the same boat. The whole idea of children makes me lose it." The word "children" sat like a boulder between us. Might as well hang it around my neck.

Camden watched the mother and child feed the ducks the last of their breadcrumbs and then rubbed his eyes wearily, as if erasing the scene. I imagined he was thinking of his own childhood, which, from the few things he'd told me, had been lonely and distracting until he'd learned to understand his visions. "If I only knew what caused this stupid talent in the first place."

"You are the Chosen One."

"It's my father's fault. I know it is. If I ever meet him, I'm going to knock him sideways. What kind of man leaves a woman pregnant and then runs off? What kind of man abandons his family? Damned irresponsible jerk."

"Maybe your father didn't know your mother was pregnant, ever think of that? If you'd let me find him, we could ask him and clear this up."

"I don't want you to find him."

"You'd rather be angry and sulk and fling things around?"

"I'd rather be normal."

"Good luck with that."

He sighed and pushed his hair out of his eyes, which had returned to their usual blue. "Guess I'd better get back."

"Have you ever thought about having a useful talent, like changing leaves into dollar bills?"

We walked back to Grace Street. Several blocks from the house, we could hear the piano. Somebody was tearing through "Dizzy Fingers." I know Kary's playing when I hear it. She wasn't playing.

"Don't tell me you're doing that, too, Camden." Then I recognized the sound. Sure enough, when we went inside, there was Charlie, pounding away at the piano. Kary watched in admiration. He finished with a spectacular run and smacked the last chord. We applauded.

Charlie bowed. "Thank you, my loyal fans. Glad to see I have a few left."

Kary beamed at him in a way that made me very nervous. "That was wonderful. I wish I could play like that."

I wondered how long he'd been here.

"Are you rehearsing here now?"

He reached for the ashtray, realized it wasn't there, and covered his mistake with a blues rift on the bass keys. "Just stopped by to help Kary pick out something to play for the pageant."

Kary picked up the stack of music books from the piano bench. "I need to find something really showy. 'Dizzy Fingers' is always a crowd-pleaser, but I can't play that. I'd have to practice for a hundred years."

Charlie pointed to a piece of music open on the piano. "We're going with 'Graceful Ghost' by William Bolcom. It's more classical and certainly difficult enough to impress the judges. And you could play 'Dizzy Fingers,' Kary. Don't sell yourself short. You can play anything you like."

"'Graceful Ghost' is more my speed, Charlie, and you know it."

The smiles, the glances, the cheerful banter—my jealousy spike-o-meter was going haywire. So I changed the subject.

"Caroline and Sandra are in town. They're coming by around five."

This, as I'd hoped, distracted Kary—although not as long as I liked. "Oh, I can't wait to see them! Charlie, have you met Ellin's sisters? They're a hoot. Why don't we work on this piece for a while, and maybe you could stay and meet them."

"I'd love to, Kary, but I need to talk to Randall, and then I'd better be getting home. Got a minute, Randall?"

"Sure. Come on into my office."

I led the way, and Charlie came in, shutting the door behind him. He sat down across from my desk. "I'm happy to help Kary, but the real reason I came over was to see you." He searched his pockets for his cigarettes. "Will it bother anyone if I smoke in here?"

"Can you stop at one?"

"I'll make every effort."

"I'd rather you didn't."

"Okay." He stopped searching his pockets. "It's about Taffy, of course. I think I know part of the problem. Lately, she's written her own songs for the band. They're—how shall I put this? They're crap. Really awful. She gets all defensive, but it's not the type of stuff we play. They're all modern and atonal." He shuddered. "Not a melody in sight."

"I don't see what I can do about that."

"Like I said, she's been putting me off, giving me all kinds of excuses. I need to know if she's seeing someone else, or if it has to do with her music."

"Just because she's writing her own songs doesn't necessarily mean she's cheating on you."

"That's what it feels like. I feel betrayed, you know? Like, she's always been into the old tunes, and now she's turning her back on them and on the band and on me."

"But she still sings with J.J.'s."

"I think she's singing with another band."

"Charlie, she can sing with as many bands as she likes. A voice like that is going to be in demand."

"Yeah, but I'm afraid she's going to leave us, and then I'll lose her. I think somebody told her those crappy songs are good. Could you follow her one day and see where she goes?"

If you'll leave Kary alone, I wanted to say. But I knew he was—pardon the pun—stuck on Taffy, and I wanted to make sure they stayed together.

"Okay. I'll see what I can find out."

"Thanks."

I wanted him to leave. I thought he was going to leave, but he went back to the piano. When I came out, he and Kary were sitting side-by-side on the piano bench, their hands intertwined as they worked on "Graceful Ghost." Fortunately, he had to go before five o'clock and the Attack of the Belton Women.

I followed Kary as she went into the kitchen to make more iced tea. She was her usual calm self—on the outside. I could tell something was bothering her. She knows we keep the tea bags in the far left cabinet, but she opened several other cabinets, as if searching for the tea. When she found them, she dropped a few on the counter, but quickly scooped them up.

"What do you think of that song, David? Does it sound difficult enough?"

"Graceful Ghost." The image of Lindsey dancing so proudly in her recitals filled my mind, her smile beaming brighter than any light on stage. "Yeah, it's great."

She filled the iced tea maker with water and put the tea bags in. "I'm glad Charlie could help me out. And here's some good news. I heard the pageant prize money is six thousand dollars this year instead of five."

She kept her gaze on the tea maker. Was she thinking of her own little graceful ghost? I'd always imagined her daughter as a tiny version of Kary, blond and brown-eyed, a budding ballerina, like Lindsey. "That's great, too."

"And I asked him about Viola's cousin. He said he didn't know."

"Well, Millicent Crotty won't talk to me. Maybe you'll have better luck. And check and see if Viola recently quarreled with someone, or owed anyone money." From the looks of Viola's house, she wasn't wealthy, but people had been killed for less than twenty dollars. "There could be a long-standing feud at the theater, or someone from her past."

Now the packs of sweetener demanded all her attention. Something was on her mind, and it wasn't making tea. "And the mysterious Dahlia?"

"There are three possibilities. Nobody home on the first try. I'm going to call them again."

Kary added sweetener, turned on the tea maker, and finally faced me. "We need to discuss our Baby Love campaign."

"Actually, I'd like to discuss something else." At her look of inquiry, I decided to confront the elephant. It had been standing in the room long enough, and I was tired of it blocking my way. "You've been there for me when I wanted to talk about Lindsey. I want to be here for you and talk about Beth."

She winced and I immediately regretted bringing up her lost baby. She folded her arms tightly around her and took a few shuddering breaths. For a moment, I thought she was steeling herself to tell me, but then realized she was locking down her emotions, one by one, exactly the way I did when the grief threatened to overwhelm me. All the signs were there, the quick blinking away of tears, the defiant lift of her chin, the unavoidable catch in her throat. "I don't want to talk about her."

I had serious doubts about continuing, but I wanted her to know we were carrying the same impossibly heavy burden, and I desperately wanted to help lift hers. "It was a horrible time for you, but believe me, I understand."

"No. You think you do because of Lindsey, but there's a big difference here, David." She paused for a moment, as if deciding whether or not to explain. "I want to carry a child, feel it growing inside, and loving it as a true part of me. It goes to the deepest core of what it means to be a woman, and I can't have that."

I'd crossed over into dangerous territory. "Hold on. Having a baby doesn't define you as a woman. You're as woman as you can be."

Her gaze was hard and direct. "Are you going to stop before I get angry, or are you going to keep on until you ruin whatever this is we have between us? Because I spent a long time crawling out of a very dark hole to be able to function as a human being again, and I refuse to crawl back in."

"Kary—"

"I made one mistake. One mistake and it cost me everything. My family. My baby. Almost my life. And the only way this works is if you drop the subject and never bring it up again. Do you understand that?"

This elephant was bigger and tougher than I thought. I backed off. "All right."

The silence that followed was big and tough, too, until Kary said, "Thank you."

I sat down at the counter. I felt as if I'd run a marathon and fallen on my face right before the finish line. She wanted the subject dropped, so I dropped it and changed it. "When's the next Baby Love meeting?"

She yanked a tissue from the box on the counter and blotted away the few stray tears that had escaped, took two clean glasses from the drain board, and went to the fridge for ice. Her first attempt at a reply was unsteady. She cleared her throat and tried again. "Unfortunately, I have rehearsal the night of their next meeting, but I've thought of something else. You and I could pose as reporters doing a story on Baby Love."

"I like the couple idea better."

Ice rattled in the glasses. "But as reporters, we could get a lot of facts we could check. Doesn't the editor of the *Herald* owe you a favor?"

"I don't want to ask Chance Baseford for a favor, even if he owes me one. You know how he is."

"But he'd let us go undercover for the paper, wouldn't he? He likes exposing frauds."

"Maybe his own team of reporters could go undercover."

She set the glasses on the counter. "David, you know very well that I want to go undercover, and don't smirk like that. You know what I mean." The tea maker gave a little burp and rattled, distracting her for a moment. "What is wrong with this thing? I thought Cam fixed it." She unplugged it and then plugged it back in. The red light came back on. "There." She faced me, all traces of that fierce emotion gone. "So let's do it."

What could I say? "Undercover it is."

Chapter Seven

"She'll have a booming boisterous family."

Even though she'd warned me off, I was trying to think of a way to apologize to Kary when Camden padded downstairs, still barefoot, rolling up the sleeves of a clean white shirt. He'd put on clean jeans and a gray vest with white stripes. Although nowhere near the sartorial elegance of Reg Haverson, it was a vast improvement. His transformation was just in time, too. Ellin and her mother and sisters drove up. Behind them in her peach Cadillac was Mrs. Folly Harper.

I watched as the Cadillac parked behind the Beltonmobile. "Damn. Ellin thinks you should meet this woman. You know what that means."

"Too late now."

Ellin was first in the door, all smiles and good cheer, a deadly combination. "Look who we ran into. Cam, this is Folly Harper. She's been wanting to meet you."

I glared at Ellin. Ran into, hell! Her answering glare said, Keep out of this.

Camden shook Mrs. Harper's hand. "Hello, Mrs. Harper."

Her blue eyes shone. "Oh, my dear, the pleasure is all mine! I've been wanting to meet you for ages! I had no idea this was your house."

Caroline and Sandra came in next, followed by Jean. Ellin's sisters gave glad cries of greeting to Kary and hugged her. Then Sandra gave Camden a hug.

"Ellin says you're in charge of the music. Does this mean no 'Taco Bell Canon in D'?"

"No 'Taco Bell,' no 'Jesu, Joy of Man's Desiring.'"

"I love you. I'm so bored with those numbers. Are you going to have 'Light My Fire'?"

"Yes, and 'I Want to Make it With You.'"

Sandra and Caroline laughed, but their mother looked puzzled. "Surely you're not serious."

Caroline made a face at Jean's lack of humor. "No, Mother, we're teasing. I'm sure the music will be fantastic. Cam, is there anything to drink in your house?"

"There's plenty of Coke and tea. Help yourself."

The sisters went around to the kitchen with Kary. Folly Harper had kept her high-beam gaze on Camden the whole time. He sent a questioning glance in Ellin's direction.

"Mrs. Harper has a very important matter she'd like to discuss with you," Ellin said.

Mrs. Harper clung to his hand. Maybe she thought she could wring out some information. "It is simply vital that I get my important numbers. Ellin says you are the very best at predicting the future."

Camden carefully pulled free. "I'm sorry. I don't do that kind of thing anymore."

"But I'd be happy to pay for your services." Mrs. Harper dug into her peach-colored handbag. "What do you usually charge?"

"I don't."

"Cam," Ellin said between her teeth.

Mrs. Harper brought out her checkbook. "I need to know my lucky numbers for a certain day. For someone with your talent, I'm sure it would take only a moment of your time."

Camden shook his head. "I no longer work for the Psychic Service. I'm sure there are plenty of people there who'd be glad to help you."

"I always go with the best. Name your price."

There was an audible gulp from Ellin. "No, thanks," Camden said.

Trying to keep a smile in place, Ellin spoke to Mrs. Harper. "Could you excuse us for a moment?" She took Camden's arm and propelled him toward the dining room.

This might take a while. "Mrs. Harper, were you able to get in touch with George?" I asked.

She seemed surprised I was still there. "I left a message, but he hasn't gotten back to me yet." It was obvious she was much more interested in the tense words growing louder from the dining room.

Ellin's voice was climbing up the shrill scale. "But I don't see why you couldn't do this one simple little thing."

Camden's voice was calmer, but not by much. "Because it's never one simple little thing, you know that. It grows. It engulfs. I have too much on my mind right now."

Then Caroline joined in from the kitchen. "Good grief, Ellin. Leave the guy alone."

Sandra had to express her opinion. "If I were you, Cam, I'd run for it."

I'm sure if I'd looked around the corner, I would have seen a dazzling display of fireworks.

"This is none of your business! Mother, tell them to back off!"

"Now, girls."

Folly Harper's eyes were very round, emphasized by all her mascara. "Dear me. Did I start all this with my little request?"

The quarreling voices faded to a dull roar. "No, this kind of thing happens all the time."

Folly Harper cocked her head. "I don't understand. Why doesn't Cam want to do this?"

"He just wants to live a normal life."

"But when one is blessed with such a talent, one should use it."

"Not when it gives one a headache."

She looked surprised. "Is seeing into the future painful?"

"Sometimes."

"My goodness, I can't see the pain in finding some numbers for me, especially when I can pay a considerable amount. Which reminds me, Mr. Randall. Here's the rest of your fee." She wrote a check, tore it out, and handed it to me.

I thanked her. Footsteps clumping up the stairs told me the argument was over and Camden had retreated. I looked out in time to see Kary hurrying up the stairs after him. In a few minutes, Ellin steamed past the office doorway.

"Dear me," Mrs. Harper said. "Doesn't look like I'll get my numbers today." She snapped her pocketbook shut. "But I won't give up. Tell Camden to please reconsider my offer. I'll be in touch. And thank you for your prompt action."

She went out to her car. I didn't see Ellin anywhere, but there were footprints smoking on the island carpet, and I soon heard her bell-like tones from the porch, along with her mother's surprising comments.

"But Ellin, I think it's admirable he doesn't want to exploit these people. He knows he'd be taking Folly's money under false pretenses."

I took a peek out the screen door. Ellin paced the porch.

"Don't you understand? He is never wrong! He could make a fortune!"

Jean sat down in a rocking chair. "Whatever is going on, it's obvious you can't change his mind. I've never seen him look so immovable."

"He's impossible to deal with when he gets like this."

"Well, dear, if the two of you can't work out problems in a reasonable, adult manner—"

"Mother."

"It's not the basis for a stable marriage."

Caroline and Sandra came up behind me. They peered around my shoulder.

"Shame on you for eavesdropping, David," Caroline said.

"Yeah, it's an awful habit."

Sandra snickered. "Is Mom going on about Cam's fits?"

"I think she's on his side on this issue."

Ellin paced close enough to the door to make all three of us draw back.

"Whoops," I said. "Maybe we should retire to the island."

Caroline and Sandra brought their tea and a bag of chocolate chip cookies to the sofa. Caroline passed me the cookies. "What is the deal with Mrs. Harper, anyway?"

I sat down in the blue armchair. "She's a client of mine. She's also a supporter of the Psychic Service Network, and she's hoping Camden will predict the future for her."

"But Cam doesn't want to."

"Right. He's trying to live a normal life."

"But he's going to marry Ellin. There goes the normal life."

Sandra dunked her cookie in her tea and took a bite. "It all comes down to money. You know how Ellin is."

"I don't get that," I said. "You always had plenty of money growing up, didn't you?"

"Yes, and we've got plenty of money now. Ellin wants more. Money and fame. She's always got to prove something."

Caroline looked slightly guilty. "That's partly our fault. We teased her unmercifully when we were little. Cookies, please."

I passed her the bag. "As opposed to the merciful teasing now?"

"She was so pretty and so smart. She came along when Sandra and I were at the clunky braces and pimples stage, so naturally, we resented her."

Sandra took a bite of cookie. "And despite us, she became even more beautiful and successful and she's marrying a really cute guy who honestly loves her, even though he's not the chief surgeon or presidential candidate Mom had picked out for her."

I'd never heard them speak so frankly. "But you're here to take part in the wedding. That ought to count for something with her."

Caroline smiled. "She may not believe it, but we do love her." She paused. "Shh. Listen. I don't hear anything."

"Are they dead?"

Their mother came to the door. "Are you girls ready to go? Your sister needs to get back to the TV station."

They got up. "See you later, David," Sandra said. "Can we take the rest of the cookies?"

"Of course."

As soon as they all had gone, Camden came back downstairs. He had his sneakers in his hand.

"Are you leaving town?"

He sat down on one of the island cushions to put his sneakers on. "Rehearsal tonight. Someone's giving me a ride to the theater, but can you pick me up around nine?"

"Kary's not going?"

"The director needs to reblock a few scenes, so he doesn't need the orchestra."

Kary came down the stairs next, fussing because Camden would miss dinner.

"Angie's cooking ribs tonight, Cam."

"Sorry, Kary. I'm not very hungry."

"I'll save some for you."

A member of the cast came by and took Camden to the *My Fair Lady* rehearsal. Folly Harper called to ask if Camden had changed his mind. I told her he hadn't, and five minutes later, she called again.

"No, he really hasn't changed his mind," I told her.

Right when I sat down in my office to contact the three Dahlias, she called again. I figured she'd forgotten she'd already phoned twice. "Still no change, Mrs. Harper."

She apologized for being such a bother. "But this is important."

"No problem," I said. "I promise I'll let you know."

Once Folly was off the phone, I could make my calls. Only Dahlia was home. Even though she was the youngest of the three, I wanted to talk with her. She informed me she had a Cousin Vern, a Cousin Velma, and a Cousin Vickie Sue, but no Cousin Viola. I thanked her and crossed her off my list. I tried the remaining two. Still no answer at either number. Time for dinner.

Angie fixed a hearty he-man meal: ribs, mashed potatoes, rolls, and pound cake. Although the sight of Fred mumbling through mashed potatoes could discourage the heartiest eater, I managed to make short work of the artery-clogging feast.

Rufus took another handful of rolls. True to form, he hadn't removed his cap and pieces of rib were stuck in his beard. "Nice spread, sweetie pie. More than I can say grace over."

I can always count on Rufus for a descriptive Southern saying. He once told me he was so Southern, he was related to himself.

"Thank you," Angie said. "You boys eat up, now. There's plenty more."

Rufus pointed a rib at me. "What's on Cam's mind? He looks like he's trying to carry water with no bucket."

Rufus looked slow and dull, but he didn't miss a thing. I wasn't sure if Camden wanted the rest of his odd family to know about his new power. "One of the women in the show was killed."

"Oh, that ain't good. Is he taking it hard?"

If he didn't freak out when Viola's body was found in the cellar, then he was okay, but this was a good excuse. "I think so. She wasn't a close friend, but you know how he is."

"You on the case?"

"Sort of. No one's officially hired me."

"We're both on the case," Kary said.

Rufus reached for the barbecue sauce. "Good for you, girl. When you goin' to deputize me, Randall?"

"Whenever I need a wall of muscle to cut up rough."

"I hear you. I speak 'noir,' you know."

Angie cut another piece of cake. "Well, not tonight. We're going house-hunting."

I certainly didn't want to stand in the way of that endeavor. "Have you found anything?"

"Couple of places. We'd like to stay in the neighborhood."

Kary gathered the empty plates. "You know you can stay here as long as you like."

"Yeah, but with Cam getting married and Ellin moving in, we all might be happier elsewhere. You planning to stay on, Randall?"

"As far as I know."

Rufus chuckled. "Good luck with that. We all know how Miz Ellin feels about that. Wanna know how welcome you're gonna be?"

"Enlighten me."

"As welcome as an outhouse breeze."

Chapter Eight

"One day I'll be famous!"

Around nine o'clock, after other unsuccessful attempts to contact Dahlias Two and Three, I went to the theater. Camden was waiting outside, deep in conversation with the actor who was playing Henry Higgins.

"It's okay," I heard him say. "You'll get it. Your scenes went much better tonight."

The man shook his head. "I don't know, Cam. I think this role's too much for me. I should've started out with something smaller. All this dialogue and the songs—I'm not sure I'm going to be ready by next week."

"You know your character doesn't actually have to sing."

"That's one good thing, at least."

"You're doing fine. You'll be ready."

"Guess I have to, don't I?" The man's cell phone beeped, and he checked it. "My wife's wondering where I am. Better go. Thanks for the pep talk."

Camden got into the car and we started for home.

"Is he going to make it?" I asked.

"I hope so. He's really good in the part, if he'll just relax."

"Did Viola's pal Millicent Crotty show up? Did she take Viola's part?"

"Yes, but she called in sick."

"Right now she's the only suspect I have."

"We're going to have a memorial service for Viola after rehearsal tomorrow night. I'm pretty sure Millicent will attend, and you can grill her."

At the intersection, I said, "How about changing this red light for me?"

"Don't tempt me."

"Ellin still in the dark?"

"Yes, thank goodness." The light changed on its own, and we started forward. "What's this business with Folly Harper? She strikes me as a particularly unlucky woman."

"And a persistent one. She called three times this evening to see if you'd changed your mind."

"She wants me to tell her some numbers. She could figure that out on her own."

"Do you see special Harper numbers?"

"I see a lot of numbers, but I don't know what they mean in relation to Mrs. Harper. I don't want to know what they mean. I've told Ellie I don't work that way." He sighed. "I don't suppose it matters now. I'm wondering how the hell I'm going to tell her."

I had to stop at another red light. I looked at him. "Tell her what? That the wedding's off? Been nice knowing you?"

"I don't know," he said. "I just don't know."

"I still say you're overreacting. Your own future never works out the way you see it."

I could tell by his expression he was unconvinced. "I keep seeing a pattern of black and white."

"Like a chessboard? We are all pawns in the game of life, that sort of thing?"

"No. Different shapes, stripes, circles."

"What's this got to do with your kids?"

"I have no idea." He glanced up. "The light's green."

"That's the only thing you've said tonight that makes sense." I turned the Fury smoothly onto Food Row. "Don't tell Ellin anything yet. Wait and see. This new trick of yours might be a temporary condition, like hay fever."

He wasn't in the mood to be consoled. "Or it could increase over the years until I spontaneously combust."

"Don't combust in the car, okay? I've got enough to worry about."

"I wouldn't call it a trick. I had a problem with the dishes earlier."

Camden uses dishwashing as therapy. It's one of the ways he supported himself during the years he wandered the country, learning to control all the wild pictures that popped into his mind. "What? They wouldn't go where you wanted them?"

"Oh, they went, all right. I barely had time to open the cabinets."

"Did they wash and dry themselves? That would save a lot of time."

"No. They were clean. They shot away like a flock of startled pigeons."

"I thought you said you could control this new power."

"I can, but it still takes me by surprise." He slumped in his seat. "It took me years to figure out the visions and how to keep them in line. Now this."

"We'll figure it out." I sounded more confident than I felt. I had no idea how to fix this problem.

◇◇◇

The next morning, Camden had calmed down a little, and we all went to church as usual. I'm not what you call religious, but it's certainly worth a sermon and a couple of Bible verses to sit next to Kary. She and Camden are faithful members of Victory Holiness, a friendly nondenominational little church in a rundown part of town where it really doesn't matter who you are or what you wear. Having been brought up in a cold and sterile Lutheran church in Minnesota, I found Victory Holiness as inviting as a church is likely to be, but I had too many doubts about the fairness of life to believe as easily as Kary and Camden did in an all-loving deity. But if church was important to Kary, then I would park my butt in the pew every Sunday. Still another example of how far I will go to win this woman.

For the offertory, Camden and the choir sang something about turning your eyes upon Jesus, but the only one I could turn my eyes upon was Kary. As she smiled and passed the collection plate to me, I looked into her warm brown eyes and said a special prayer. *Lord, whatever she's looking for, I hope it includes me.*

◇◇◇

After lunch, I finally managed to get a hold of Dahlia Two. Her voice was slow and languorous, as if she'd just gotten out of bed. It took me several tries to explain who I was and why I was calling. She gave a little hiccup and said she didn't have no cousins named Viola and not to call her again, especially so dag-nabbed early. One o'clock on Sunday. I apologized and hung up, making a mental note to ask Rufus what "dag-nabbed" meant. I dialed my final number and listened to the phone ring on the other end. *Okay, Dahlia Three. Where the hell are you?* I hoped she wasn't buried in her basement.

I finally gave up for a while and spent a couple of hours at the Drug Palace in disguise. I wandered the aisles with a clipboard and pen, pretending to check stock, and keeping an eye out for suspicious characters. Everyone in and around the Palace qualifies as a character. Only a few are truly suspicious. A wall-eyed geezer who likes to nap on the bench outside. A grown man who wears a propeller beanie. He always buys two copies of *Field and Stream.* Maybe he figures he needs one for the field and one for the stream. An older woman who likes to take out her teeth and click them at me in a bizarre long-distance hello. These people are harmless.

On the side of justice, I caught a couple of slack-jawed teens lifting candy bars and a pouty blond teenage girl putting a yin-yang bracelet in her purse, you know, the kind that resemble two tadpoles checking out each other's tails. No sign of anyone filching vitamins.

Ted O'Neal was a large man with a fringe of black hair around his bald head and a cheerful manner. He was even more cheerful I'd caught the shoplifters. The candy bar thieves, to my surprise, apologized to Ted and offered to pay for the candy if he wouldn't call the police. Ted agreed and let them go, but banned them from the store. The girl tried to convince us the bracelet fell into her purse. Neither Ted nor I bought this story. When she tried to run, I blocked the door until the cops showed up. She gave the policemen another tall tale about needing the bracelet for her mother who was in the hospital and wailed and cursed as they took her out.

"Honestly," Ted said. "Can you believe all that? She could've bought that bracelet and anything else she wanted in here. And those boys had money to pay for candy bars."

"They weren't your vitamin thieves, though."

"No, so you need to keep on the job."

◇◇◇

The vitamin thieves did not strike that afternoon. When my time was up at the Drug Palace, I decided to check on Taffy.

There are worse things to do than tail Taffinia O'Brien. I knew she lived on Parkland View Avenue, but she wasn't home. I knew she worked at the cosmetics counter in Myers, a large department store in Friendly Shopping Center, but she wasn't there, either. A coworker at the store said she thought Taffy was meeting friends at Parkland Center for lunch, so I circled around Parkland Center, where enterprising folks are remodeling the older stores downtown, and caught my first break of the day. Taffy came out of a dark building on the corner of Main and Meade. Since the Fury is well-known in town, I swung into the nearest parking spot and continued on foot. I was halfway down the block when Taffy whirled around and pointed an accusing finger.

"Are you following me?"

"Who isn't?"

"What's the deal, Randall?"

"Can't I just enjoy the view?"

The finger stabbed closer. "Charlie sent you, didn't he?"

"I'm working a case on this side of town and happened to see you." She looked as if she didn't believe me. "Why would Charlie send me?"

She shrugged. "Forget it. I was headed for Insteps for lunch. Join me?"

"It would be my pleasure."

Insteps is a tiny, trendy little café inside a remodeled train station. It has a shoe theme. Why shoes and not trains is something I can't figure out. We sat in the Pump Room on two high, cushioned stools. I helped Taffy take off her light yellow jacket. She was wearing a short green dress covered in sequins, so I got a great view as she crossed her legs. The dress looked too short and fancy for midday.

"Going someplace special?"

"No."

"Coming back from someplace special?"

She picked up the menu. "Maybe I like wearing this dress."

People on their way to illegal trysts tend to dress down. I tried to remember what was in the neighborhood and realized that dark building she'd come out of was Spider's Web, an exclusive nightclub that was open every other weekend. The Web catered to the snootier strata of Parkland society. I couldn't imagine the patrons lining up to hear "Ain't Misbehavin'."

"They take you on at the Web?"

A lovely rush of pink colored her cheeks, not quite the spectacular sunrise of Kary's, but a guilty rush. "What if they did?"

"Just curious."

"Don't you dare tell Charlie."

"Hey, what you do with your spare time is your business."

Our conversation paused when the waitress came for our orders. I decided on the Sling-back Special, and Taffy ordered a High Heel Highball. When the waitress left, Taffy said, "I'm not singing there yet. I had an audition."

"Did you dazzle them with 'Lovin' Sam the Sheik of Alabam'?"

Her glare almost reached Ellin intensity. "I sang my own songs."

"I didn't know you wrote songs."

"J.J. doesn't want to hear them. He says they're awful."

"You know J.J.'s musical tastes, like mine, stop round the late forties."

She tossed back her hair. "He won't even give me a chance. I love the old songs, but I've got all this other music in me, too. The Tempo's a great club, but I have my career to think of, you know."

As far as I knew, Taffy's job at Myers consisted of looking gorgeous as she stood behind glass cabinets full of outrageously priced beauty products. I knew her main ambition was to be a singer, but she doesn't have the annoying screeches and four octave trills of a modern pop star. Since her choices in town are limited, I couldn't blame her for trying something besides the Tempo.

"So I'm guessing Charlie doesn't like your new songs?"

"He wouldn't set foot in a club like the Web."

"I don't see why you have to keep it a secret. The Web isn't open that often, and the Hot Six doesn't play every night. You can do both."

"I don't want to hear Charlie gripe about it."

"Do you really care what he thinks?"

She hesitated before replying. "No."

Our drinks arrived. My Sling-Back Special was pretty good. Taffy took a sip of her High Heel Highball. Something else was bothering her, I could tell. "You two sounded really good on 'Sweet Man' the other night."

"Thanks. It would be even better if he'd agree to accompany me on my songs."

"Have you asked him?"

"Several times. He refuses to listen to anything but jazz. It's like he's got a mental block or something. Manny's done some good arrangements for me. Charlie could play them if he wanted to."

"Manny?"

"Manuel Estaban. My teacher."

Uh-ho. "What's he teaching you?"

I watched for another guilty blush, but Taffy's cheeks were blush-free. "Over at Parkland Community College they have a songwriting class. Manny says I have an excellent grasp of rhythm and lyrics. He says I'm wasting my talents doing nothing but traditional songs. He's all for experimenting."

I'll bet he is.

"Manny says music should be an expression of your heart. He loves my work."

Somehow I felt Manny would love Taffy's work even if she used only one note.

She spun an ice cube around with her finger. "Guess how many songs I've written."

"Twelve?"

"Twenty-six. And J.J. won't let me sing a single one."

I set my drink down. "Have you thought about writing a song that sounds more like the songs he likes? Kind of ease him into your other stuff?"

"But I like my music so much better. Why can't he bend a little?"

I didn't have an answer. I listen only to traditional jazz myself. There are a few classical pieces Kary plays that aren't bad, and the occasional rock tune from my past conjures up a memory or two, but I had to side with J.J. and Charlie. Of course, I hadn't heard any of Taffy's songs.

"When will you hear from the folks at the Web?"

"They're supposed to let me know something tomorrow."

"How about a little sample?"

She glanced around the restaurant. It wasn't crowded, and our table was off by itself by the window. "All right. I wrote this one yesterday. It's called 'My Unformed Wish.'"

The title should've warned me. Taffy kept her voice low, but I could still hear how painfully bad the song was. No tune. No particular rhythm. And the words flopped between teen angst and stream of consciousness:

> *"It isn't that. It isn't what you think.*
> *I tear at the walls of my existence to find a solace.*
> *Solace, what's that?*
> *Outside my window a moon that only I can see destroys*
>   *my visions."*

As she droned on, I kept an expression of polite interest. Good lord, what a waste of a perfectly good voice. Was this the same gal who could belt out "Some of These Days" and "All of Me"? Even my tie was getting soggy.

"How can I keep what lies beneath a secret?
The red walls surround me in a cocoon of unhappiness.
What is a wish that cannot be fulfilled?
That cannot be fulfilled."

It took me a moment to realize she'd finished. "Wow. What can I say?"

"You see what I mean, David? You see why this is so important to me?"

"Then I wish you the best of luck."

"Thanks." She shook her wrist so her bracelet watch slid around. "I've got to get back to work." She reached for her pocketbook.

I picked up the check. "It's my treat, please."

"Thank you." Before she left, she held up a warning finger. "Not one word of this to Charlie."

"Okay."

It was going to be several words.

Chapter Nine

"But now it's time to sleep."

I was half way to Parkland Community College when I realized this was Sunday afternoon and Manuel Estaban probably wasn't there. But as luck would have it, the college was having some sort of May celebration. There were people everywhere. I managed to find a parking spot, and a student pointed out Manuel Estaban. I'd hoped Mr. Estaban would be a gray-haired grandfatherly figure, but he was a tall dashing man in an expensive-looking suit. His glossy black hair was tied back in a ponytail. On most men, a ponytail looks silly, but on Estaban, the hairstyle accented his movie star cheekbones and profile. He was talking to a group of young women who giggled and hurried off as I approached.

"Manuel Estaban?"

"Yes. Good afternoon."

"Good afternoon," I said. "I'm looking around the campus, thinking of taking a few classes this summer."

He shook my hand. "I teach music appreciation and song-writing. Are you interested in music? We will be offering several courses next semester."

"Songwriting sounds interesting. How do you go about teaching someone how to write a song?"

"Ah, well, you must have a little talent in that direction, of course, but it is not difficult. A simple melody, some words from your heart." He spread his hands. "There. You have a song. In my classroom, I have a chart that shows you how everything connects. You can start with a tune, or with your lyrics. It is very simple."

Up to now, I was thinking the guy had dazzled Taffy with his good looks and expertise. Then he said something else.

"I am also available after class for private sessions."

Private sessions, eh? "Do many students take advantage of that?"

"A few of the more gifted."

"Seems like that would take a great deal of your time."

"Oh, no. It is a pleasure to nurture talent."

Is that what you call it? "Do you have any students who show special talent?"

His smile widened. "Indeed I do. There is one young lady in particular that I predict will go far. Not only does she have an exceptional voice, she has a soul that cries out to be heard. I have encouraged her to find an outlet for her talents. She hopes one of the local nightclubs will hire her to perform her songs."

Taffy, for certain. "That's a huge step."

"Yes, I am very proud of her."

"Are any of your other students making this kind of progress?"

"I have high hopes for all of them."

Okay, so maybe he was sincere. Maybe I was reading too much into his idea of "special talent." Maybe Charlie's future with Taffy was doomed. "Thanks for the information, Mr. Estaban."

He shook my hand again. "I hope to see you in one of my classes very soon. Will you stay for the celebration? There are refreshments, cold drinks."

"Thanks. I'm going to speak to a few more teachers."

"This is a fine community college. You will be happy here."

No, I'll be happy to get Charlie and Taffy back together, which was shaping up to be trickier than I thought.

◇◇◇

There was still no answer at Dahlia Three's. According to my information, she lived in Brooksboro, North Carolina, which was a full day's drive away. Still, it would be worth a shot. I decided to go by the house first and pick up a few things, but I almost had heart failure when I came up on the porch and found Kary crying.

"What's wrong?"

She wiped her face. "Jordan came and got Cam. They found Fred in the park. I'm afraid he's dead."

"Are you okay?" I never thought Fred meant anything to her other than the garrulous old nuisance he was to everybody.

"I feel so bad for Cam. You know how he feels about Fred."

"He'll be okay. You come in and sit down."

We were not alone for long. A police car drove up. Jordan gave me a wave as Camden got out. Kary hurried down the steps and took Camden's arm.

"Are you all right?"

"Yes. Jordan took Fred over to the funeral home for me. I had a talk about funeral arrangements."

"And funeral costs," I said. "I'm guessing Fred didn't have anything even closely resembling insurance."

"Nothing. Except the ring."

The one treasure Fred had saved was his wife's ring, which he'd insisted Camden give to Ellin.

"He had no family. Nothing." Camden looked distracted. "I need to find something for him to wear."

We went up to Fred's room. Besides the twin bed, plain wooden dresser, and a straight chair, there were pictures of the planets and articles on the space shuttle. A model of the *Enterprise* balanced on the dresser next to a stack of *Space Explorer* and *Discover* magazines. An attempt had been made to brighten the little room, but no amount of cheer could take away the stale air of defeat. Life had given up on Fred years ago.

Camden looked through the closet. "I wish I had something better than these old sweaters and things. Maybe one of the shirts I got for Christmas."

Since Fred in life was a wizened little troll, and Fred in death was probably even more shriveled, my clothes would be of no use. "We'll buy something."

"With what? I don't know how I'm going to pay for even the simplest casket." He sat down on the edge of the small bed. "Well, yes, I do."

I knew, too. "Folly Harper."

"Looks like I don't have a choice."

"At least she doesn't want you to summon a dead relative. She only wants a few lucky numbers. You could make those up."

Camden stared at the wall calendar. It was May, but Fred hadn't changed the picture since February. I wondered if Camden was thinking of the father he'd never known, if Fred had been any sort of substitute. This was highly unlikely. If anything, Fred had been the aimless cousin no one wanted to claim.

"You did all you could," I said. "He had a place to sleep, food, company if he wanted it. Hell, I hope you look after me when I get that destitute."

There was the ghost of a smile. "What do you think I'm doing now?" Even this faint smile faded. "Damn it, Randall, I should have seen this coming. I was so wrapped up in my own problems—"

"Don't start with that. Fred was sick and old, that's all there is to it. You took care of him way better than anyone else would. End of story."

He sighed. "Yeah. End of story." He glanced once more around the room, pausing for a long look at one photograph. I realized it was the only black and white picture in the room, a photograph of a spiral galaxy.

A pattern of black and white. "You did see it coming."

He stared at the photo a few more moments. "I suppose so." He got up and looked in the dresser drawers. We found a reasonably new shirt. I convinced Camden we could find a suit somewhere that would look like an Armani compared to anything Fred owned and finally pried him from the depressing little bedroom.

◇◇◇

We held a family council at the dinner table that evening. Rufus said he'd be glad to help out with funeral expenses, but there'd been a lot of rain this month and not much construction work. He couldn't contribute a lot in the way of money. Angie expressed sympathy, but shook her huge head.

"Cam, honey, I'm scraping the bottom this month. Three people still owe me for alteration jobs from April. I'll be lucky to have the rent."

"It's okay," he said. "You didn't really know Fred, and I'll admit he didn't have the sunniest personality. I've decided to take Folly Harper's offer. That way, I might have enough to do the right thing for Fred."

Rufus's brow was already low, but he managed to get it down a few more inches. "This Harper woman doesn't have any dead relatives libel to pop up in you, does she?"

"She wants me to tell her lucky numbers."

Kary reached across to pat his hand. "We know you don't like doing that kind of thing, Cam, but this doesn't look dangerous, does it?"

"No," he said, "and it's going to make Ellie deliriously happy."

Everyone sat back as if relieved. "That can't be a bad thing," Rufus said. "Do your stuff, get some dough, everybody's happy, and Fred's taken care of."

We had several visitors from the church that evening. I don't think Fred ever darkened the door of Victory Holiness, but word got around that a friend of Camden's had died, and that was a good enough excuse for church folks to descend bearing casseroles.

The smell of ham and cheese and the sight of carefully wrapped dishes made me think of my mother. Mom's a New Yorker of Italian descent. She must have seemed like an exotic hothouse flower growing in the pale wheat and endless corn of Elbert Falls, Minnesota. But her overwhelming good nature won over the cautious farmers and their wives. She'd made pies and cakes for all the church socials, and whenever there was a wedding or funeral, she was first in the door with her offering of food.

My dad loved her. If they quarreled, I never heard it. But he had an eye for the ladies. When I was older, Dad told me his secret.

"It's just sex, Davey. It doesn't mean anything. You know I love your mother. She's the one I come home to."

Made sense to me. I never heard Mom criticize him, so I figured it made sense to her, too. Several years and two wives later, I began to perceive a flaw in this theory. Women wanted commitment. They wanted honesty. That did not mean screwing around on the side. So I had changed my ways.

Rufus stood with a group of men in the backyard, most of them chewing and spitting. Angie was in the kitchen, helping the church ladies organize all the trays, baking dishes, and plastic containers of food. I watched Kary as she put her arm around Camden's shoulder and said comforting things. If she wasn't an angel, she was the next best thing.

The house full of well-meaning strangers carrying food brought back a lot of memories I wanted to forget, but Camden was having a harder time. It took my thick head a while to realize he probably hadn't gone through this delightful little ritual before. His foster parents had died while he was out traveling the country. His birth mother was still alive, but lived in Richmond. He didn't know anything about his father. This was the first close relative to die—if he thought of Fred as a relative. Fred was something, though, and Camden had taken care of him. When the women moved into the island to admire the array of flowers one of the neighbors had sent, I found Camden at the back window looking out as if he were on a spaceship and his home planet had exploded.

I stood beside him. "Pretty weird, huh?"

"I don't understand. Things are backwards. People keep coming up, telling me how sorry they are Fred's gone, and I have to make them feel better. They want me to tell the story over and over, how sick he was, how the police found him."

"Yep, they want all the gory details."

He gave me a look full of compassion. "It must have been hell for you, Randall."

"Still is, pal. Come on. Enough comforting." I steered him out the back door. "Kary's doing a great job with the guests. Let's take a walk."

He didn't argue. We walked down the sidewalk. Neither of us said anything for a long while until Camden asked how my cases were coming along.

"Already found George Mark McMillan. Case solved."

"That didn't take long."

"Hey, I'm good. Want me to get rid of this telekinesis for you?"

"Oh, that. Sure. Why not?"

We reached the corner of Grace. To the right up Park Street past Temple would take us to Food Row, which was noisy and full of traffic, so we turned left to take the quiet route around the block. "Are you going to tell Ellin?" I asked.

"I keep hoping it will go away."

"Well, all I have to do now is get Charlie and Taffy back together."

"I didn't think that was a problem."

"I thought it was their usual quarrel, too, but there's a Spaniard in the works."

"You're going to have to explain that."

"It'll take at least another block."

We walked the rest of the way down Park Street, turned left again and started up Willow, a street similar to Grace, but with fewer trees. No willows, though.

"I followed Taffy today and found her coming out of the Spider's Web nightclub on Main and Meade," I said. "She'd had an audition there. She sang one of her songs for me, and it's a whole lot worse than I imagined. Seems she's taking a songwriting course at PCC. The instructor's a dashing Latino who thinks Taffy has special talent. You can take it from there."

"Does Charlie know this?"

"Not yet."

"He's going to explode."

"Probably." We sidestepped three trashcans left on the walk. "It would be different if Taffy's songs were good."

"You heard only one. Maybe the others aren't so bad."

"Even if they're all horrible—and I'm pretty sure they are—he could pretend to like them. Hell, I've made all sorts of sacrifices for women. So have you."

"Yes, but there's a limit. You know how Ellie is about having me as a permanent member of the PSN team. That's one thing I won't do."

We made the next left onto Meadow Street, which always makes me wonder if there really was once a meadow in the neighborhood. There are a lot of empty houses on Meadow, grass and vines reclaiming the land. Maybe one day, it'll be a meadow again.

I pointed out a little fact to Camden. "You're going to help Folly Harper."

"That's different."

"That's one step closer to TV fame."

"No, it's not."

"Welcome to our newest PSN program, 'Camden's Corner.' No psychic request denied. No question too stupid."

He punched my arm. "Shut up."

I punched him back. "You shut up."

We made the last left turn back onto Grace. Most of church ladies' cars were gone. We went up the front steps. Camden sat down in the porch swing. I took one of the rocking chairs.

"Thanks," he said.

"No problem."

Moths danced and bumped against the porch lights, and high in one corner, a fat gray spider worked on her web. Camden watched the spider for a while and then looked off toward the park where tomorrow Oscar would sit in his regular spot and wonder where his sparring partner was. Then he looked out on Grace Street, the light from the street lamps gleaming through the leaves of the oak trees. Change. Upheaval. He didn't like it, but nobody could control it. We all had to deal with it sooner or later.

Chapter Ten

"That's all the time you've got."

Early Monday morning, I finally got in touch with the third Dahlia. She was indeed Viola's cousin, and she apologized for being so hard to reach.

"I've been in Europe for three weeks and returned home yesterday. The police were here all day about Viola. I don't know what I could tell you that I haven't told them already. I have every confidence they can find her murderer, so I will not require your services, although I thank you for the offer."

There was a stiffness in her tone that told me she considered me an ambulance chaser. "Mrs. Mitchell, I realize this is a personal matter, but my friend found your cousin, and I'd like to help solve this crime."

"Then you'll do it on your own time and pay your own expenses. I can't afford to hire you, and quite frankly, I don't know what I could tell you that would be of any use. Viola and I were not close. She spent an inordinate amount of time with amateur theatricals, and the one play I saw was not to my taste at all. I'm afraid that choosing to associate with people of such loose morals was her undoing."

Dahlia appeared to be as old-fashioned as her name. "Was that the last time you saw her?"

"Yes, and I haven't time to answer any more of your impertinent questions. Good day."

With a decisive click, she hung up. No cell phone for Dahlia. Probably had one of those wooden boxes hanging on the wall.

Camden came to my door. "No luck, huh?"

"She was not impressed by my charm or my professionalism and believes Viola's theatrical career led her astray. What do you know about *Arsenic and Old Lace*? Is it filled with sex and nudity?"

"I'm not familiar with the play, but the Little Theater wouldn't do anything x-rated."

"Dahlia was scandalized. Maybe one of the actresses showed an ankle. Damn, I really wanted to solve this case."

Camden came in and sat down in the chair I have for clients. "I'll hire you."

"Seriously?"

"Except for one uninterested cousin, Viola doesn't have any family. I can relate. Despite all her pets, there was a great deal of loneliness in her house. And she took in all those animals. How could you not like someone who rescues animals?"

"Can you afford to pay my extravagant fee?"

"Let's see. I could waive your rent until you solve the mystery."

"That might not encourage me to work very hard."

"Except you owe me for two months already, so get busy."

I reached across the desk to shake his hand. "Deal."

He had a sudden worried look. "Speaking of animals, who's looking after Viola's pets now? I hope they weren't taken to the pound."

I took out my phone. "An excellent reason to call Jordan."

Jordan sounded gruffer than usual. "We are in charge of this case, Randall. You don't have a dog in this fight."

"Odd you should mention animals. Camden wants to know if anyone's taking care of Viola's pets."

There was a brief pause, and I imaged the noise I heard was steam hissing from Jordan's ears. "You win, Randall. That's the flimsiest excuse ever."

"Oh, and he's hired me to find Viola's killer."

"Who's hired you? Cam? Now you're really pushing it. Let me have a word with him."

I handed my phone to Camden. "You might want to hold this away from your ear."

Camden listened, occasionally saying things like, "Yes, I did," and "No, it was my idea," and "I promise he won't get in the way," which we all knew was a big fat lie.

"Ask him if we can have another look in her house," I said.

"Could we have another look in Viola's house? I might be able to pick up some more clues." He listened. "There was a 'sold' sign at the house. What did the realtor say? And what about the animals? Oh, okay, thanks. No, we'll be careful, I promise. You want to talk to Randall?" He glanced at me and shook his head. "Yeah, I'll tell him. Maybe not in those words, exactly." He returned my phone. "Jordan said the neighbor is taking care of the pets, and that you are a pain in the ass."

"That makes it official. I'm on the case. What about the house?"

"The buyer's still interested in it, even though the realtor explained about the murder."

"Then we need to have another look before they move in and spread their vibes all over."

"Let me call Folly Harper and see what I can do for her and get that out of the way."

Camden called Folly Harper and asked her to come over whenever it was convenient. She was on the doorstep before we'd finished breakfast. She wasn't so excited that she forgot to offer her sympathies. Being a true Southern woman, she had to hear all the details, but once this was taken care of, she was ready to get down to business.

"I can't tell you how pleased I am you've reconsidered. So what do we do? How does this work?" She was fluttering around like a peach-colored hen.

Camden drank the last of his tea and suggested they go out to the porch. I had funeral ham biscuits and a handful of potato chips to eat, so I brought my plate with me to the porch.

Camden offered Mrs. Harper a seat in one of the rocking chairs and sat down on the porch swing. "It's really very simple, Mrs. Harper. I'll hold your hand a few minutes, and we'll see what comes up. Now, you're specifically looking for some numbers?"

"Yes, dear. Very important numbers."

"Okay."

He took her plump little hand and was off somewhere beyond, his blue eyes zeroing in on whatever it is he sees. After a while, he came back. "I see thirty-six, eighteen, twenty, and two. Do any of those mean anything to you?"

Folly Harper scrabbled in her purse for pencil and paper. "Thirty-six, eighteen, twenty, and two. This is wonderful! And you were so fast! Let me write those down. Did you see any others?"

Another long moment of silence. "Just those."

I knew he wasn't lying, but it would be ridiculously simple to make up a string of numbers, take the money and run. Folly Harper would have believed anything he told her.

She beamed at him. "That's wonderful. I can't tell you how help-ful this will be! But we didn't settle on a price. How many readings would you be willing to give me for, say, five hundred dollars?"

Five hundred bucks! As many as you want.

Camden looked as surprised as I was. "That's way too much—"

"Now, now, dear, don't be modest. Why don't we start with five hundred, and if these numbers are as good as I'm sure they are, we'll go up from there?"

"Mrs. Harper—"

"Folly, dear. You're the first person to take me seriously about this, and I appreciate it."

Camden tried one more time. "I take everyone's request seriously."

"I'm sure you do." Her windswept hair leaned toward him, her hand on his arm. "Dear, I know you and Ellin are getting married, and newlyweds need lots of things. Let's not argue about money. Here's five hundred. Take it." She practically slapped the bills into his hand.

Camden gulped. "Thank you."

"No, no, thank you, dear. I can't wait to get home and try out my numbers."

I waited until she had driven off before making any comment. "Okay, I give up. What is she doing with those numbers?"

He was still sitting in the swing with the money in his hand. "I don't know. I thought she might be working out a horoscope or something."

"Playing the lottery?"

"No. She should never gamble, by the way. Her luck is terrible."

"So you didn't sense anything illegal?"

"She likes to have her lucky numbers."

I indicated the pile of bills in his hand. "Looks like you've got a few lucky numbers there, yourself."

"I have to admit it'll help." He stood up and put the money in his pocket. "On our way to Viola's, let's stop by the shopping center."

◇◇◇

As it turned out, Suit City had a suit a customer ordered and never picked up. We checked on it and decided it would do for Fred, and the price was right. Then I took Camden by the funeral home where he made the final arrangements, including financing.

I thought we might have to break into Viola's house, but as luck would have it, we arrived the same time the neighbor came over to feed the animals. I explained that I'd been hired to find Viola's killer and needed another look around.

"That's good news," she said. "I hate to think of someone like that still out there. Everyone in the neighborhood's been jumpy since Viola was found."

She took care of the birds while the cats told Camden God knows what. I made a careful search of the living room, finding only pet memorabilia. Camden didn't want to go back to the basement, so I checked it out. Still nothing but cold stone and dirt. I returned to Viola's pink bedroom. The books on her nightstand were all biographies of famous actors and actresses and histories of the theater, specifically musicals. In her bureau drawers, I found what women usually keep: undergarments, jewelry, scarves, and neatly folded sweaters. In the closet, her dresses and suits were arranged according to color, her shoes in boxes with labels. But also in the closet I discovered large stacks of scrapbooks, Viola's entire theatrical career, every newspaper article, every picture, every program, every ticket, and every poster organized by date, starting in the late fifties, when she had the role of Julie Jordan in *Carousel*. I put the scrapbooks on the bed and went through them until I found the latest one. Here were the roles I'd seen mentioned on the theater webpage—Mother Superior, Aunt Eller, and even a newspaper account of the casting of *My Fair Lady*, with "perennial favorite Viola Mitchell has been cast as Henry Higgins' mother" underlined in red ink and carefully pasted into the book.

Camden came to the door. One of the cats ran in and jumped on the bed. "Find anything?"

I moved the cat out of the way. "Viola's scrapbooks. Looks like she saved all her programs and publicity, but I don't see anything about *Arsenic and Old Lace*. There are two blank pages right before her *My Fair Lady* pages, so maybe something was here and taken out. That was the play before this musical, right?"

"Yes."

"As meticulous as Viola was, she would've saved the program, at least."

"Maybe she hadn't had time to put that in."

"Maybe. You have any luck?"

"No, the cats are thinking only of food, there's no way to tell what the birds are thinking, the lizard's asleep, and the neighbor's ready to lock up."

We looked around Viola's room one last time in the hopes of finding anything she might have saved from *Arsenic and Old Lace*, but found nothing. I put the scrapbooks back up in the closet.

"Someone from the theater might like these. There's a lot of history in them."

"I didn't see any pictures of friends or relatives anywhere," Camden said. "Her whole life is in those books."

"Don't you find all this pink a little odd? It reminds me of a teenage girl's room. And check out the stuff lined up on her dressing table. There must be two dozen lipsticks, perfumes, powders."

"Any BeautiQueen?"

"All pink, no peach."

Camden picked up a bottle of cream labeled "Eternal Loveliness." "Maybe Viola was trying to recapture her youth. Women think they have to look younger." He held the bottle a little longer. "She hated growing old. She hated playing the mother or the school teacher. She wanted the glamorous roles, like the ones she'd had before. Maggie in *Cat on a Hot Tin Roof*, or Maria in *Sound of Music*."

"You're getting all this from a bottle?"

"Pretty much." He picked up a jar labeled "Turn Back the Clock," and then a container of "Everlasting Radiance." After a few minutes, he said, "Yep. They're all tuned to that same frequency."

None of this helped my case. "All that proves is Viola, like millions of women, didn't like getting old."

◇◇◇

As we got in the car, I wondered if Taffy had heard from the Spider's Web. "Care to take a side trip to Myers? I want to see if Taffy got the job."

Taffy was at the cosmetic counter in Myers, earnestly assuring a skeptical woman about the latest makeup trends. When she saw us, she waved us over.

"Randall, Cam, tell Mrs. Hoover how good she looks in April Rose and Velvet Magic."

Since I didn't know what Mrs. Hoover looked like without the alien pink cheeks and too much eyeliner, it was hard to judge. Camden thought of a tactful answer.

"That's a very complimentary shade."

Mrs. Hoover preened for a while in one of the counter mirrors and must have been satisfied with what she saw. "I'll take it."

Taffy took her money and put her purchases in a bag. "Thank you." As soon as Mrs. Hoover left, she beamed. "I got the job!"

"That's great, congratulations," I said.

She started closing lids on little round containers. Mrs. Hoover must have tried the entire line of exotic rouges. "Cam, you mustn't tell Charlie, but I'm performing at the Spider's Web Saturday night."

"Don't you think Charlie would like to know?"

"He'll only cause a fuss. If it isn't jazz, he's not interested." One of the containers slipped. Camden caught it as it skittered across the counter.

"You're not leaving the group, are you?"

"I haven't decided what I want to do. It's important for me to branch out and try new things." She took the container. "Thanks. Do you think Ellin would be interested in this color? It's Sweetheart Pink."

"Ellie and I are having a little difference of opinion right now."

"It can't possibly be as different as me and Charlie."

Not unless Charlie is making the piano play by itself. I picked up one of the little tubes of lipstick. It was called Windswept Coral. I had no idea the wind swept underwater. "Taffy, what do you know about BeautiQueen?"

"We don't carry it. You have to buy it at one of their parties."

"But so far as quality how does it compare with the brands you have here?"

She shrugged. "It's all right. I would say their skin care products are very good. That's what they're known for mainly. That and the distinctive peach color."

A woman came up to the counter. Her makeup had such a high gloss finish, she glowed like a pearl. "Do you have any High Five Fingernail Polish?"

"Yes, ma'am. I'll show you." Taffy gave us a little wave. "Gotta get back to work, fellas. Remember, the gig at the Web is a secret."

We went back to the car. "Lunch at Baxter's?"

Camden hesitated. "We've got all that food at home."

"But we don't have any Baxter's barbecue."

◇◇◇

Baxter's is an ordinary little brick building with plain wooden chairs and tables, a few plastic booths, paper napkins, and plastic forks and knives. You'd never guess this restaurant served the world's best melt in your mouth barbecue. We settled into our favorite booth and ordered two lunch specials.

Camden reached for the sugar packets. "You going to tell Charlie about Taffy's new job?"

"I'm going to try to convince him to come to the show. I think if Taffy sees him there, she'll be happy he made the effort."

"What if it throws her off?"

"I'm pretty sure this is too important to her. If he's sitting there, smiling, offering support, then my work will be done."

"And if she tries to behead him with the mike stand?"

"Then I'll step in for the rescue."

Our order came. We spent the next few minutes in barbecue heaven.

Camden wiped barbecue sauce off his mouth and chin. "Don't let me go home without a paper for Fred." He stopped. "Oh, man. I can't believe I just said that."

"It's okay."

He pushed the rest of his lunch aside. "I keep thinking it's some sort of joke. I'll get home and Fred'll be there, cranky as ever. It's like a test. Let's see how you react to someone's death. Okay, you passed. We were only kidding. He's really alive. Here he is."

"It can be pretty unreal."

"I miss him, Randall. I know he grumbled a lot and was set in his ways, but you knew Fred was going to be Fred, no matter what. He was part of the family. Part of my family."

His carefully constructed family that kept changing. "Want me to find you another old codger?"

I thought my flippancy might be too much, but he gave a slight grin. "You'll do for now."

Our waitress paused at the booth, a pitcher of iced tea in her hand. "Something wrong with the order, Cam? You're usually ready for seconds by now."

"No, it's fine, thanks." He handed her the tray. "Could you wrap it up for me? I'll take it home."

"Sure thing. More tea?"

"Yes, thanks."

She filled our tea glasses, took the tray, and left.

I got up. "I'll get a paper anyway. I want to check the sports page."

Outside Baxter's was a row of newspaper machines featuring the *Parkland Herald*, as well as smaller papers like the *Masonville Tribune* and the *Celosia News*. The headline in the *Tribune* declared "Council Locked on Pork Issue," which sounded kind of messy. "Local Man Grows Big Tomatoes" was the lead story in the *Celosia News*. But the headline that caught my eye was in the *Herald*: "Parkland Man Found Dead in Hotel." The name George Mark McMillan leaped off the page. I quickly scanned the article, my heart somewhere around my shoes. McMillan had been found dead at the Green Palms Hotel. The official report was suicide.

Damn.

I hurried back inside, sat down in the booth, and folded back the page. "Look at this."

Camden read the article, his eyes growing wide. "Good lord."

"Apparently, I wasn't the only one looking for George."

"It says the police believe he shot himself."

"And how likely is that? Steal a big pile of cash and then kill yourself?"

"We need to let Folly know right away."

I called Mrs. Harper, hoping to hell she didn't have anything to do with this. But then, wouldn't Camden have picked up on it? Maybe not. His brain was concerned with the wedding, the show, this telekinesis thing. Maybe she should have given some of those lucky numbers to George.

She sounded properly shocked. "Oh, my God. Mr. Randall, what on earth is going on?"

"That's what I'd like to know. You said you left a message for George. Did he ever get back to you?"

"Yes, he did. I told him I was sadly disappointed in his behavior and I expected him to come home with the full amount he'd stolen, that he couldn't get away with it, and I was willing to give him a second chance. He seemed very surprised I'd been able to find him, which was what I'd wanted."

"What did he say?"

"He sounded very contrite. He said he never meant to cause me such anxiety. He still had all the money, and he said it wasn't what I thought, at all. He was going to explain everything when he got back." She choked on a sob. "I can't believe he's dead."

"Do you want me to find out more about this?"

"Oh, my, could you? Yes, by all means. I want you to find out exactly what happened. Please go to Clearwater. I'll reimburse you for your travel expenses."

I closed my cell phone. "George called her and apologized and said he was going to explain when he got back to Parkland. She wants me to investigate. We've got to put Viola's case on hold for a while. Are you going to be okay with the funeral and everything?"

"I can handle it."

We went home, I packed an overnight bag, went to the airport, and caught the first available flight to Clearwater.

Chapter Eleven

"How kind of you to let me come."

To get to Clearwater from Parkland, I had to fly to Tampa by way of Atlanta and then drive twenty miles. I got to Clearwater around five thirty. The hotel clerk at the Green Palms wasn't the man I'd spoken to on the phone, but a perky little redhead, who was very forthcoming in more ways than one.

She leaned over the desk, giving me an unobstructed view of cleavage. "I've never seen such excitement. There was all this commotion, and reporters everywhere and people wanting to check out, like they thought they'd be next. It was real exciting."

"How did he die?"

"It was really gross. He shot himself. I don't think there was much left of him. The newspaper printed these pictures." She pulled a brightly colored tabloid from under the desk. "See?"

"Shotgun Suicide," the lurid headline read. The story inside didn't add much to the existing facts. There were pictures of George before and after. More gore than I cared to look at.

"Do you remember Mr. McMillan? Did you ever speak with him?"

"Oh, I remember him," she said. "He had the worst pickup lines I've ever heard. One time he even stroked his moustache like some villain in an old movie and said, 'May I get you drunk, my fine young thing?' And he kept going on and on about this beauty cream he was inventing that would keep women from ever having wrinkles again. What a character."

"Did he have any visitors? Anybody ask about him?"

"A woman called and asked to leave a message."

That would've been Folly Harper.

The clerk rearranged her bosom in case it had escaped my notice. "And one time there was this man he was talking to."

"Did either of them seem angry or upset?"

"No, just talking. They acted like they were old friends. I thought they might even be brothers. They were going fishing. Then Mr. McMillan came over to the desk to say something stupid to me." She batted her eyes. "I'll bet you don't ever say anything stupid."

"Oh, you wouldn't believe how stupid I've been." I glanced at the tabloid again. Another article about a dog that channeled Elvis made me remember George's doberman. "You've been very helpful, thank you." Leaving the clerk with her breasts intact, I stopped by Happy Tails to inquire about Danger.

◇◇◇

The waiting room at Happy Tails looked like finals for the Westminster Dog Show, one of every breed yapping, whining, or quivering in their carriers, a pug, a beagle, a poodle, even a Great Dane sitting majestically in the corner.

I had to raise my voice so the receptionist could hear me over the racket. "I'm a friend of Mr. McMillan's. I wanted to check on Danger. Has anyone come for his dog?"

"I'm sure someone did." She checked her computer. "Yes, his cousin, Mrs. Lucy Warner, picked up Danger yesterday. Terrible thing to happen. The world today. People are crazy, you know?"

A cousin? "Well, that's a relief. Thanks very much." And where might she be? "Did she say she was taking Danger back to Kansas with her?"

"No, she said something about North Carolina."

"Oh, yes. I keep forgetting she moved. Thanks."

On my way out, I sidestepped a basset hound and a fuzzy terrier that made a lunge for my ankle. So George had a relative in NC. That made things easier. As for the man he met at the hotel, his fishing buddy, I'd check and see if George did have a brother. If so, why didn't the brother ID George and claim his dog?

◇◇◇

The first thing I did when I got back to my hotel room was call Folly to ask about George's family. She told me George was an only child, and she didn't know any cousins, but she thought there might be a relative living in Parkland. I hoped this relative was Lucy Warner, as it would make my investigation a whole lot simpler. I told her I was still gathering information and would give her a complete report when I returned. Later that night, as I watched the news, I found out a few more details. George McMillan had been alone at the time of the shooting, and the lower part of his head was missing. His hands had been badly burned, a result, the report said, of the gun exploding as he shot himself. Damn, what a cheery little detail. I wondered if George really meant to make such a mess, if he really meant to commit suicide, or if there might be something missing in this case besides his chin.

George's body, personal effects, and his SUV had been claimed by Lucy Warner. The police were satisfied that this had been a suicide. Florida wasn't my territory, and I didn't have a Jordan Finley on the Tampa police force to grudgingly let me snoop around. At the moment, there was nothing else for me to do except go home.

◇◇◇

The early flight out of Tampa was delayed, so I didn't get back to Parkland until after three on Tuesday. I'd missed Fred's funeral and Viola's memorial service.

Kary and Camden were sitting on the porch. The yellow signs the funeral home had put in the street with "Slow – Funeral" and "Thank You" had been taken away, but the wreath of white flowers was still on the door. Kary was in a rocking chair, and Camden sat in his usual place in the porch swing. They looked weary but calm, as if they'd run a long way together and finally crossed the finish line. I'd often thought they could be sister and brother. That's how they felt about each other.

Kary looked perfect, as always, in a black dress with little lacy sleeves, her hair up in a sleek bun. One hour is Camden's limit for neatness. His jacket and shoes were off, his tie undone, shirtsleeves rolled up. He was unraveling even as we spoke.

I sat down in another rocking chair. "Sorry I missed the funeral."

"It was the perfect service for Fred," Kary said. "All of his friends from the park showed up, even Oscar. Pastor Mark took care of everything. Our church sent flowers, and Mimosa played hymns I think Fred would've liked. 'The Old Rugged Cross.' 'Abide With Me.'"

Camden looked out across the front lawn, past the trees, and way beyond. "Before I found Grace Street, when I was wandering aimlessly across America, trying to make sense of this talent of mine, I often told myself I wanted a home and a family. I didn't care where or what kind, but I was going to stay in one place and always have them around." His gaze came back to me. "Doesn't work that way, does it?"

"Nope." I had no problem relating to this. "I'm afraid not."

He pushed his hair out of his eyes. "I want everything to stay the way it is. That's selfish. I know it is." He rubbed his face tiredly. "Too many things changing too fast."

We sat for a while in silence, listening to the birds in the trees, the faint hum of traffic from Food Row, the slight creak of the porch swing. Kary reached up to undo her hair. "What did you find out about George?"

"Looks like he really did try to swallow a shotgun. There's a relative nearby I'm going to talk to. Did you get a chance to talk to Millicent?"

"She came to Viola's memorial service, and I got to speak to her for a few minutes. She said Viola didn't have an enemy in the world."

"She had at least one. No big blowouts back stage? No one angry that she got the part in *My Fair Lady*?"

She shook her head, and that glorious hair spilled over her shoulders. "Not that Millicent could recall. I'm not sure she's going to be a reliable source. She told me the same story three times about how she and Viola got rave reviews for their performance in *The Cherry Orchard* years ago."

"When was the last time she saw Viola?"

"She was the one who gave Viola a ride home Wednesday night after rehearsal, and I did overhear that, as we suspected, there was poison in the wine."

"A gift from a friend."

"Maybe the friend didn't know it was poisoned."

"There still isn't a motive." And what was the motive behind George McMillan's death? I took out my phone. "I need to call Folly and tell her the grim news."

Camden took a deep breath. "I'm going to clean out Fred's room." He started to get out of the swing, but Kary stood and motioned him to sit back down. "I'll take care of it, Cam."

Not fifteen minutes after I called Folly, her peach-colored Cadillac screeched to a halt in our driveway. Folly hopped out of her car. As she came around in front, it began to roll toward her. In her agitation, she must have forgotten to put it in park.

I started down the steps. "Hey, look out!"

The car stopped just shy of grazing her leg. She did a little side step and stared at the Cadillac as if it were a stray dog trying to sniff up her skirt. I glanced at Camden. His eyes were on the car, his jaw set.

"One second, Folly." I went out to her car. As I thought, it was in neutral and quivering like a racehorse ready for the starting gun. I put it in park, turned it off, and saw Camden relax his grip on the porch railing.

"Is something wrong with my car?" Folly asked when I returned to the porch.

"You forgot to put it in park. It's okay now. Come have a seat. There's bad news about George's death."

She sat down in one of the rocking chairs and looked up at me anxiously.

"Folly, it looks like he committed suicide." As I told her the details, her peach complexion slowly drained to white. She reached into her purse and brought out a letter.

"Mr. Randall, this came for me today, from George. I didn't want to read it by myself. Would you mind?"

I took the letter, opened it, and took out one sheet of paper. A quick glance told me this was a suicide note. "Do you want me to read it out loud?" She nodded. "'Dear Folly, by the time you receive this, I'll be dead. I can't bear the shame of what I've done. I took our formula for the new skin cream and planned to sell it to Perfecto Face.'"

Here, Folly gave a little gasp.

"'But at the last moment, I couldn't go through with it. I can't come back to BeautiQueen and to our partnership, not after my traitorous actions. You'll never be able to trust me again. I can't even trust myself. It's better this way. Your money is safely back in our account. Forgive me. George.'"

I folded the letter and put it back in the envelope. "I'm really sorry, Folly."

She took a peach-colored handkerchief from her purse and wiped her eyes. "Selling our formula to the competition is a terrible thing, but not terrible enough to die for. I wish he'd come home. I would've forgiven him." She fixed me with an intense stare. "I don't believe George was the type of person who would kill himself. I want you to continue the investigation. I want you to find out what really happened to him."

"The Tampa police told me his cousin Lucy Warner identified the body. Could she be the relative in town?"

"I suppose so. I never met any of George's family." She dug into her purse. "I want you to find out who killed George."

I was beginning to wonder how dangerous the cosmetics business could be. "Would someone murder George for this formula?"

"Entirely possible. You have no idea what women will pay for younger, smoother skin." She wrote another check and handed it to me. "Up until he stole that money, he was a good employee and, as I've said, like a son to me. Please find out all you can."

She then turned her sorrowful face to Camden and held out her hand. "I need some very lucky numbers today, Cam."

He took her hand. In a few moments, he said, "Twenty-eight, six, fifteen, three, and sixty-two."

"Thank you so much, dear."

He patted her hand. "Let me get you a drink. Would you like iced tea? Coke?"

She dabbed her eyes. "Tea would be fine."

He went into the house. Folly wiped more tears away. "David, I suppose I should call this Lucy Warner and offer to help. I feel terrible about this. Maybe if I hadn't made such a fuss about George taking the money, this never would've happened."

"Don't start talking like that," I said. "I'm going to find out what's going on."

"What can I do to help?"

"I'd like to visit your company and talk to George's coworkers."

"How about nine tomorrow? Everyone will be there."

"That's fine. And let me talk to Lucy Warner first and see if she has any more information about what happened to George."

Camden brought her a glass of tea, and they sat for a while, sympathizing with each other over their recent losses. After Folly left, I went to my office and accessed my phone directory. When Lucy Warner answered the phone, her voice sounded hoarse, as if she had been crying.

"Yes? Who's calling, please?"

"Mrs. Warner, my name is David Randall, and I've been hired by Folly Harper to investigate the death of your cousin, George MacMillan. I realize this might not be a good time. My sympathies on your loss."

"Thank you. How very kind of Folly, but there's really nothing to investigate."

"I'd still like to talk with you."

"All right. I live on Marshall Street. Four ninety-four. If you'd like to come now, I could spare a few minutes."

Wait—what? Four ninety-four Marshall Street? That was

Viola's address. "Excuse me, Mrs. Warner, did you just move into that house?"

"How in the world did you know that?"

"I knew the woman who lived there."

"Tragic, wasn't it? I suppose some people might be afraid to move into a house where the owner had been murdered, but I don't have that kind of imagination. The house is exactly what I've been looking for, and I love the neighborhood."

"If you don't mind me asking, do you know what happened to Mrs. Mitchell's pets?"

"Oh, I decided to keep them. I love animals. They all get along extremely well with George's dog, even the lizard. Come on now, if you like."

I thanked her and went back to the porch. Cindy had joined Camden on the swing, probably offering her condolences. "How's this for an odd coincidence? Lucy Warner bought Viola's house and is looking after all her animals."

Camden stopped swinging. "That's really odd. Does she know what happened to Viola?"

"Doesn't seem to bother her. Oh, by the way, nice trick with the car. You're improving."

He looked depressed. "Improving. Do you know how much effort it took to hold that car? None."

"Great. Soon you'll be able to leap tall buildings in a single bound."

He slumped in the swing. "I've been thinking about it all day. I'm going to have to tell Ellie the wedding's off."

"Okay. Who's going to pay for your funeral?"

"If I knew what was going to happen next, maybe I could manage, but this talent is so unpredictable."

"What's the worst thing that could happen? You grow a big head and an extra finger? Come on! You've managed so far, haven't you?"

He gave me the Deep Look. "You want to marry Kary, and she wants lots of children. Have you decided how you're going to manage?"

He had me there. Despite having made my peace with Lindsey, I could still feel the tightness in my throat, the raw ache, the hole in my life that would never be filled. "I'll cross that bridge when I come to it. Tell Ellin what's going on. She'll be thrilled to have psychic children."

Camden shook his head. "An entire family of psychics, except for Mom? I don't think she'll be thrilled at all." He pushed his hair out of his eyes. "She's coming by in a little while. I'll have to tell her something."

"Escape with me to Viola's house."

"I appreciate the offer, but I can't put this off too much longer. And some people from the church called and said they wanted to visit. They're on their way."

"How am I going to know what the cats are saying? They might have already solved the murder. I hear cats can do that, right, Cindy? Have you figured it out?" The cat looked at me intently. "What's she saying now?"

"'Who are you?'"

"Seriously."

"She saying you're on your own."

Chapter Twelve

"Just you wait!"

At Viola's house, I parked in the driveway behind a light blue minivan. I walked up the short paved walk to the front door of the small brick house. I rang the doorbell. Deep barks from inside told me Danger was on the job. Lucy Warner came to the door. She looked like any one of a million middle-aged women—short dark curly hair streaked with gray, a yellow tee shirt with a collar and matching slacks, glasses, and one of those grandchild necklaces, the kind with little photos of the kids. She reminded me of my high school tennis coach, a square-shaped woman with wide shoulders and sturdy legs. She had on a thick layer of the famous peach BeautiQueen makeup.

"Yes?"

"Mrs. Lucy Warner?" I showed her my ID. "I'm David Randall. We spoke on the phone a few minutes ago. I wanted to ask you a few more questions about George McMillan, if you don't mind."

"Yes, of course. Come in."

The place still reeked of animals. The birds all squawked and whistled from their cages. The cats wound about the well-chewed furniture. The loud deep barks continued to echo from another room.

"I keep Danger in the kitchen," Lucy Warner said. "He's still very nervous. He's usually a good dog, but this whole thing has upset him dreadfully. Have a seat."

I looked to see if there was a spot not covered in pet hair and decided on a chair near the love seat occupied by the other cats. A small round table next to the chair held a collection of pet photos and an ashtray shaped like a bone. Another look at her necklace, and I could see the little photos were of dogs and cats, not kids. "You're certainly the animal lover, Mrs. Warner, to take on all these pets."

"You probably think I'm a little crazy, but the fact that the former owner had all these pets was a big selling point for me." She sat down on the sofa and was immediately engulfed by the cats. "I came right away when I heard about George. I knew no one would think of Danger, and the poor thing might be taken to the pound if she wasn't claimed." She reached into the lizard's cage, picked it up and set it on her shoulder where it drooped lethargically. "A terrible thing, simply terrible."

I couldn't tell if she meant George's suicide or the abandoned dog.

"Folly Harper is convinced George was murdered. Did he have any enemies? Anyone who would have a grudge against him? Did he owe anyone money?"

Another cat decided my leg would make an excellent scratching post.

Mrs. Warner shook her finger at the cat. "Bootsy, stop that." The cat looked insulted and moved away. "No, I'm afraid I don't know much about George at all." She coughed. "Excuse me, please. I think I'm allergic to something."

Can't imagine what. I could feel animal hairs clogging my pores.

Lucy Warner rearranged the lizard. "He was my second cousin. I know he worked for that crazy woman, selling cosmetics of all things. Folly Harper doesn't make a move unless she's consulted her lucky numbers. From what I hear, she's involved in some very strange things."

"What do you mean, strange?"

She stroked the nearest cat. "Alpha-hydroxy."

For a minute, I thought she was speaking a bizarre cat language to the two in her lap. "Alpha what?"

"Everyone knows that lipids are the only way to go. Alpha hydroxy can be very damaging to the skin, especially in the summer."

Now I understood. "You're talking about cosmetics."

She looked at me as if I'd dropped a half-eaten mole on the carpet. "Didn't I just say Folly Harper was crazy? Still, I shouldn't complain. George gets me lots of free samples—excuse me, George used to get me free samples." She sniffed sadly. "I don't mean to sound heartless. I didn't really know him too well."

I made an attempt to get the conversation back on course. "George was traveling with a large sum of money Mrs. Harper said he stole from her. He wrote Mrs. Harper a letter saying he was going to sell their secret skin care formula to a rival company, but then he had second thoughts. Do you know anything about that?"

"I can't imagine George going over to another company. He was always ridiculously loyal to BeautiQueen, even when that Folly woman made disastrous decisions."

"Such as?"

"I'd call putting out a spring line in nothing but peach a disaster. Not everyone looks good in peach, although this does suit me well enough."

She had on enough, that's for sure. "It seems an odd reason to commit suicide over."

One cat yowled, so she set it down. "Poor George was probably trying to protect her. From what I hear, BeautiQueen may be in financial trouble."

I made a mental note to check the finances of both BeautiQueen and Perfecto Face. "When was the last time you saw George?"

"At a family reunion this past Christmas. That's when he told me about her peculiar habits."

"Besides George, who else works for Folly?"

"Hundreds of people. Anybody can have a makeup show in her house and become a BeautiQueen salesperson. But at the top level, I'd have to say Folly and George ran the show. After all, BeautiQueen isn't some big famous cosmetics company like Mary Kay or Clinique."

I started to ask if Folly Harper had enemies in the other local cosmetic camps when Danger managed to get out of the kitchen and headed for me as if I were the last bag of Doberman Chow in the grocery store. The cats and the lizard scattered.

"Danger!" Lucy Warner said sharply and the dog skidded to a stop. It came to her, little stub of a tail wagging furiously.

I was glad to be intact. "The dog certainly likes you."

She rubbed Danger behind the ears. "Oh, yes, Danger and I are old friends. She was mine at first, before George decided to take her. Poor thing. If only she could speak, maybe she could tell us what in the world happened to George."

The dog looked perfectly content to be with Lucy Warner. She even let me give her a pat on the head. So much for loyal Fido howling at his master's grave. I didn't need Camden to tell me what was on Danger's mind—I love whoever feeds me.

"I'm sure George would be glad to know his dog is taken care of."

"Well, I love all kinds of animals. I'm so glad I could take care of that poor woman's pets. I certainly hope they catch whoever killed her."

"How did you hear about this house?"

"Several weeks ago, I made an offer the owner was considering. Of course, the realtor called and explained all about the murder, and said she'd understand if I wanted to withdraw, but with Danger here, I don't think I have to worry. As soon as the police did whatever they needed to do and the people from Goodwill cleared out the woman's personal effects, I was told I could move in." She peered at me over her glasses. "I hope you don't think that's too ghoulish, Mr. Randall."

"No. A little unusual, maybe. Mrs. Mitchell was murdered, and there's a possibility your cousin George was murdered, too."

"Do you believe there's a connection? I never heard George mention a Mrs. Mitchell, but then, I saw him infrequently."

Maybe there wasn't a connection, only an odd coincidence. Maybe someone at BeautiQueen could tell me more.

◇◇◇

When I got home, Camden was on the porch saying good-bye to the church people. Of course, they all had to stop and talk to me and continue their futile attempts to get me to join a Sunday school class. After they left, I started to tell Camden what I'd learned at Lucy Wharton's when a burst of piano music made me stop. I knew that sound.

"How long has Charlie been here?"

"Not long. He and Kary have been working on some music."

"Oh, yeah?"

Charlie put the finishing touches on a telling little number called "Since My Best Gal Turned Me Down" and joined us on the porch. He looked cheerful. Too cheerful.

"You and Taffy come to an agreement?" I asked.

"No, and you know what? I've decided that doesn't really matter."

Camden gave me a worried look. I didn't have to be psychic to pick up the message.

Charlie sat on the porch rail. "Randall, I have to tell you, Kary is an angel. I've never had a woman listen to me like that."

I didn't like the sound of this. "She's used to dealing with small children."

"I told her all about me and Taffy. She's so sympathetic. I feel so calm being around her. You know, I haven't had a cigarette since I got here? 'Course, I didn't want to smoke in your house. You guys don't mind if I light up?"

"Go ahead." My concern was growing. Charlie was also a borderline alcoholic who smoked like a freight train, but already there were signs of Kary's influence. I could see her reforming him, helping him quit smoking, getting him into AA, leading him into a life of health.

The snap of Charlie lighting a match jarred me out of this depressing daydream. "What about Taffy?" I asked him.

He lit his cigarette and shook out the match. "Why should I waste my time on her? She's made it pretty plain she doesn't want me—unless you've found out something different."

"I think you need to give it a little more time."

"I think she's not only planning to leave me, she's planning to leave the Hot Six. I think she's found another band."

"You're close. She had an audition at the Spider's Web downtown, and she performs this Friday night."

"I knew it! Damn! It's those songs of hers, those weird, tuneless songs. The words don't make sense. There's no melody. Why would she want to sing them when there're so many great old songs around?"

Camden, as usual, tried to be diplomatic. "Maybe she just wants to try something different."

"And forget the good stuff? She's crazy. Nobody'll listen to that weird music except dried-up nutballs from the college."

I had to grin at the dramatics. "Tell us how you really feel."

"If this is the reason she's been so standoffish, I understand."

"Well, there might be another problem."

He took a long drag on the cigarette. "Tell me."

"You're right about the nutballs from the college, only they aren't weird and dried up. Taffy's been taking a songwriting course at PCC, and the instructor is muy macho."

"A songwriting course? Oh, I'll bet he goes on and on about how wonderful her songs are."

"He seems to think she's got talent."

"Who is this guy?"

"Manuel Estaban."

Charlie dropped his cigarette and ground it out with his shoe. "Well, that's just dandy."

"I have a plan, if you'd care to hear it."

He folded his arms. "Go ahead."

"Come to her concert. Sit on the front row. Smile and act like you're enjoying yourself. It can't fail."

"Sit through a whole evening of those songs? My teeth are aching already."

"Do it for her. She'll love you for it."

He took a long moment to consider. "It's this Friday night?"

"Yes."

"That's opening night. I couldn't possibly go."

"Kary can play the show, right? What's more important?"

Another long pause. "A whole program, like, two hours?"

"At least."

He took out his cigarettes. "I don't know, Randall."

"I can't stand soap operas, but I let Kary tell me whole plots. And there isn't enough time to go into the sacrifices Camden has made for Ellin, but I think he signed his soul away a couple of years back."

Camden gave me a dark look. "I still have my soul, thanks."

"Okay, but that's all you have left. Sometimes you have to give a little, Charlie. You can afford to give up one Friday night. Put those away. You just had one."

He stuffed the pack of cigarettes back into his pocket. "She doesn't understand what music means to me."

"You don't understand what it means to her. You're even. Be a man and come to the concert."

"Let me get back to you on that. See you later, guys."

He got in his car and drove off.

I watched him go. "Think he'll challenge Estaban to a duel?"

"I hope not," Camden said.

"He'd better go to that concert. I can't have him hanging around Kary every day."

Kary came out to the porch in time to hear me say this. "Can't have who hanging around?"

Damn. "Oh, nothing. I was just mentioning to Camden that Charlie's been spending a lot of time here lately."

"And there's nothing wrong with that."

"No, no. Not a thing." There was an uncomfortable silence. "He said he'd talked to you about Taffy."

She gave me a long, considering look. "Yes, it's too bad when two people can't be completely honest with each other."

I knew I'd better tread carefully. "If he'll go to one of her concerts, she'll see he cares about her music."

"Then I hope he does." Thankfully, she changed the subject. "Cam said you went to talk to George's cousin. What did she say?"

"The cousin, Lucy Warner, identified George's body and brought his doberman, Danger, to her new home, which just happens to be Viola's home on Marshall Street."

"That's bizarre."

"She said she'd decided to buy the house before all this happened. The good thing is she's looking after Viola's pets."

"She does know a murder was committed there?"

"Doesn't seem to bother her in the slightest. She told me she didn't know George very well, but couldn't imagine him having any enemies or being disloyal to BeautiQueen. She said the company may be in financial trouble, which I will check on. Right now there doesn't seem to be any reason for George's suicide, but he may have stumbled across a formula a rival company would kill to have."

Kary thought a moment. "But George's cousin moving into Viola's house is too much of a coincidence, don't you think?"

"It is a little strange."

"We should find out if there's a connection between George and Viola, and even more importantly, we need to work on our cover story for the Baby Love affair."

We had to get that over with. "We can go undercover any time. Now, if you like."

"Well, not right now." She checked her watch. "I have a student coming for a piano lesson. Is it your turn to cook, David?"

"I'll choose something from our vast array of funeral food."

"Cam, are we expecting any more guests?"

"Just Ellie."

The way he said this made Kary frown. "What now?"

"He's calling off the wedding," I said. "Get out the dustpan and get ready to sweep up the pieces."

Her eyes widened. "Are you serious? Cam, have you lost your mind?"

"I wish I could! I can't marry her and risk passing on this crazy talent to our children."

"I thought you had worked that out."

"Not exactly. There's something else." I could see the debate in his eyes. "Something I haven't told you."

"So tell me."

He pushed out of the swing. "Watch this."

The large plastic trash cans came hopping around the corner, lids flapping. They made a circle of the yard and clumped back to their place at the side of the house. Kary's mouth fell open.

"And this."

All the branches that had fallen during the last thunderstorm rolled down to the curb and stacked themselves in a neat pile.

His voice was on the rise. "And this!"

Before he could topple the oak trees or peel off the gutters, Kary caught his arm. "Stop." She pulled him back into the swing and sat down beside him. "Oh, my God. When did this start?"

He caught his breath. "A few days ago."

"Do you have any idea what caused it?"

"Being born."

"Born alien," I said.

"Yes, my weird alien powers continue to manifest."

"'Manifest.' Excellent choice."

Kary gave me a quick Teacher Look and returned to her consoling. "All right, it's weird and spooky and bizarre, but you can control it."

"For now, yes. But who knows what it'll do next?"

"That's just it, Cam. No one knows. It could go away. It could skip a generation."

"It could grow until you destroy the earth," I said. "That's my theory."

"Very funny. Look how hard I'm laughing."

Kary put her hand on his shoulder. "Cam, Ellin loves you. She'll stick by you no matter what."

"But you know her. She'll go crazy. Tee-shirts, action figures, the works." He pushed his hair out of his eyes. "And here's the really scary part. Our three children—I know they're going to be psychic. What if they have all these strange talents, too? I don't know what to do. I think we ought to wait until I can control it better before we get married."

"How long did it take you to learn how to control all the visions?"

He paused. "Two years."

"Is Ellin going to wait two years? She's not going to wait two minutes. Marry her and then deal with the problem." He put his head down in his hands, and she patted him on the back. "You've just had Fred's funeral, and you're anxious about the wedding. All this emotional upheaval is causing a little short circuit, that's all."

"I hope so," he said.

"What else have you moved?"

"The other day, I stopped Folly's car from running into her."

"So it's a useful talent."

"I appreciate your efforts to look on the bright side, but this power is getting stronger, and I don't want to hurt anyone."

"You would never hurt anyone, and you know it."

"But does this power know it?"

Neither Kary nor I had an answer for that.

"It's no use," Camden said. "I have to call off the wedding."

◇◇◇

We couldn't convince him to abort his suicide mission. With Ellin coming over, I didn't want to be within a fifty-mile radius of the house, but it was my turn to fix supper. Kary's student came for his lesson, and afterwards, she went upstairs to finish packing Fred's meager belongings. I was in the kitchen checking through the many casseroles when Ellin arrived. I could hear her talking to Camden in the island. After a few minutes of kind words for old Fred, she was chattering away about how pleased Folly was with his help and flowers and candles for the wedding when he interrupted.

"Ellie, we have to talk."

Here we go. Stop, drop and roll.

"About what?"

Camden took a breath and took the plunge. "We can't get married."

I didn't hear anything, so I risked a peek around the corner. I was surprised to see Ellin still in place instead of catapulting to the ceiling.

"Cam." She put her arms around him. "This is probably a case of pre-wedding jitters. I have them, too. It's a big step for both of us."

"No. It's not that."

"What, then? You're not taking what Mother says to heart, are you? She really loves you. She just has her own screwy ideas on what my life should be."

"This isn't about your mother. It's about me. We need to wait."

Her voice slid up an octave. "Wait?"

"Something's happened. I don't know how to explain it."

She pushed him away. "What are you talking about? We can't wait. Everything is planned. Everything is ready. Come hell or high water, the wedding is May thirty-first." There was a pause as if something had occurred to her. "Oh, my God. You see something, don't you? Something disastrous happening at the wedding. What is it? Can it be avoided?"

From my vantage point, I saw the blue armchair quivering as if readying for takeoff. Camden saw it, too. He took a careful step to the side to keep Ellin's back to the chair and set his mouth in a firm line. The chair remained in place.

"If things could be avoided, believe me, I'd take care of it. You have no idea."

"What are you saying? Are we destined for divorce? Is one of us going to die?"

This time, the lamp in the corner began to rise. Camden shot it a quick look, and it settled back down. "God, I hope not."

I thought she'd really blow a fuse, but she surprised me again. She touched his arm and turned him to face her. "Cam, look at me. What is it? Whatever it is, I'll understand. We'll find an answer. You've got me imagining all the worst things. It can't be that bad, can it? Are you freaking out because of your change issues? Everything changes, Cam. You have to deal with it."

His glance scanned the room on the lookout for more levitations. "Too many things are changing too fast."

"No, they're not. We've been living together for months, and I know you like it. Just because we marry doesn't mean you have to stop eating Pop-Tarts, or stop singing, or stop wearing your god-awful sloppy clothes. Well, I may have to trash your clothes, but that's for another day."

With the room in control, he brought his gaze back to her. "I've had a lot to deal with, Ellie. I just lost Fred, and seeing Viola buried in her basement is going to haunt me for a long time. When they find a house, Rufus and Angie are moving out. Everything's moving in all directions. I feel like I'm standing in the middle of a tornado."

This was as close as he could get to telling her the truth.

"Isn't that why I'm here? Or do you love me only for my vision-erasing capability?"

"Don't go there. You know that's not the only reason."

"Then man up and tell me what's wrong."

"I've told you I'm concerned about the kids—"

The famous Belton patience was fraying. "We are not going to have children! And if we do, *you* are going to take care of them. Tell me what's wrong, or I'm walking out that door and never coming back."

Come on, Camden. You don't want that, do you? That's what I want, sure, but I'm not the one who's telekinetic.

Before he could say anything, she thought of something else. "Cam, this better not have anything to do with the fact that I'm not psychic."

Let's see you get around this one, buddy.

"Trust me, Ellie, you would not want any sort of supernatural power. You've got enough natural power of your own."

She put her arms around him again. "You know I love you, and if you get possessed by another nutty musician, or have flashbacks to murders, or go wandering off after UFOs, or feel overwhelmed by all the changes, I'll be here for you, you know that, blocking out the harmful rays. That's one thing your pal Randall can't do."

For God's sake, tell her, Camden. She'll never be this agreeable again.

He must have thought he needed to protect her, or else the memories of his psychic childhood were too awful and he dreaded putting his children through that trauma. He hesitated a moment too long.

She'd had enough. "Fine. You have until May thirty-first to get over whatever this is, do you hear me? Get over it!"

The front door slammed. I waited a moment and then looked around the corner. Camden stood in the middle of the room. All around him, all the items from the coffee table and a couple of kittens were hovering in the air in a sad little circle.

Chapter Thirteen

"I'm an ordinary man."

Wednesday morning, before my visit to BeautiQueen, I went online and was surprised to discover Folly Harper listed as a member of the board of Tecknilabs, as well as First Federal Bank and Burlson and Rawls Industries. The woman was loaded. No wonder it was no problem to write those peach-colored checks. According to the latest *Business Weekly* report, BeautiQueen products were up fifty percent. That's a lot of eyeliner. But nothing indicated any sort of financial trouble. If George thought Folly was being foolish with the company funds, all he had to do was check. As far as I could see, BeautiQueen showed no signs of aging. So why take the money and run? If he needed dough, all he had to do was ask.

Folly greeted me at the office of BeautiQueen. "I can give you the full tour, David. Where would you like to begin?"

"Wherever you like."

As we walked down peach colored corridors, Folly sniffed and dabbed her eyes with her peach handkerchief. "I'm so sorry. I can't stop thinking about poor George. Who in the world could have killed him? Did his cousin have any ideas?"

"No. She said she didn't know George all that well."

"This is so upsetting."

We passed a wall of framed photographs displaying Employees of the Month and Top Sales People of the Year. George had won these awards several times. Was it possible a jealous coworker had decided George didn't deserve the glory? "I'd like to talk to your employees. Maybe George had enemies you didn't know about."

"He worked mostly with Mary Montague in Production and Design. We can stop there first. They were all dear friends, though."

Production and Design was a large peach colored room with three desks and a larger space filled with posters, charts, and graphs. Mary Montague was a rail-thin blonde with a severe haircut and dark eyes.

"I couldn't believe the news about George," she said. "He wasn't the suicidal type."

"So he got along well with everyone?"

"Oh, yes. He was a little intense about his ideas sometimes, but we're all that way. Everything was for the good of the company."

"What's this you're working on?"

Mary Montague picked up a shiny poster from her desk. "Our Spring Forward campaign."

The poster showed a cute peach-colored frog jumping into green water, an array of circles spreading out like ripples in the pond. Different boxes and bottles sat in each circle.

Mary pointed to the slogan. "'Spring Forward With BeautiQueen.' We've finished with the copy." She indicated her computer. "You might like to check over it, Folly."

"Thank you." Folly sat down at Mary's desk.

The third desk by the window was piled with folders. I walked over to have a look. "Was this George's desk?"

"Yes. We haven't touched anything."

"Was there someone in line to replace him, someone who wanted his job?"

"George and Mary were the only ones really interested in this part of the business," Folly said.

No motive there, then. "What are all these folders?"

Mary hesitated. "George had lots of ideas. The filing cabinet was full, so he started keeping them in stacks on his desk."

"He didn't keep all this on his computer?"

"He didn't trust the computer. He was always afraid someone might hack in and steal his ideas."

"Is it possible there's someone in the company who might be capable of that?"

"Go ahead and read through them. I think you'll understand."

I opened the first folder and read all about Revita-Face, the first self-revitalizing cream, guaranteed to give you a new face each morning. All you had to do was peel off your old face. The second folder told the amazing secret of orange peels to reduce wrinkles. The third outlined a clarifying technique involving rubber bands and a tuning fork.

I closed the folder. "Was he serious about these?"

"Oh, yes," Mary said. "But now you see why no one would want to steal them."

I'd dealt with frustrated artists before. They tend to be super sensitive about their work. "Did people make fun of him?"

"No, actually, everyone understood he was trying to do his best for BeautiQueen."

She handed me another folder. "And he did occasionally come up with something we could use. This is his idea for Peach Glitter Surprise Mascara. The young girls love it."

The photograph inside the folder showed three pre-teen girls, their eyelashes sparkling. "Was there a special project, something he really wanted to make?"

"We all want to find a product that reverses the aging process. That's the Holy Grail of the cosmetics industry, a cream or lotion that makes you look twenty again. George did some work on that, but I can't really say it was a pet project."

Folly had finished reading the advertising copy. She got up from the desk. "That's fine, Mary. How's the First Blush campaign coming along?"

"We should have that done by next week."

"Excellent! David, did you have any more questions?"

"Not right now, thanks."

I spoke to a few more employees at BeautiQueen. All seemed genuinely shocked and sorry about George's death, and all agreed that, although some of his ideas could be screwy, they admired him for trying to push the company in new directions.

Folly and I returned to the front door. "That's all I can do here, Folly. Do you have a key to George's house? There might be some clues there."

"Yes, I do. Let me get it for you."

While I waited, Mary Montague came up. "Mr. Randall, I would like to mention one other thing, if it can help your case. I didn't want to say anything in front of Folly, but sometimes George could be—how shall I put this?—a little too friendly in the workplace."

"He harassed you?"

"Oh, I set him straight right away, but he saw himself as a ladies' man, and sometimes this annoyed the female employees."

"Did anyone file a complaint?"

"No, if we told him to stop, he'd stop, but, I don't know, I thought he might have had a girlfriend in Florida, and things went wrong. Oh, here comes Folly. Please don't worry her with this. It could mean nothing."

Folly handed me George's house key. "Mary, did you need to see me?"

"I wanted to thank Mr. Randall for being on this case."

Folly patted my arm. "I know you'll solve this. I can't imagine who'd want to harm poor George."

Mary gave me a look that said, "I can."

After what the receptionist at the hotel told me about George's clumsy advances and now Mary's information, I was beginning to believe, as Mary did, that George put the moves on the wrong woman.

◇◇◇

I drove to George's ordinary little house on Hauser Street and let myself in. George's house, like his office, was filled with ideas. Six filing cabinets full of ideas. Otherwise, George had lived a

Spartan life. He had a sofa, a chair, the usual kitchen appliances, a bed, a nightstand, and a desk. There were no pictures, books, magazines, or photo albums, just a large stack of flat BeautiQueen boxes, unassembled. He might as well have lived in a hotel.

The backyard was fenced in, and there was a doghouse for Danger. I couldn't find any dog food in the house, or a leash, or squeaky toys. Probably Lucy Warner came by and got them.

I opened one of the file drawers and looked through the files. Wrinkle Re-Duce. Eye Lift Deluxe. Por-Sa-Lynn Face Cream. The only things worse than George's ideas were the titles he gave them. There were several pages of stuff I didn't understand. What the heck was pentyleneglycol? Or cyclopentasiloxane? If I had to guess, I'd say ingredients for cosmetics. Either that, or George had been shooting for a Scrabble championship.

I'd read through three drawers before I found a folder marked "Rejections." Inside this folder was a thick stack of rejection letters from various pharmaceutical companies. So George had been shopping his ideas around and no one was interested. Why keep a folder full of rejections? Was George the type of person who liked to wallow in failure?

I gave Folly a call. "I'm here in George's house looking at rejection letters he received from other companies. Did you know he was sending his ideas to other people?"

"Why, no, I didn't. He never said anything about that to me." She sounded hurt. "He certainly had a right to, but usually we discussed things like that."

"Is there anyone else at BeautiQueen who would've taken offense at this, perhaps seen it as a betrayal?"

"I can't imagine who."

"Think about it. I'll check with you later."

I took the rejection folder back to my office to contact the companies. The few I managed to reach vaguely recalled George and his ideas.

"We get hundreds of inquiries from inventors and scientists, Mr. Randall," one secretary told me. "Unless an idea or product is revolutionary, we can't use it."

"What would be considered a revolutionary idea?"

"Anything that makes you live longer and look better without harmful side effects."

"Eat right and exercise?"

She laughed. "Now that's revolutionary."

My next stop was Perfecto Face, Incorporated, the company George mentioned in his suicide note. I was greeted by a lovely woman with the melodic name of Amelia Tilley. Perfecto Face obviously worked well for Ms. Tilley. Her skin was flawless caramel, her eyebrows arched perfectly over huge brown eyes, and her lips gleamed like rich pink roses.

"What can I do for you, Mr. Randall?"

"I'm with the *Parkland Herald*. I'd like to write an article about Perfecto Face for our next Sunday supplement. Do you have time to answer a few questions?"

"Of course." She indicated a chair and took her seat behind a large beige desk. The entire office was decorated in shades of beige, tan, and brown. Several framed photographs of Amelia Tilley were arranged on a table by the window. The photos showed her in a variety of sparkly gowns and tiaras.

I can recognize a beauty queen when I see one. "Are you a pageant winner?"

"Yes, I am."

I took a closer look at the photos. According to her decorative sashes, Amelia Tilley had been Miss Celosia, Miss Summer Squash, Miss Winsome Valley, and Miss Elbow Macaroni. I had to chuckle at that one.

Ms. Tilley grinned. "That's an actual pageant. It's part of the Best Pasta Festival in Far Valley."

I came back to my seat. "Have you entered the Miss Parkland Pageant?"

"Yes, I have."

"Then I'd like to wish you good luck."

"Thank you." Ms. Tilley handed me a beige brochure. "Now, about Perfecto Face. We're a small local company with an emphasis on cosmetics and grooming aids for women of all colors. We're pleased to have any publicity."

I took out my tape recorder and set it on the desk. "Would you describe your spring line?"

She handed me another brochure. "We have a full range of pinks this spring. We're calling it Think Pink."

I glanced at the brochure. Women of all races smiled back, all thinking pink. "How would you describe your sales?"

"Very positive. Sales are up twenty percent."

I'd checked into that, too, and she was correct. "And your research into products such as alpha hydroxy. How does that work?"

"We're starting new research. We've been fully occupied with the spring line and our standard products, but we expect to reveal an exciting new skin care cream this fall. I can't give you any specific details, you understand, but it involves gamma hydroxy, the latest scientific breakthrough."

What happened to beta hydroxy? "I see." I took another look at the Think Pink brochure. "These are beautiful shades. Do you have much problem with other companies trying to steal your ideas?"

"I like to think we have a good professional relationship with our rivals. Perfecto Face is one of the few companies devoted to women of color, so we're competing for a different section of the market."

"Do you know Folly Harper of BeautiQueen cosmetics?"

"Yes, I know Folly. She's an inspiration to our younger sales-people on how to get ahead."

"And her partner, George McMillan, did you know him?"

Ms. Tilley's smile faded. "He killed himself, didn't he? I heard that on the news."

"When I interviewed him for a previous article, he said something to me about joining Perfecto Face."

"I'd met him and we discussed that, but his ideas didn't fit the vision of our company."

"Something about a new face cream?"

"I don't think he'd done enough research. Besides that, I didn't want to cause any trouble between Perfecto Face and

BeautiQueen. As I said, I admire Folly Harper. There's plenty of room for our two companies. We cater to different clienteles." She looked puzzled by the turn in conversation, so I headed back to the gamma hydroxy quadrant.

"This shade here, this Sun-Kissed Rose. Who comes up with such descriptive names?"

◇◇◇

After a half hour thinking pink, I thanked Ms. Tilley and went back to my car. My phone beeped with a text from Kary saying she was having a hot dog at Janice's to celebrate the last of the end of grade testing and did I want to join her?

As I slid into the booth at the little restaurant, Janice caught my eye and nodded. She'd bring me the usual two dogs all the way.

I pulled a handful of napkins from the dispenser. "Are you free at last?"

"Two more workdays to go."

"Congratulations. I'll buy lunch."

"Thanks." Kary pulled the paper off her straw and plunked it into her diet soda. "I'm still looking for a connection between George and Viola, but meanwhile, I may be able to get some information about Folly. One of the women in the pageant is Amelia Tilley. She runs her own cosmetics company, so she should know Folly."

"She does. I talked to her this morning. Perfecto-Face is the company George was going to sell BeautiQueen secrets to."

"Rats! I thought I had the inside story. What did she say?"

"That he wanted to join her company, but his ideas didn't fit. I've read some of George's ideas. She was being very polite."

"So she knows Folly?"

"She said Folly was an inspiration. Something else about George, though. His co-worker at BeautiQueen said he was an expert in unwanted attention."

"He harassed her?"

"I think he tried his dubious charm on Ms. Tilley, too. She appeared to be upset about his death, but she could be hiding something. Maybe she and George had a secret deal. You might be able to find out more."

"Oh, yes. There's a lot of talk about men in the dressing rooms."

Janice brought our hot dogs, a plate of fries, and my drink. Then she hurried off to help another customer. The little restaurant teemed with college students, businessmen on lunch break, and mothers with babies in strollers. I moved my fries over and spent a few minutes writing "Marry Me" in ketchup. I turned my plate so Kary could see.

She took one of her fries and gave the letters a gentle swipe. "You get more creative every day."

"I won't give up."

"Back to the case, please."

I knew when to make a strategic retreat. "I checked out George's house, too. Loads of really bad ideas everywhere and rejection letters from cosmetic companies."

"So maybe he did commit suicide. He might have gotten tired of all that rejection."

"I don't know. The more I learn about George, the more I believe he was too full of himself to pull the trigger."

"Maybe someone else killed him and made it look like suicide."

"He sure as hell wasn't killed for his ideas."

"If he was such a masher, maybe some woman got tired of his advances."

"But you deal with that every day, don't you?" Someone as attractive as Kary had to.

She munched another fry before answering. "It doesn't make me mad enough to kill. I try to ignore it, or make a joke, and if a guy gets too fresh, I give him my Teacher Look."

I'd reached for my drink, but paused in mock fear. "Not the Teacher Look."

"Only as a last resort."

We ate for a while, and then I couldn't help but ask about Charlie. "How's the show coming along? Charlie staying sober?"

"I told him he'd better."

"All he has to do is attend Taffy's concert, and she'll love him forever."

"I said I could handle the piano part on Friday night. We've been taking turns as it is. What time is her show?"

"I believe she goes on at nine-thirty."

"Then he could easily play the first act and get there in plenty of time."

"Keep reminding him. Use the Look, if necessary."

"I will." She used it on me. "Now about Baby Love. I have a plan for our undercover operation."

Of course she hadn't forgotten this. "Would you marry me first? You know, so we'd be a legal couple."

"Hmm. Something to consider." Her smile was impish. "But if Baby Love's an illegal company, that won't matter."

"It would matter to me. It would give my acting verisimilitude."

Her eyes went wide. "Wow!"

"You like that? I've been saving it up."

"I am so impressed. I don't think I've ever heard anyone use that word in a sentence."

"Plenty more where that came from. Marry me, and I promise a spectacular six-syllable word a day."

"That sounds very educational," she said. "But I must respectfully decline. I think going in as reporters from the *Herald* is our best bet. I've thought it over, and I don't think we'd need the paper's permission. After all, we're not going to actually print a story. If we find anything illegal, we'll call Jordan and let the police handle it."

"You want to go after lunch?"

"Unfortunately, I have to get back to school."

"After school, then."

"All right." There was a sparkle in her eyes that I knew and feared. "Meet me at the corner of Hanley and Berry at three o'clock, and we'll put my plan into action."

◇◇◇

I amused Kary by trying to spell "Marry Me" with leftover bits of slaw. Then I paid the check and we went our separate ways. Kary headed back to school to finish filling in the test information, and I went over to the Drug Palace to put in a few hours wandering the aisles with my clipboard, pretending to be checking inventory. I'd politely asked a woman not to open the boxes of tampons until she'd bought them—I mean, come on, couldn't she tell what was inside?—when Ellin came down the aisle. I headed her off by the picture frames on the corner. She didn't waste time or breath.

"You put him up to this."

I knew eventually she'd blame me for Camden's panic attack. "Yes, of course. As an expert in break ups, I spent days planning to destroy your marriage. And why would I do a thing like that?"

"Because you see me as a threat to your secure little setup at the house."

"I have no problem co-existing with you. If you'll relax and enjoy it, 302 Grace is a great place."

She glanced at the picture frames as if trying to decide which size would do the most damage to my skull. "You know the reason Cam is acting this way."

"I do?"

"Yes, you do."

"Are you talking about our super secret brain link?"

She wasn't going to admit to any psychic connection. "Don't be ridiculous. I mean you two tell each other everything."

"Whoa." I made the time out sign with my hands. "Hold on. Time. Women tell each other everything. Guys only share the important info, like who's bringing the beer."

"Like why one of them is calling off the wedding. You must have some idea."

Yes, but Camden doesn't want you to know his latest trick. Not that you can't levitate on your own. "It's between you and Camden. If he doesn't want to get married, there must be a damn good reason."

"And if you're such a damn good detective, you'll find out. I'm hiring you."

I felt my eyes bulge. "What?"

"I'm hiring you. Solve the mystery. Find out why Cam won't marry me." She whacked a pile of bills onto my clipboard. "And since you already know, this will be the easiest money you ever made."

I tried to catch the money as it spilled over the clipboard. "Wait a minute. Ellin, I can't take this case."

"Because you already know the answer."

"Because this is something Camden has to work out."

She leaned in, blue eyes glittering. The glass in the picture frames trembled. "You're such a pal. You help him work it out. You have until two o'clock, Sunday, May 31st."

As she stalked out, I heard a chuckle one aisle over. "Randall, you sure have a way with the ladies."

I managed to corral the last of the dollar bills. "That one is not mine."

Ted came around the corner, hands in the pockets of his white smock. "She hired you."

"And I'm giving her money back."

"So what's with Cam? Cold feet? I thought he and Ellin were a sure thing."

"He's a little nervous, that's all. He'll marry her. The show must go on."

◇◇◇

The show must go on, indeed. At three o'clock, I met Kary at the appointed rendezvous place. She parked Turbo beside the Fury in the large public lot across from the Sears warehouse and got out. She was carrying an attaché case and an expensive looking camera.

"I borrowed this from one of the teachers," she said. "He showed me how to use it. I thought I'd pretend to take pictures for this imaginary article we're writing."

"Good idea. I use John Fisher when I'm playing reporter. Have you made up a convincing handle like Cynthia Scoop or Fiona Factfinder?"

"How about Liz Hunt?"

"Perfect. Now where's this hideout?"

She pointed to an innocuous row of offices on Berry Street. "The second one."

"Looks harmless."

Kary's face was serious. "We'll see."

The only thing that distinguished the Baby Love office from the other offices was a sign on the door that read: "Baby Love, a Mothers United Organization Dedicated to Creating Future Families."

"Follow my lead," Kary said as I opened the door for her.

The office was just as plain and unremarkable inside. There was a small table with stacks of brochures and a faded plastic flower arrangement, a bulletin board filled with birth announcements, pictures of babies, and church events. A young woman was seated at a large metal desk. She looked up from her computer. "May I help you?"

"Good afternoon," Kary said. "My name is Liz Hunt, and this is my associate, John Fisher. We're from the *Parkland Herald*, and we'd like to do a story on Baby Love. Would that be possible today?"

"I'm sure I could answer any questions you have," she said.

"And do you mind if we take a few pictures?"

"There's not a lot to photograph in here, but go ahead."

While Kary quizzed the woman about Baby Love's practices, I read the bulletin board. Everything looked completely legal. Happy thank you letters to Baby Love for fulfilling baby dreams. Photos of fat, healthy babies in the arms of their new beaming parents. A list of satisfied customers with addresses and phone numbers. I copied a few of these into my notebook, and tuned back into the conversation to hear Kary ask about age limits for prospective parents.

"We like for our parents to be at least no younger than twenty-one and no older than sixty, but we have made exceptions," the woman answered. "As long as someone is in good health and can support a child and give it a loving home, then age is no barrier."

I couldn't help but think of Viola and all those death-defying products on her dresser. Age was a barrier for her theater career.

She fought it as hard as she could. But why would someone kill her? Was there another actress out there seething with rage because Viola got all the mother and teacher roles? Jealousy over glamorous lead roles I could understand. Or maybe Viola had some dirt on someone and was killed to keep her from talking. But since as far as I could tell, Viola's world consisted of the theater and her pets. I was having a hard time finding a motive.

I brought my attention back to Kary, who had now moved into the dangerous territory of single parent adoption. From her intense look, she was about to sign up and start looking through the catalog.

"Ms. Hunt," I said. "We have another appointment at four thirty."

She gave a little start as if she'd realized why she was there. "Thank you. Let me get a picture or two and we'll go."

The woman posed for a photo, and Kary took several shots from different angles. I wrote down the woman's name, thanked her for her time, and escorted Kary out.

"Whew," she said as we walked back to our cars. "I was almost sucked in. Did you find out anything?"

"Two things. One, there's a list of people on the bulletin board with names, addresses, and phone numbers prominently displayed. I took down a few for you to follow up on. And two, the woman didn't ask for our ID. That's something you might want to consider."

She unlocked her car and put the camera on the passenger's seat. "I don't know, David. Everything looks legit. Maybe I overreacted."

"You've still got some info if you want to pursue this. You were very convincing, by the way."

She was still pensive. "Thanks."

Was this the time to confront the elephant? Could I bring up Beth without having Kary dissolve into tears? Could we discuss our lost daughters, find some kind of comfort in our mutual grief? Something told me to hold back. Standing beside our cars on a hot sidewalk wasn't the place, and Kary was ready to go.

"I'd better return the camera. See you at home."

She got into Turbo and cranked the little car into life. I watched until the Festiva turned the corner and was gone. There had to be some way around this problem, or we would always be stuck in the elephant's graveyard, eyes shut tight so we couldn't see the bones.

Chapter Fourteen

"What could've depressed her?"

Rufus had decided it was his turn to cook dinner, so he'd fired up the grill in the backyard and was roasting huge slabs of hamburger while Angie was in the kitchen, filling a bowl with potato salad. She called out a cheerful hello.

"We'll be ready to eat here directly."

"Thanks," I said. "Where's Camden?"

"Doing laundry."

Camden was down the hallway behind the stairs taking towels out of the washing machine.

"Why are you doing that the old fashioned way?" I said. "Levitate them into the dryer."

"So far, nothing has gone flying today. Anything new on Viola?"

"No, but I visited BeautiQueen and found out George came this close to charges of sexual harassment, checked out his house and found his many weird makeup ideas and rejection letters from cosmetic companies, talked to a lovely woman named Amelia Tilley, who looks up to Folly as an example of a successful businesswoman, was ambushed by Ellin in the Drug Palace and hired to find out what's wrong with you, and I investigated Baby Love with Kary in disguise as reporters for the *Herald*."

He'd been tossing towels into the dryer. He paused. "Ellie's hired you to find out what's wrong with me?"

"Paid me real money."

"That could take years."

"She seemed a bit insistent."

He threw the last towel in and shut the dryer door. "Well, if I knew what was wrong, I could save everybody a lot of trouble. Did you and Kary find out anything about Baby Love?"

"I know she wants to uncover some big scam, but I think they're okay."

We were going to eat outside, but a stray shower came by as Rufus finished cooking the last hamburger. He came in with a mountain of meat on a platter and set it on the counter. "Well, there's my supper. I don't know what ya'll are gonna eat."

This was an old joke and easily ignored. We wrangled the large burgers onto buns and sat down at the dining room table. Angie passed the bowl of potato salad, and Kary poured iced tea for everyone. There was cheese, of course, ketchup, mustard, and mayo, as well as a jar of pickles Angie's sister had sent over.

"Thought we needed something other than funeral food," Rufus said.

Camden managed to get a two handed grip on his burger. "Thanks, Rufus."

"Still some cakes left and one or two casseroles." He took a huge bite, chewed and swallowed in one gulp. "What's going on I should know about?"

Kary had decided to cut her huge hamburger into three smaller pieces. "Looks like I need a new crusade. Baby Love isn't the evil corporation I'd hoped it was."

"Did you look up those parents?" I asked.

"Yes, and every one checks out. The company's not scamming anyone."

Rufus took another bite. "Something else will come up. Randall here attracts trouble like a donkey attracts flies. What you got, two dead people now?"

"Yep. Do you know George McMillan or Viola Mitchell?"

"Can't say that I do."

"George worked with Folly Harper at BeautiQueen cosmetics and, according to her, would not have killed himself. Viola was the grand dame of the community theater, and someone poisoned her and buried her in the basement. So a possible murder and a definite murder."

Rufus wiped his mouth with the back of his hand. "Sounds like business as usual around here. Who wants another burger?"

Kary thanked him and said she had plenty. Camden said it was taking more time than he had to finish his first one. "Kary and I have to get to rehearsal. I might have another for a late night snack."

"If Millicent Crotty is there tonight, find an excuse to hold her hand and see if you get any useful vibes," I told him.

◇◇◇

After cleaning up the kitchen, Rufus took Angie out for a ride around the neighborhood to scope out any possible houses. I had emails to sort through and phone calls to make, and thought I'd have a peaceful evening working in my office. It was peaceful until I had an unexpected visitor.

"Hello? Cam? Anyone home?"

"Just me," I called.

Ellin came to my door. "Where is everybody?"

"Rufus and Angie are looking at houses, and Kary and Camden had a final dress rehearsal tonight. There's a preview performance tomorrow."

"Oh, that's right. I've been so busy with wedding details I forgot the show is this weekend." She came in and stood behind the chair I have for clients, gripping the back as if to prepare for bad news. "Do you have any answers for me?"

"I think once the show's over Camden will be able to concentrate better on wedding plans."

"He doesn't have to plan anything."

"He'll be there, I promise."

She deflated a little and sat down. "My sisters are driving me crazy. If Cam doesn't show up, I'll never hear the end of it."

"Ellin, he'll be there."

"What's happening with his psychic ability? He said he never knew what it was going to do next. Is he having trouble controlling it? Is that the problem?"

"He's dealing with a few glitches, but he'll take care of it."

"What kind of glitches?"

"The kind you would love to exploit on TV."

That brought the fire back in her eyes. "You think that's all I care about, don't you?"

"Let me think about that. Yes."

"Well, you're wrong. I want to marry Cam and live happily ever after, or at least, as happily as we can, whether he has psychic powers or not."

While this was good to hear, I wasn't sure I believed it. "You'll work it out."

"What sort of insane cases do you have going now, and how deeply is Cam involved?"

Ellin's focus is all on the PSN, so she usually isn't around for our family gatherings. "I'd better get you caught up. Folly Harper wanted Camden to see some lucky numbers for her, which he did. We're still not sure what those numbers are for, but the bigger problem is the apparent suicide of her coworker, George McMillan. He ran off with company funds, intending to sell company secrets, but he felt guilty and killed himself, or at least, that's what it looks like. She's hired me to investigate. My one link to George is his cousin Lucy, who oddly enough has moved into Viola Mitchell's house."

"Viola Mitchell from the theater? Cam told me he found her body in the basement." She sat back in the chair. "That has to be why he's acting so strangely."

"He's also hired me to find her killer. And I'm trying to get Charlie Valentine and Taffinia O'Brien together and help Kary prove Baby Love is a legal operation. So to answer your question, I have four insane cases going, and Camden's involved in two of them. Once you're married and move in, you can be involved, too."

"No, thank you," she said. "I have enough trouble keeping Cam from going over the edge every time he sees death and destruction."

Ellin had no psychic powers of her own, but she can erase Camden's worst visions by holding his hand. "See? You're made for each other."

She had definitely mixed feelings about this talent. "Because my mind is so blank." She sighed and rubbed the back of her neck. "It really is blank today with all the wedding plans and Reg's screwy ideas for PSN programs and my sisters and my mother—" She paused. "Why am I talking to you?"

"Because I have on my listening face."

She must have been tired because she gave a slight laugh. "It's very convincing."

"You're my client, remember?"

"And you'd better have some results for me soon." Abruptly, she changed the subject. "I couldn't leave the network to go to Fred's funeral. How was it?"

"I was in Florida, tracking down George. Kary said it was a service Fred would've liked."

"Cam hasn't said anything about the funeral to me. I know that's part of why he's upset. I never understood why he took Fred in. Kary he met through a mutual friend, but he practically picked Fred up off the street. I'm surprised the house isn't filled with more homeless men."

I raised my hand. "I qualify."

"And you can have this house all to yourself because I don't intend to live here."

That would be fine with me, but I had to remind her 302 Grace Street might be the deal breaker. "Camden's not going to live anywhere else."

She gave me a look that made Kary's Teacher Look seem like heartfelt gaze from a puppy. "We'll see about that."

◇◇◇

Ellin had matters to deal with at the PSN, so she wasn't there when Camden and Kary came home from the *My Fair Lady* dress rehearsal around eleven. Kary went on to bed, but Camden wanted another piece of giant hamburger. We heated one up in the microwave, divided it into two he-man chunks, and took our feast to the island.

Camden sat cross-legged on the sofa and unwrapped a slice of cheese for his burger. "I didn't get a chance to hold Millicent's hand tonight, but I got some very odd vibes concerning her face and her hands."

I kicked off my shoes and made myself comfortable in the blue arm chair. "Age related? Arthritis, maybe?"

"I asked her if she was feeling all right, and she assured me absolutely nothing was wrong and how dare I ask. Things got even stranger when the black and white pattern joined in."

I can usually make sense of Camden's visions, but this black and white thing had me stumped. I shrugged and took a bite of burger. "How old is Millicent? Maybe she was born before color was discovered."

"Late seventies, I believe."

"I could use some more ketchup. Would you levitate the bottle around the corner for me?"

"It's in the fridge."

"Bring the fridge around, then."

Camden put his burger on the coffee table and picked up his plastic cup full of Coke. "Everything stayed put at the theater tonight, thank goodness. During the Ascot race scene, a piece of the set fell over, and I thought I'd caused it, but the flat hadn't been properly anchored."

"You've got your windstorms, and I've got mine. I really stirred things up with Kary the other day."

His blue gaze went right through me. "Did you bring up her baby?"

"If we don't talk about these things, how can our relationship progress?"

"I told you she'd talk about Beth when she was ready."

"She needs to talk about Beth now. I can see it's killing her. She never talks to you about it?"

"She doesn't have to."

Of course not. He was able to feel her emotions, just as he felt mine. "Maybe I can't be strong enough for me, but I can be strong enough for her."

"So you've got everything worked out concerning Lindsey?"

Why even attempt to lie? "No." I don't usually ask Camden about my future because I don't want to know, but this time had I gone too far? "Have I ruined any chance I might have had with Kary?"

"I wish I could be more definite," he said, "but that's up to her."

◇◇◇

To keep from thinking about my vast stupidity, I spent most of Thursday morning at the Drug Palace, foiling evildoers and talking on the phone to other cosmetic companies. Only one remembered being contacted by George and said his ideas were so preposterous she'd posted a copy of his letter in the company break room where it had been a source of great amusement for the staff.

I remembered to call Lucy Warner to ask about Viola's scrapbooks. She assured me that someone from the theater had retrieved them. She had no further information about George.

"Did you find any other programs or posters in the house?"

"No. A cousin called to make sure everything else was donated to Goodwill."

Good old Dahlia, not wanting to be involved in any way. I thanked Lucy and walked back up the aisle to the pharmacy to report to Ted that all was well in the Palace. Then Kary called with another invitation to lunch, which filled me with such relief I stopped breathing for a moment. We met at the Elms, a classy little restaurant near Friendly Shopping Center. Although there are no elms, each table is sheltered by its own little grove of palm and fichus trees in ornamental pots, so diners have privacy. Green and white tablecloths, real silverware, and fresh flowers in glass vases add to the garden theme. I was glad for the opportunity to let her in on what had happened.

Kary looked through the menu. "So there was nothing in Viola's house or her scrapbook about *Arsenic and Old Lace*?"

"There was a place for it, right before the *My Fair Lady* stuff. I don't believe Viola left them out. These scrapbooks were a well organized record of her life in the theater. I think someone took the *Arsenic* mementoes."

"To cover up the crime?"

"Possibly. If a member of the cast was responsible, they wouldn't want us to make that connection."

Kary took out her phone. "The *Herald* might have had an online review." She had to pause her search to give our waiter her order. Then she looked up the newspaper's website and read for a while. Her eyes widened. "David, you're not going to believe this. There isn't a review, but I looked up a description of the play. *Arsenic and Old Lace* is a comedy about a man who finds out his two aunts are poisoning lonely old men with elderberry wine and burying them in the cellar."

"What? You're kidding." She handed me her phone so I could read the synopsis.

Arsenic and Old Lace had been written in 1939 by Joseph Kesselring. The hero of the play, Mortimer Brewster, not only had two murderous little old aunts, but one brother who believed he was Teddy Roosevelt, and another evil brother on the run from the law who'd had plastic surgery to look like Boris Karloff, the actor who played the original Frankenstein's monster. The play was considered a farce and a black comedy. "This is too much of a coincidence. Now I definitely need to find out who was in that play."

"When the murderer was in Viola's house, he or she must have gone through the scrapbooks and removed any mention of *Arsenic and Old Lace* so no one would find a connection."

"But there's bound to be some sort of record of the play at the theater. Don't they have a website?"

"Here." Kary took back her phone. "Let me see." She made another search and scrolled down the page. "Okay, here's all the info on *My Fair Lady*, dates and times of performances, cast list. Why isn't there anything about *Arsenic and Old Lace*? They just did it in February."

"Who's responsible for putting information on the website?"

"I don't know, but I'll find out." Our orders came, and she put away her phone. "I needed this, David."

"What? Chicken salad on whole wheat? It does look good."

"This case! Something else to do besides running into dead ends like Baby Love."

"I'm sure you'll find another shady company to bring down."

"Thanks for letting me help you."

"There's one simple way to become a permanent member of the Randall Detective Agency, you know."

She indicated my soup and sandwich. "Are you going to spell it out with crackers?"

"Do I need to spell it out?"

"No." She took a few bites of her chicken salad and then put her fork down. She gave me a long look and came to some sort of decision. "I want to apologize."

"For what?"

"For going off on you the other day about Beth."

"You don't need to apologize. I was out of line."

"You were trying to help me. I shouldn't keep everything so tightly locked away. I should say her name out loud every day until it no longer hurts so bad." Tears formed in her eyes. "I know her little soul is at peace. My soul needs to be at peace, too, but it's so hard."

It took me a long time before I could even think about Lindsey. Even longer to look at her picture or watch her dance. Kary didn't have any pictures of Beth. There had been nothing to see, nothing to hold.

I reached for her hand. "I wish I'd been there for you."

She wiped her eyes on her napkin. "You're here for me now. Thank you."

"I'll always be here for you."

She thanked me again, blew out a shaky breath, and picked up her fork as if to say, that's done. That's all I can manage at this time. "I'll check that website as soon as I get home."

One elephant had been slowly pushed away. I was determined another would not take its place.

Chapter Fifteen

"I could've danced all night."

Despite the prevailing icy conditions surrounding Camden and Ellin, *My Fair Lady* opened for a preview audience that night. I brought Rufus and Angie with me to the theater. Ellin was there, too, along with her mother and sisters and most of the congregation from Victory Holiness. The show was a hundred times better than the last time I'd seen it, but the fellow playing Henry Higgins had a bad case of opening night jitters. He made it through the first scene okay, the one where Higgins meets Eliza on the street and makes a bet with his cronies that he can teach her to speak proper English, but even I could tell he was missing lines and wasn't sure where he needed to be standing. From his slightly unsteady stance, I had the suspicion he'd had a little too much to drink before the show. As he exited, he nearly toppled into the orchestra pit. He seesawed a bit then abruptly had his balance. The audience laughed as if this were part of the show and applauded as he went off stage, but I'd seen a very similar trick at home.

At intermission, I went in search of Camden. I found him around back, standing outside with all the actors who needed a smoke. He looked pretty snazzy in the old-fashioned gray suit and striped ascot. His Freddy haircut was mostly at the back, so he still had plenty to run his hands through.

"Was it too obvious, Randall? There wasn't enough time to reach him."

"He looked tipsy, that's all," I said. "The audience thought it was part of the show."

"Thank God. We've got him in the dressing room, filling him with coffee. The poor guy was so nervous he must have had way too much."

"Will he be able to finish the show?"

"His understudy's standing by." Camden indicated another man dressed like Higgins going over a script with the stage manager. "Did Ellie come?"

"Oh, yes. I'm still on the case to find out what's wrong with you."

"I hope you can."

"I think you ought to tell her. Maybe you won't even have kids. You've always said your own future never comes in clearly. What if you're wrong? You want to risk losing Ellin over this?"

"There's still this—this moving things to contend with. She'll go nuts."

"Yeah, she'll have a field day. But that's a chance you oughta take. If she wants to marry you, she'll have to back off."

"Back off?" Ellin's voice said, and we both jumped. She approached, her expression puzzled and annoyed. "Field day? What the hell are you talking about?"

"Just doing my job, ma'am," I said. "Grilling a suspect." Damn! How much had she heard?

Enough, evidently. "Cam, what do you mean, 'She'll go nuts'? And what's all this about moving things?"

I could hear the synapses firing frantically. "In the house," Camden said. "To make room for your stuff."

"Why should that matter if we're not getting married?"

Camden had come to the end of this burst of creativity. He started to stammer something else as I groped for an explanation. We were rescued by the stage manager.

"Places, everyone!"

Camden dashed back inside. As I headed back around the auditorium, Ellin ran after me. "Randall."

I stopped and faced her. "I'm sure he'll tell you everything when he's ready."

"Oh, that's real comforting. That's what I pay you the big bucks to say."

"It's all I've got right now."

"Moving things?"

"Like he said, to make room for your stuff."

"I'm not going to live there. If anything, he should be packing his stuff."

"One problem at a time, Ellin."

She gave me one of her deadliest stares. "You might want to think about packing your stuff, too."

"No way. If you and Camden leave, the house is mine."

She wasn't about to cut me any slack. "We'll see about that."

◇◇◇

The second act went without a hitch. The original Higgins pulled himself together and did a credible job. In Act One, "On the Street Where You Live" stopped the show, and Camden sang part of it again in act two. Despite whatever else might be happening in his life, when it comes to singing, Camden always manages to come through. His clear tenor voice filled the auditorium, and when he came to the part about wanting to be nowhere on earth but Eliza's street, I saw Ellin give her cheeks a rough swipe.

I noticed that in one scene in the first act, the scene at the racetrack, everybody had on black and white. I thought I'd mention that to Camden, in case he hadn't noticed. Black and white figured prominently in weddings, too, so maybe he was having flashbacks, or flashforwards I should say, to the happy day—if it ever happened.

After the show, we went backstage to congratulate everyone. Camden and Ellin made polite conversation, as if they'd just met. I heard her say, "Have you had enough time to think?" in a tone that could have easily made it rain in Spain. He shook his head. I couldn't hear his reply.

I looked around for Kary and found her and Charlie still down in the orchestra pit going over a section of "I Could've

Danced All Night" that apparently hadn't gone the way they wanted it to during the performance. When they finished, I said, "Great show, guys."

Charlie jotted a note in his book. "Thanks. I wanted to make sure Kary knew the repeat we added. She's in charge tomorrow night."

Kary also marked the place in her music. "Charlie's agreed to go hear Taffy sing."

I couldn't believe how relieved I was. "Good news."

Charlie didn't look happy. "We'll see."

"What could go wrong?" Kary said.

Oh, so many things, I thought.

He turned off the piano and the light. "I don't know, Kary. These songs of hers are really awful."

"Either she'll be glad you made the effort, or you'll find out for sure if your relationship is in trouble. And you can come tell me all about it."

That took care of my relief. Back to anxious worry.

The cast had to stay for pictures, so I took Rufus and Angie home and came back for Camden. The photo shoot was over, and he was in the dressing room he shared with Higgins and Pickering. He had on his jeans and shirt and was wiping off the last streaks of makeup.

"Stop, stop," I said. "For the first time in your life, you have a tan."

He grimaced. "I have to put on two layers, otherwise, I'm invisible. I don't see how women stand this stuff. It's like wearing a mask."

"I think that's the whole idea."

He went to the sink and washed his face and hands. "I wish I could wash away this talent this easily. If I only knew what it was going to do, how strong it's going to be." He dried his face, now back to its original color: pale. "As soon as the show's over, I'm going to tell her."

"Wise move. If you tell her now, they'd be hard pressed to find another Freddy."

Camden wanted to make sure he left matinee tickets for some friends at the box office, so we went up the aisle to the lobby. While he talked with the girl behind the counter, I checked out the photos and plaques decorating the walls. I didn't think I'd find a picture from *Arsenic and Old Lace*, so I was surprised to see one and even more surprised to recognize a familiar moustache. George McMillan stood with the other cast members of the play. He was dressed as Teddy Roosevelt. Everyone was smiling except George, and that included Viola Mitchell and Millicent Crotty.

A connection.

"Camden, come have a look at this." He came over. "Recognize anyone else in the photo besides Millicent who would know both Viola and George?"

The cast of *Arsenic and Old Lace* was nowhere near as large as the *My Fair Lady* cast. "I don't see anyone who's in our show."

"I can't believe there's a picture here. We haven't been able to find anything about this play."

"Let me ask Emma."

He went back to the box office and talked briefly with the girl before returning. "That photo was just put up today. Emma says the fellow who does the frames for them had misplaced it in his studio."

A lucky break for me. Whoever was covering his or her *Arsenic* tracks missed this one. "Well, now I have a connection between George and Viola, and apparently, someone was after them both."

"The stage manager might know more about it, if he's still here."

We went back into the theater and found the stage manager walking along the rows of seats and picking up discarded programs. "Yeah, I remember George," he said. "He did only that one play. He did it as a favor to the director. He wasn't all that good, but he looked the part, and they didn't have anyone else who could play Teddy. They had a heck of a time getting him to rehearse, plus he made a nuisance of himself with the ladies."

Good old dependable George. "In what way?" I asked.

"Thought he was hot stuff. I was dating the girl who played Elaine Harper, and I had to tell him several times to back off."

"So he didn't get any action. You figure that's why he didn't try out for another play?"

"Maybe. All he had to do was yell, 'Charge!' and run up the stairs, but you would've thought he was the biggest thing to ever hit the stage. I guess he thought the theater was the local passion pit and being in a show would make him a stud."

"Did he ever talk about his job at BeautiQueen cosmetics?"

"I heard him bragging a time or two how he was going to invent some kind of cream that would revolutionize the world, but, like everything else he talked about, he was pretty much an old windbag. We were glad to see him go."

"Who was the director for that show?"

"We had a guest director from the college, Wesley Lennox. I think he's still there."

I thanked the man for the information, and Camden and I walked back up the aisle.

"I had the same report from one of George's co-workers and from the clerk at the Green Palms Hotel," I said. "George was an expert at unwanted attention."

"Maybe he hit on the wrong woman at the wrong time."

"And she hit back."

Chapter Sixteen

"And up to his old tricks."

Friday morning, I went to the University of North Carolina at Parkland campus and found Wesley Lennox. Lennox was a big broad-shouldered man who looked more like a football coach than a drama professor. He met me in his office on the second floor of the university's huge auditorium. Framed posters of past shows fought for space on the walls, and stacks of plays filled every corner of the room.

"See if you can find a spot to sit, Mr. Randall." Lennox wedged himself behind his desk, which was also overflowing with scripts and notebooks. "How can I help you?"

I moved text books from a folding chair and sat down. "I'm investigating the deaths of George McMillan and Viola Mitchell."

"I could hardly believe what happened to Viola. She was a feisty old gal, but I didn't think anyone hated her. And you don't think George committed suicide?"

"I'm checking all possibilities. I was told you directed *Arsenic and Old Lace* at the Parkland Little Theater and Viola and George were both in the show. I understand George played Teddy as a favor for you."

"Sort of." Lennox moved another stack of papers so he could lean his arms on his desk. "We went to college together right here at UNC-P, but over the years, we'd lost touch. The folks at Little Theater called me to direct *Arsenic*, but nobody showed up at auditions who looked anything like Teddy. Then I remembered George and his moustache and gave him a call. Teddy's an easy role, lots of fun."

I thought of George scowling in the cast picture. "Did he enjoy it?"

Lennox rubbed his chin. "Not really. I'm not sure what he expected. If you haven't done a play before, you don't realize what a commitment it can be. Blocking is a tedious process, rehearsals can go on much longer than you planned, and of course, sometimes you get a fractious cast."

"Is that what happened?"

"My two leading ladies, Viola and Millicent, were divas, and George didn't help matters. I should have remembered from our college days that he thought he was God's gift to women."

"But he wasn't successful?"

"Not in college and not during the show. He always tried too hard. No one in the cast liked him. It got to where he wouldn't come to rehearsals. He did the show, though, and did as well as I could've wanted. That's the last I saw of him."

"Did you know his plans for a new face cream for BeautiQueen cosmetics?"

"I knew he worked for a cosmetic company. He seemed to think that would impress the ladies."

"But he didn't tell you his ideas?"

"He bragged about revolutionizing the world of makeup. I didn't pay him any attention. I just wanted him to know his cues. I remember one night Viola threatened to quit if he didn't straighten up. Usually nothing kept her off that stage. She was a trouper."

It was beginning to sound like Viola would've killed George, if she wasn't already dead. "Besides Viola, do you recall anyone having a serious quarrel with George?"

"No, but he didn't make any friends." He pulled out his desk drawer. I expected papers to fly out in all directions, but he reached in and brought out a folder, which he searched through until he found what he wanted. "Here's a picture of the cast."

This was different from the one I'd seen. Viola and Millicent Crotty stood side by side. They wore long old fashioned dresses and shawls, Viola towering over the shorter, stouter Millicent. Both had on little lace caps and looked a hundred years old. There was George in his Teddy Roosevelt outfit, a younger man in a suit, and a pretty young woman. The stage manager's girl friend, I guessed. There was an actor dressed as a policeman, someone who looked like a mad scientist, and a looming man in dark clothes who reminded me of Frankenstein.

"I understand this play is about two little old ladies who murder people with poisoned wine."

"Yes, they think they're doing a kindness to lonely old men. Their nephew finds out about all the bodies buried in the cellar and hilarity ensues."

"You realize Viola was poisoned with wine and buried in her basement."

"A very sick joke. You think it was someone in the cast?"

"Someone who knew the play, for sure. I need the names of all these people."

Lennox had a cast list in the folder, including their contact information. Besides Viola, Millicent, and George, there were eight names. "We kept losing cast members for one reason or another, so the fellow playing Reverend Harper also played Mr. Gibbs, and the fellow playing Mr. Witherspoon played Officer O'Hara. Then I had to fill in as Officer Brophy because the actor got another role and decided not to honor his obligation to our show."

Eight people, all of whom had good reason to hate George McMillan and possibly Viola Mitchell, as well. "Can I have a copy of this list?"

"I'll make you a copy."

Lennox went down the hall to the copy machine. When he came back, he handed me my copy. "If I were you, I'd start with Millicent Crotty. She'll tell you George was unprofessional and a pest. I had to hear her say that a thousand times."

◇◇◇

"Unprofessional and a pest," Millicent Crotty said when I called her from my car. I had to explain who I was twice, but she still didn't remember me calling to ask about Viola. In this case, her memory loss worked to my advantage, because she didn't remember refusing to talk to me, either. She did remember George and gave me an earful. "I've worked with amateurs before, and he was by far the worst. What's he done now?"

"I'm investigating his alleged suicide." If I thought that would make her pause, I was wrong.

"I'm not in the least surprised. He was obviously an unhappy man."

"Do you have any idea why?"

"He was incredibly moody. He got upset if we didn't laugh at his crappy jokes. He was always bragging about his work at that cosmetics company as if his ideas were going to save the world. And he actually thought I would go out with him! I set him straight. He tried that nonsense with Viola, too, and she was pushing seventy at the time. You'd think the smell of those cats would've put him off, but no, he kept pestering her. Even though she said she never took her costume home, I swear I could smell cat on it. She'd lived with the damned things so long, they all smelled the same. I don't know what happened to the cats. She was probably buried with them, like some Egyptian queen."

"About George," I said.

"I certainly tried at first to help the man. I showed him how to project and keep himself open to the audience and how to properly apply stage makeup, if you can believe that. You'd think he'd know something about makeup since he was such a big shot at BeautiQueen! I told Wesley Lennox I didn't care if McMillan was a friend of his. He'd better not cast him in any show I was in ever again."

She sounded as if she could continue like this for the rest of the day. I waited until she took a breath and changed the subject. "Mrs. Crotty, when was the last time you saw Viola?"

"That was Wednesday night after rehearsal. I gave her a ride home."

"Did she have any enemies, anyone who might want to harm her?"

"Viola had an abrupt manner and always spoke her mind, but she was never cruel to anyone. Her murder shocked everyone in the theater community."

"Were you aware her death was arranged like the plot of *Arsenic and Old Lace*?"

"Poisoned wine and buried in the cellar. Someone out there is very disturbed."

"Someone who knew the play."

There was a brief silence on Millicent's end of the line. "Aside from McMillan, the cast was very congenial and supportive. We had several folks quit, and other cast members stepped up and took extra parts. Even Lennox had to take a lead."

"I understand you've taken Viola's part in *My Fair Lady*."

"Yes, and don't go thinking for one minute I coveted that part! It was Viola's from day one of auditions, and I never begrudged her that. She was perfect for the role. We never fought over any part in any play. She was very tall, you see, and I'm short and plump. Directors are always looking for certain physical types. Henry Higgins' mother needed to be tall and imposing. I'm neither. They're just going to have to deal with that. But no matter what happens, the show must go on."

Once Millicent began talking theater stuff, it was hard to get in a word, but I managed to ask about all the other people in Lennox's production. She'd worked with most of them and gave me succinct views on their appearances and their characters, both on stage and off. Everyone had loved Viola, so Millicent was certain I could mark them off the suspect list for Viola's murder.

"And as for McMillan, I would say the men tolerated him, and that lovely little girl playing Elaine laughed off his advances. Her boyfriend was our stage manager, so George didn't try anything with her. After a while, he stopped coming to rehearsals, and as far as I was concerned, the problem was solved."

"But he did the show."

"Oh, yes, he did every single performance and didn't miss a line or an entrance, not that Teddy has a lot to do."

I thanked Millicent for her time and all the information and managed to hang up without cutting off another stream of backstage gossip. Next I called the man who had played Mortimer Brewster, the lead, then the two villains of the play, and the man who had filled two parts. All told me abbreviated versions of Millicent's story. Viola had been a tough old gal, a real queen of the theater, someone they respected. They were very sorry she was dead and hoped I could catch her murderer. George McMillan was full of himself, cocky, and at first, they feared he was unreliable. But he'd come through and done the part, so they didn't consider him a total loss.

"Sometimes in community theater you have to take whatever you can get," the man who had played Dr. Einstein said. "You get people who've never been up in front of a crowd before and they freeze on stage. You get people who drink and fool around backstage and walk right through the scenery. You get people who fall into the orchestra pit. I've seen it all. McMillan didn't bother me."

Since I'd seen a similar incident during the performance of *My Fair Lady*, I knew what he was talking about. As for George's performance, there was a general consensus among the actors I talked with. He did his job. They'd worked with worse. Why would any of them track down George, travel to Florida, and shoot him?

◇◇◇

I returned to 302 Grace to review what I had so far. George McMillan, failed pickup artist, tried to sell a secret face cream formula to rival companies, then stole BeautiQueen money and ran off to Florida where, tired of being a screwup and filled with remorse over his evil deeds, supposedly committed suicide. So far, I didn't have much of a case.

Rufus clumped by the office door on his way to the porch. He had a beer in one hand and a kitten in the other. "How're things goin'?"

"Not real good. You leave any beer?"

"Yeah, there's a couple."

I joined Rufus on the porch. Over the dim rush of traffic noise from Food Row, we could hear a chorus of little frogs cheeping from the park. The kitten snuggled in Rufus's huge hand and began to purr.

"How's your house hunting going?" I asked.

Rufus shifted the wad of tobacco to his other cheek. "We've 'bout decided on the one on River Street. It needs work, but Cam said he'd help out. 'Course it don't seem like he's gonna be available to do repairs if he calls off the wedding. Ellin'll stomp a mud hole in him and walk him dry."

"I think he'll reconsider."

"Don't know what's going on around here. Him and Ellin, Charlie and Taffy, Charlie and Kary."

Even though Rufus isn't psychic, he seems to know everything that happens in the house. "Don't start."

"Somebody needs to, and it ain't me. When the wind blows hard enough, even turkeys can fly."

I stared at him for a minute and then had to laugh. "Damn, where do you come up with these sayings?"

"Don't come up with them, Yankee boy. Everybody round here knows 'em."

"I never hear Camden talking like that."

"That's cause he didn't have the proper raising." He took a drink and wiped his mouth with the back of his hand. "Bet he knows some, though."

The spider up in the corner had snagged a fat moth. Rufus gestured to the web. "Wonder if Cam knows what he's getting into. Never can see his future, you know."

I can't see my future, either. I'm not sure I want to. "It's what he's always wanted. A home, a family." That's what I wanted, too.

"Yeah. Guess that's what everybody wants." When a car drove up with Ellin's sisters waving out the windows, he grinned. "Now here's some gals who know how to have fun. Oughta get yourself hitched to one of them."

Caroline and Sandra got out of their car and bounded up the porch steps.

Caroline said, "David, you're the very man we want to see."

"That's what I like to hear."

"This is serious. Hi, Rufus."

He touched the brim of his cap. "Afternoon, ladies."

I offered my rocking chair, but Caroline sat on the swing, and Sandra sat on the railing. She leaned closer.

"What's all this with Cam calling off the wedding? Does he have a death wish?"

I'd been wondering when the sisters would hear the news. "He's a little edgy, that's all."

"Ellin hired you to straighten him out, so do it."

"I'm working on it."

"And his bachelor party? Have you planned that yet?"

"No, I hadn't thought that far."

Caroline reached over to punch my arm. "Do we have to do everything?"

"Yeah, sure, go ahead."

"I got that under control," Rufus said.

"Then it ought to be legendary. No, really, David, what's the problem?"

I didn't see any reason not to tell them an abbreviated version. "Okay, it's like this. Camden's having a little trouble controlling a certain element of his talent. He's afraid to pass this on to his children. I've tried to explain to him that if he does have psychic kids, he can help them understand what's going on."

"And Ellin can exploit them on TV."

"Exactly. Once he's calmed down, he'll be fine. He loves Ellin. He's not going to let her get away."

The sisters exchanged a glance. Sometimes I think they're psychic. "We've never seen Ellin so upset," Sandra said. "We had to come see what was going on. Is Cam here?"

"He's taking a nap," Rufus said. "Got another show tonight."

Caroline got up. "We came to warn him that Mother plans to stop by later. She's not pleased."

"I'll tell him."

"We could only distract her for so long. There was a screwup with the church fellowship hall being booked for a reunion the same time as the reception, so that kept her busy for a while, but now she's out for his blood."

Sandra checked her watch. "We've got to go change the ring bearer's pillow. It's the wrong shade of green."

"Ring bearer? I thought Ellin didn't want any kids in the wedding."

The sisters shared an evil grin. "She doesn't," Caroline said. "See you later!"

Rufus chuckled as the sisters drove off. "Them two's got more than their share of sass." He shifted the kitten to his other hand where it promptly attacked his thumb. "And speaking of sass, we gotta find homes for these little monsters. Why don't you take care of that? Maybe that Folly woman would take one."

"She would if it was peach-colored."

"What about your other clients? They likely to take one?"

I didn't think Charlie would be a responsible pet owner. Lucy Warner, however, even though she wasn't a client, might be a very good choice. "I've recently met someone who loves animals. She has a doberman, though."

Rufus shook the kitten off his thumb. "Damn. I think this one could hold its own."

Chapter Seventeen

"Ding, dong, the bells are gonna chime."

Around noon, I decided to take a break from the alien casseroles and have a peanut butter sandwich. Camden got up from his nap in time to join me and Rufus in the kitchen for lunch.

I tossed him the jar of peanut butter. "The sisters came by to tell you Mom is on the warpath."

"I'm not surprised."

"Rufus and I can probably smuggle you out of the country."

"No, thanks. I'll take my chances." He made a sandwich and brought it to the counter where Rufus was chowing down on what looked like a ham and potato casserole. "There's still some of that left?"

Rufus swallowed. "And a couple more in the freezer. This one's not too bad. Got something in it I don't quite recognize, but it's good and chewy."

Which was why I opted for peanut butter. I sat down at the counter. "I talked with Wesley Lennox this morning. He confirms that George was a lousy actor and even lousier with the ladies. Then I finally got in touch with Millicent Crotty. She'd still be griping about him if I hadn't hung up. Other cast members confirm what she told me."

Rufus took another big spoonful of casserole. "Sounds like this guy was universally disliked."

Camden and I both paused. My eyebrows went up. "'Universally'?"

"Reckon that earns me ten points."

"Nice one, Rufus."

"Was gonna use unequivocally, but that'd just be showin' off."

Camden passed me the chips. "So what's next?"

"I've got some more cosmetics companies to talk to and Drug Palace patrol." And I've got to get Charlie and Taffy back together, I added to myself, although I'm sure Camden heard me. "And there's the little matter of my other client and her Case of the Reluctant Bridegroom."

"I'll work it out."

Rufus spoke through a mouthful of casserole. "What's the problem? Afraid she'll go nuts 'bout you movin' stuff around?"

Again we both stared at him.

He wiped his beard with the back of his hand. "I live here, you know."

"Rufus, when did you see me moving stuff around?"

"Wasn't you sleepwalkin' last night?"

Camden looked wary. "I haven't done that in a long time."

"It was either you or Casper the Friendly Ghost. You walked right past my door, and all these little things was followin' you. Coupla of magazines, a plastic cup, some of Ellin's seashells. I turned you around and sent you and your parade back upstairs."

"You're sure you weren't dreaming?"

"Not the way Angie was snorin' last night. I was wide awake, but you weren't. Ellin's bound to see something like that sooner or later. Might as well come clean. Sure, she'll want you on that show of hers, but you've held out so far."

"The safest thing is not to marry her."

"Now you're just being stupid. You'll still be levitatin' things whether you're married or not."

"But I'm worried about our kids."

"You can have kids whether you're married or not, too, have you thought of that? If you ain't careful, it could happen any time."

I put my sandwich down. "Rufus has the perfect saying for this occasion. How does that go again? Something about the wind and turkeys?"

"Naw, I got a better one, 'cause Cam ain't been thinkin' this through."

Camden sighed. "Lay it on me."

"You're worryin' 'bout things that may never happen." Rufus pointed a large finger at him. "That's all foam and no beer."

◇◇◇

Rufus went off to meet Angie at another house. Camden had housekeeping chores to do. I worked in my office until I heard a car drive up. I thought it might be Ellin, but it was her mother. No need to guess why she was here.

Camden met her at the door. "Good afternoon, Jean."

"Cam, dear, I hope you're not busy. I need to speak to you."

"No, please come in. I was just washing the dishes. Come have a seat."

I got up and peered around the corner. Jean didn't look or sound very bloodthirsty. They went into the island where she spoke in an earnest tone.

"Now, dear, I've heard all this nonsense about you wanting to call off the wedding, and I want you to reconsider. Besides all the trouble and expense, it would be vastly unfair to Ellin to back out now and so embarrassing to the family."

I couldn't believe it. Was she trying to talk him into going through with the wedding? I thought she'd be thrilled to have him out of the picture.

This obviously threw Camden for a loop. He took a long moment to reply. "I'm sorry. I don't have any control over this situation."

"What situation? If there's another woman—"

"Oh, no. No. Ellie is the only one for me. She always has been."

"Then for heaven's sake, what is the problem?"

He sounded understandably puzzled. "I thought you'd be happy. I know you don't really approve of me. I've had to make my own family. I have no formal education, no steady job. I see things no one else can see. Ellie deserves better."

"Maybe she does, but she's in love with you. You can't help the fact your mother gave you up. You can take classes if you want more education, and you can certainly find a decent job if you try. But you'd damn well better get yourself to Parkland Memorial Methodist on the 31st, or tell me why."

You see where Ellin gets all her charm? I angled myself for a better view of the island and caught a glimpse of Camden's face. He looked disconcerted, as if Jean Belton had leveled a killer gaze of her own into his brain. This is your future mother-in-law, I wanted to say. Do you know what you're doing?

She put her hand on his shoulder. "Cam, you may not be what I had in mind for Ellin, but you're a decent young man with a good reputation. I think you'll make a fine husband for my daughter. And now I want you to tell me what's bothering you."

For a moment, I thought he would refuse, but he'd said he was going to tell Ellin everything. Might as well share the news with Mom. Besides, she was being frighteningly understanding. He might not ever have another chance like this.

"Jean, how do you feel about grandchildren?"

"I'd love to have grandchildren."

"What if they were like me? Clairvoyant."

"Seems to me that's a bit far-fetched, isn't it?"

"What if they could do other things?" he said. "Things that aren't considered normal?"

"Dear, if you're worried about children having problems, let me assure you, not a one of mine is normal. It wouldn't bother me in the slightest."

"But it would bother Ellie."

Mrs. Belton considered this for a moment. "Oh, well, she'll just have to deal with it, won't she? And really, Cam, this clair-voyance you say you have—don't you think it's about time you grew out of it? Even if you have it, and I'm not sure you do, the children could be like Ellin."

"They're not going to be."

"You can't know that."

"I'm afraid I can," he said. "I've been getting stronger and clearer visions for days. You're going to have three grandchildren, two girls and a boy. All clairvoyant."

"I can't believe that." Another pat on his shoulder. "Dear, I really think all of this is just in your mind."

"That's exactly where it is," Camden said.

Her exasperated sigh was exactly like Ellin's. "And this is the reason you want to call off the wedding? That's nonsense. No one can predict how many children they're going to have and what they're going to be or how they're going to be. You and Ellin will have your hands full dealing with each other the first few years, believe me." She started for the door, stopped and leveled another stare. "I'll tell her you want to talk to her. You do want to talk to her, don't you?"

Camden wasn't crazy. "Yes, I do."

"Those are the very words I'd better hear on May 31st."

Jean left. Camden stood for a while and then turned his head. "I know you heard that, Randall."

"Yup," I said. "Decide right now these Belton women are going to drive you insane."

◇◇◇

As an antidote to all the wedding drama, Camden decided he needed to watch some mindless TV. I was trying to convince him that *Plan 9 From Outer Space* would be an ideal choice when Kary came home.

"I took the rest of Fred's things to the church, Cam. Someone will be able to use them."

He reached for the remote and muted the sound. "Thanks, Kary."

"David, it took some doing, but I found out why there's nothing about *Arsenic and Old Lace* on the website. I made a bunch of phone calls and finally got a hold of the woman who takes care of the site. She said someone hacked into it and deleted all references to the show. She figures it was one of the teenagers who helped run lights trying to impress a girlfriend. She'd heard them bragging about their computer skills."

"Or it was someone who doesn't want a connection known."

"Yes. Could be our murderer." She looked at Camden. "Are you okay? You look a little frazzled."

"Jean stopped by. Against all possible reason, she's decided I'm the right man for her daughter."

"Well, that's very good news, isn't it?"

He turned off the TV and set the remote on the coffee table. "Ellie's hired Randall to find out what's wrong with me."

Kary couldn't help but chuckle. "She hired you, David? She must be desperate."

"It's more of an angry desperation."

Kary turned back to Camden. "You have to tell her. Sooner or later she'll find out, and the longer you keep it from her the angrier she'll be. You can't start off your married life keeping this huge secret."

"I know. I hope and pray there'll be the right time."

"If this new talent suddenly appeared, maybe it'll suddenly go away."

"I hope and pray that happens, too."

"I still say it came on because you're nervous and excited about the wedding."

"Let's call it that."

I filled Kary in on my morning activities and what I'd learned from Wesley Lennox and Millicent Crotty. "I talked with cast members of the play, but I haven't come up with any real suspects. And I've just thought of something. Did Jordan and his team ever find the wine bottle? Camden, you said you saw a bottle of wine with a note, right? But where's the bottle?"

I wasn't sure Jordan would tell me, but when I called to ask, he must have been in a good mood.

"No wine bottle, but it would've been very easy for the murderer to smash it up and throw it away. Do you have any leads?"

He was playing nice, so I did, too. "I have a list of cast members who were in *Arsenic and Old Lace* with Viola."

"Thanks, but we've checked them out. Anything else?"

"Her best friend Millicent Crotty was the last one to see her alive. She gave Viola a ride home Wednesday after rehearsal."

"Checked that, too."

"Was she poisoned?"

"Yes, with arsenic. The coroner estimates she'd been dead approximately forty-eight hours when Camden discovered her. How's he doing, by the way?"

Oh, he's got bigger problems than a little flashback or two to the murder. "Nervous about the wedding."

Jordan gave a short bark of laughter. "I would be, too, if I was marrying Ellin Belton. Keep in touch."

He hung up. I closed my phone. "Jordan has everything except the George McMillan connection, which is something we're still trying to figure out."

"Maybe we're looking in the wrong place," Kary said. "What about Millicent? You said she hated George."

"But would she go all the way to Florida and shoot him?"

"She could've hired someone. I'm just trying out ideas here."

"And I appreciate your ideas, but I think the killer is someone who hated George and Viola."

"Still, I'll keep on Millicent. She may know something yet."

"If she remembers."

Chapter Eighteen

"She completely done me in."

That night, Kary and Camden went to their performance, and I dragged Charlie with me to the Spider's Web for Taffy's opening night. He argued all the way.

"I can't stand this music."

"Put your brain in neutral, smile, and look interested. It won't cost you a thing."

"Just my sanity."

"You've already lost that."

The Spider's Web was a dark little club like the Tempo, but much fancier with black silk draperies and small round glass-topped tables surrounded by slick chrome chairs. The bar was a long piece of chrome decorated with twinkly silver lights. The stage featured black silk curtains with a lacy overlay depicting spider webs. On stage, a single spotlight shone on a chrome stool and matching microphone. Once inside, I could tell Charlie was waiting for the opportunity to bolt. I steered him to a table right up front.

"Sit."

It was worth all the aggravation to see the look on Taffy's face. She beamed at Charlie in a way that had to calm any fears he had about their relationship. She took her place on the stool and adjusted the microphone. She wore a short black dress, silver high heels, and a silver jacket. Charlie waved at her and smiled. His smile soon faded as she began her set.

> *"The dejection of my heart sends waves of fragrant longing.*
> *I call to you, but there's no answer, no answer.*
> *How can the emergence of effusion pass the borders of expression?*
> *Is there a remedy for such perfidy that ransacks my soul?"'*

I saw Charlie's fist tighten on the table. I hoped he wasn't planning to leap up and run out.

> *"'I find myself in a perplexing ditch with no sides.*
> *I long for the hyperphysical heart that can pull me, a restless cipher, from the winding stream.'"*

"Randall."

"Concentrate on her legs. That's what I'm doing."

Taffy did look stunning in her black and silver outfit. Charlie took a deep breath and shifted his gaze. At the same time, Taffy flung her arms wide. Her voice went up three octaves. Everyone in the place jumped.

> *"'Woe! My life is saturated at last! Leave me! I am fulfilled!'"*

She stopped, lowered her arms, and bowed her head. The crowd applauded. Charlie managed to unclench his fists to join in.

"This is worse than I thought."

"But the crowd loves her. Be happy for her success. Otherwise, you're going to drive her away."

"I need a cigarette."

Taffy started her second song. Charlie sighed and sat back, his expression resigned. She sang seven songs, each one hideous. When she'd finished and taken her bows, she came straight for Charlie.

He gulped and spoke under his breath, "My God, that was awful, Randall. What am I going to say?"

"Say you're glad to see her. Say she looks great and you're happy for her."

Taffy hugged him and gave him a big kiss. "I saw you out here and I couldn't believe it!"

"You look great, Taffy. I'm so happy for you."

She beamed and gave him another kiss. "Oh, that means so much to me. What did you think of 'Evening Star'? I've been working on that song forever."

Charlie glanced at me for help. Fortunately, a long thin man squeezed through the tables to pat Taffy's arm and give his opinion.

"Lovely songs, dear. I'm such a fan. 'Evening Star' was immensely satisfying, a true aperitif for the soul."

As he drifted off, Taffy chuckled. Charlie said, "I couldn't agree more."

"Was it your favorite? Or did you like 'Candy Floss' better?"

"I think I liked the last one the best."

"Really? I love that one, too. I'm so glad you came! And you, too, David. I've got to get a drink before the next set. You're staying, aren't you?"

"Yes, of course," Charlie said.

She kissed him for the third time and hurried off. He turned to me with a rueful smile. "I'm going to get a drink, too."

He had two drinks and made a great pretense of listening to the rest of Taffy's program, which was slightly less painful than the first part. When she finished, we applauded with the crowd. I turned to Charlie. "Now, that wasn't so bad, was it?"

"It was the worst thing I ever sat through," he said, "but I'm glad I came. I concentrated on how beautiful she looked up there in the spotlight. I really never get to see her sing when I play for her. I'm always over to one side or behind her." He sighed. "The things we do for love."

I thought the evening had gone well. That was before I saw Manuel Estaban. As Taffy stepped off the stage, Estaban came to her, arms outstretched.

"Taffinia! You were magnificent!" He kissed her on both cheeks. "Fantastico! I wish the whole class could have been here. Your use of the plural negative was inspired."

Charlie stared at him. "Is that the teacher?"

"'Fraid so."

He didn't say anything else, but as Estaban continued his praises, I could see the steam building behind Charlie's eyes.

Taffy took Estaban by the arm and pulled him over to our table. "Manny, this is Charlie Valentine and David Randall."

Estaban shook my hand. "Ah, yes. Mr. Randall came by the school the other day. He is also interested in songwriting, are you not, Mr. Randall?"

Taffy frowned. "Are you? I didn't know that."

Estaban then shook Charlie's hand. If Charlie's grip was a little intense, the teacher didn't seem to notice. "And you, Mr. Valentine, are you also a songwriter?"

"I play piano with J.J.'s Hot Six at the Tempo. Taffy sings with us."

"I shall have to come hear you there, as well, Taffinia."

Unfortunately, by this time, she'd worked things out. "Randall, did you come by the school to check up on me?"

"Why would I do that?"

"Did Charlie send you? You told him, didn't you?"

I tried to avoid an explosion. "Your songwriting wasn't a secret, really, was it? Otherwise, he might not have known about your concert tonight."

Things might have been okay if Charlie hadn't decided to join in. "Otherwise, I might not have known about Senior Slick here, either."

Taffy's eyes flamed almost as hot as Ellin's. "I knew you'd try to make something of this! Manny is a very good friend and an excellent teacher. You have no right to insinuate anything else."

Estaban, to his credit, took the high road. "It is quite all right. I understand completely why Mr. Valentine would feel jealous. You are a beautiful young woman. If you will excuse me." He gave a little bow and walked away.

I caught Charlie's sleeve as he started to follow. "Calm down."

Taffy gave Charlie a slap on the shoulder. "How dare you insult Manny! How dare you try to make a scene on my big night?

"I'm here, aren't I? That ought to count for something."

"No one's keeping score here, Charlie! You either came because you wanted to, or Randall made you come."

"Thank God I did. I see what's going on now."

"Nothing's going on!"

Their quarrel was attracting attention. "Look," I said. "You two sit down, have a drink, and talk this out."

But Taffy had had enough. "No. I'm going to apologize to Manny, and then I'm going home."

She made her way out through the crowd, pausing to accept congratulations. Charlie watched her go. Then he slumped into his chair.

"You're an idiot," I said.

"I know, I know." He put his head down in his hands and clutched his hair. "She drives me crazy."

"All you had to do was smile and say you liked her program."

"I didn't like it. It was shit."

"I'm trying to help you here." I didn't add that I was trying to help myself, too. If things continued to deteriorate between Charlie and Taffy, Charlie would head back to Kary. "Call her tonight and say you're sorry."

"No."

"Okay, I give up. Be miserable." I put my money on the table and prepared to leave.

Charlie raised his head. "Wait. Will you do one more thing? Will you see how serious she is about Estaban?"

"Only if you agree to call her tonight."

"All right."

I found Taffy and Manuel Estaban outside the club. He was kissing her hand, but it was a good-bye kiss.

"Such a triumphant evening, my dear. Congratulations again. I will see you in class."

He got in his car and drove away. Taffy turned and saw me.

"I should think you'd get tired of being a spy."

"Charlie's sorry. You know how his temper is."

"Why didn't he come tell me that himself?"

"I didn't want him punching Estaban unless there's a good reason."

There was a long pause. "Did he like any of the songs at all?"

"Taffy, whether he did or not, you know what a sacrifice it was for him to come. Does he have to like your songs to like you?"

"But they're such a part of me."

"There's bound to be a part of Charlie you don't like."

"He's so damn stubborn."

"So are you."

"I don't want to see him for a while. I need my space."

In your perplexing ditch with no sides? "Okay. I'll tell him."

Back at the table, Charlie was on his fourth beer.

"What did she say, Randall?"

"She needs a little space."

He raised his glass in salute. "Woe, my life is saturated at last."

Chapter Nineteen

"Show me."

Saturday morning, Kary slept late, so I didn't get a chance to ask her about Operation Millicent. I spent the morning at the Drug Palace, where I caught another teenage girl shoplifting another bracelet.

"Damn," I said to Ted as a policeman conferred with the teen and her mom. "What is it with these bracelets? Why don't you just give one to every customer?"

He took the bracelet and hung it back on the revolving rack. "It's the latest fad. In another week or two, they'll all be after something else."

"You'd think they'd want something prettier than this."

He shrugged. "You never know what's going to catch on with the kids."

"If I catch many more kids, I'll have all the shoplifters in Parkland."

Ted went back behind the counter and started straightening the boxes of film. I leaned on the counter. "What do you know about BeautiQueen cosmetics?"

"My wife uses it. She says it's good stuff. A little pricey."

"Any complaints or scandals?"

"None that I know of."

He finished straightening the film and moved down to the rows of cigarettes. "Now that I think of it, my wife's going to a makeup party this afternoon."

The perfect spying job for Kary. "A BeautiQueen party?"

"Yeah, at one of her friend's." Ted wrote the address down and handed it to me. "What do you think's going on, Randall?"

I wish I knew. "I'm trying to learn all I can."

◇◇◇

I got home around noon. As I came up the porch steps, the slow firm pounding of a scale meant another one of Kary's students was here. I glanced at her student, a little girl, ten or twelve, dressed in white shorts and the latest Disney cartoon tee shirt, her long brown hair tied back with a matching ribbon. After a few deep breaths, the pressure in my chest eased. I was getting better at this, but the occasional glimpse of a child who reminded me of Lindsey could still freeze my heart.

I sat down in my office and stared at the starburst patterns of my screen saver. Outside my window, Camden was mowing the front yard with his old-fashioned push mower, the kind you really push. The blades made a steady whirring sound, sort of like my brain trying to process all the information about my cases. Inside, the piano notes marched up the scale slowly and deliberately, the way I'd mounted my campaign to win Kary's heart. After our talk at the Elms, my heart was considerably lighter, and I had to believe things would improve, but like a sudden jarringly wrong note, my plans could all fall apart.

After Kary's student had gone, I heard her talking to Angie, asking her to help with a lace trim on a pageant dress and how the house hunting had gone.

"Pretty good," Angie's voice replied from the island. "We're going to put in an offer for the one on River Street. Most of the places we looked at were way out of our range, and there were plenty of dumps we could afford, but this one's a good choice for us."

"I still wish you'd stay here. The house won't be the same without you and Rufus."

"Aww, that's right sweet of you, but Rufe and I need our own place. Why don't you heat up one of those casseroles for lunch?"

In thirty minutes, the smell of something cheesy filled the house. When I came around to the island, I found Angie taking up most of the sofa, her sausage-sized fingers delicately pulling threads through the lace of a short pink gown. In the kitchen, Kary pulled a large dish out of the oven and set it on top.

"Mystery casserole number three is ready."

I rummaged in the fridge for a soda. "It smells good."

"I think it's supposed to be a taco casserole. See the little bits of chips?"

"Why don't you try it first?"

Kary spooned out a portion onto her plate and tasted a small bite. "Not bad."

We brought our plates to the table. "Learn anything from Millicent?" I asked.

"I had a few moments to talk with her after the show. She told me quite a bit about George, and then she went off on a tangent about how he wanted to make up for his bad behavior and brought everyone gifts from BeautiQueen. She doesn't like peach, by the way."

"So, nothing we can use."

"Not really. But I'll keep trying."

"Well, I have a mission for you. Ted's wife is going to a BeautiQueen party this afternoon at a friend's house. You can go and get the scoop on the company and its products."

"It's this afternoon?"

"Oh, hell, I forgot. You have a matinee."

"When is the party?"

"Three o'clock."

"The show is at two, so orchestra members need to be there by one thirty at the very latest. Shoot a monkey! This is exactly the kind of thing I could do."

"'Shoot a monkey'?"

"It's one of Rufus's cleaner expressions."

Angie lumbered up to the table, still carrying the lace dress. She pulled out a chair and sat down. "I'll go."

"You will?" I was taken aback.

"To a BeautiQueen party? Sure. I use that stuff."

I straightened in my chair to get a better look at her. She was still the same three hundred fifty-pound woman, tiny bright eyes above cheek bubbles of fat, a shapeless dress like a tent covering God knows how many rolls of arm and middle. No doubt my expression was slightly skeptical.

But Kary looked pleased. "Angie, that's a great idea."

"I'd be happy to go."

I still wasn't sure. "It's a secret mission."

"Oh, and Kary wouldn't stand out?"

"You may have a point." Actually, now that I thought about it, Angie might be a better choice. Everyone would be staring at her, wondering how many gallons of base coat she would need.

She snapped off a thread. "What's the deal with this makeup? You figure somebody's smuggling heroin in jars of overnight cream?"

"Nothing quite so dramatic. I need more information on Folly Harper and BeautiQueen products. There's a party this afternoon, and I need a ringer."

Her grin made her eyes disappear. "Ding dong."

I had deputized various members of the household before with good results. Angie looked like Queen of the White Trash Mamas, but I knew beneath that tonnage lurked a shrewd mind. I also knew she could take care of herself, and she could move a lot faster than anyone would suspect.

"Okay," I said. "Your assignment, should you choose to accept, is to infiltrate the BeautiQueen party, and gossip your little heart out. I need the inside scoop on Folly, stuff I can't learn checking financial reports, stuff you women love to dish out."

She pulled another thread. "I'll need some money. You can't go to one of these things and not buy something."

I took out my wallet. "Twenty-five be enough?"

Her snort made the furniture rattle. "If I want one little tube of lipstick, yeah." I know I looked startled. "Honey, a complete skin care system can run you a hundred and fifty to two hundred and beyond. Eyeshadow's six bucks, regeneration cream's thirty, not to mention moisturizers, toners, peels, gels, scrubs—"

"Okay, okay, I get the picture." I took out more bills. "Here's fifty-five. Make it last. I haven't got any more."

She folded the money and put it into the pocket of her immense smock. "It's a start. I need lipstick, maybe a little eye cream, maybe some Secret Passion."

"Secret Passion? This is already kinkier than I imagined."

If I could have seen her little eyes, I'm sure they were rolling at my stupidity. "My favorite perfume, but they don't always have it. See, what burns me up is when you've got a favorite fragrance, or a lipstick color you really like, and the company discontinues it."

"I thought pink was pink. Can't you find the same shade in another brand?"

"It's not the same. You'd be surprised how many shades of pink there are. One company can't duplicate another's formula exactly. There's a knockoff perfume called Secret Desire, supposed to smell the same for less. No way. I can tell the difference, and so can anyone else who's loyal to Secret Passion."

"Then I hope they have it. Dare I ask how much it is?"

"Don't worry. I'll get a small bottle." She held the dress up to examine her handiwork. "So I get the lowdown on Folly Harper and the company, is that it?"

"That's it." I dug out the address Ted had given me. "Twenty-nine Ash Grove Court at three o'clock."

"I'll have Rufus drop me off."

"Don't let him serenade the ladies."

She set the pink dress aside. "Okay, now answer me another question. What's all this about Cam calling off the wedding? Wouldn't have anything to do with the dishes I saw hopping around here yesterday, would it?"

I exchanged a glance with Kary and tried to stall. "Dishes hopping around?"

"Yeah, there was a big stack from the other night when we had all that company, and he was putting them up, only they fell, or started to fall. Next thing I know, they're all on the counter, like he pulled them back with a string. Then they was flapping toward the cabinets, and he let 'em in like birds come home to roost." She gave me a level stare. For once, I could see her eyes. "What the hell is he up to now?"

I wasn't sure Camden wanted her to know. "I have no idea."

She gave another elephant snort. "The kid's telekinetic, too, right? Honest to God, if he isn't a piece of work."

I shouldn't have been surprised she figured it out. "It's a recent development."

"And what does Blondie think of this?"

"She doesn't know, and Camden doesn't want her to know," Kary said. "Not yet."

"Gee, I wonder why. Don't worry. I won't rat on him. So how powerful is it? I mean, can he move mountains?"

"It's pretty strong," I said. "He kept Folly's car from bashing into her the other day. But it's driving him crazy. He's afraid the kids will inherit it."

"Kids? Does Ellin strike you as the maternal type? I don't think he has to worry about kids."

"I told him he can't depend on his own future, but he's decided the best thing to do is not marry her."

"Well, I think it's the best thing, too, but anyone can see he's nuts about her, and in her strange twisted way, she's nuts about him. So, what'll we do?"

"'We'?" I said. "What's this 'we' business? You're hired for the BeautiQueen job, that's all. Let the two of them thrash it out."

◇◇◇

Speaking of thrashing, I hadn't heard from Charlie lately. When I called his number, he wasn't home. I called the Tempo. He wasn't there, either. I tried J.J.

J.J. sighed. "Yeah, he's here. Crashing on my couch."

"Did he tell you what happened Friday night?"

"Said something about the worst evening ever and how some foreigner was stealing his girl. Didn't make much sense. Course he was sloshed at the time."

I leaned back in my office chair. "He made it through Taffy's program pretty well, but her song writing teacher was there, one of those dashing Latin types. Charlie tried to start a fight."

J.J. chuckled. "That ain't the way he tells it."

"How hung over is he?"

"It'll be tomorrow before he's coherent. You'd better tell Kary she's got to cover the show again this afternoon."

Great. Way to go, Charlie. "She can handle it. Do you know if he called Taffy?"

"I don't think so."

I thanked J.J. and hung up. Charlie must have been born with his own self-destruct button. Until he sobered up, called Taffy and apologized, there wasn't much more I could do for this broken romance.

As for Camden's broken romance, I didn't have to wait long for the next installment. Ellin's silver Lexus drove up and parked.

Camden must have sensed she was there because he met her in the island. She circled cautiously, like a plane that's not sure the runway's safe. "Mother said something about grandchildren. Are you still seeing that?"

I angled my swivel chair so I could see. Camden sat down on the sofa. He took a long time before he answered. "I see three children for us. Two girls and a boy." Another long pause. "There's a very good chance they'll inherit my talent."

I hadn't imagined Ellin could be this quiet. She sat down beside him. I could see the sparkle of her diamond and emerald engagement ring and wondered if she knew it had once belonged to Fred's wife, the one treasure Fred had.

"I want you to have it," he'd told Camden, "to give to that girl of yours. She's ornery, but so was my Cora."

Camden's ornery girl was trying to understand. "You're not marrying me because of that?"

"There's something else. I'll show you, but you have to promise me you won't go crazy."

"I won't."

"Keep your eye on the pear."

The pear-shaped glass paperweight was in its usual place on the coffee table on top of a stack of coupons. Today it did a little dance, hopped down on the carpet, and then hopped back to its place. It gave a little pear bow, and was still.

Ellin gazed at him with wide eyes. "Oh, my God. Did you do that?"

"I'm afraid so."

"Is this what you couldn't tell me? When did this start?"

"A few days ago."

She picked up the pear as if to assure herself it had no moving parts. I could see the delighted sparkle in her eyes. "This is fantastic."

"Ellie—"

Too late. She was up and rolling. "Fantastic! I can't believe it! Do you realize what this means? This is absolutely the most wonderful example of psychic ability I've ever seen."

"It's not wonderful. It's scary as hell."

"How can you say that? This is so exciting!"

"You're not the one who has it."

She went all stone-faced. "Well, of course not. When did I ever get anything remotely psychic? You can bet if this were happening to me, I'd be thrilled."

"Thrilled to have freaky powers you don't understand? I can control it now, but what if it gets away from me?"

"You're overreacting."

"No, you're overreacting," he said. "You promised you wouldn't go crazy. This is exactly what I was talking about."

She put both hands out, palms forward. "Okay, okay. I'll settle down. Let's talk this through. What does this have to do with us getting married and having our three children?"

"Don't you see? Our kids could have this power, or worse."

"They could be like me—duds."

"Don't say that. You're not a dud."

"Yes, I am."

"No, you're not."

I lost interest in the argument. They could go on for quite a while like this. At least he had the guts to tell her his big secret. Rustling noises in my trash can made me turn to investigate. Two kittens were in the can, wrestling with crumpled pieces of computer paper. When I untangled them, one of them bit me.

"Ow!" Damn sharp little teeth. "You bite me again, I'll pull out those teeth."

Teeth.

Wait a minute. With the lower half of his head gone, and his hands burned, making fingerprinting inconclusive, how did anyone know for sure that body in Clearwater belonged to George Mark McMillan? No teeth. No way to check dental records. What had the coroner used to make a positive ID?

I called Jordan. "If there are no teeth, how does the coroner identify a badly damaged body?"

"Fingerprints, DNA."

"Let's assume the fingers are too messed up for prints, and don't DNA results take a while?"

"At least two weeks. There are always scars and birthmarks. A family member usually knows enough about the victim for a positive ID."

"So if somebody's really mangled, but Aunt Susie says, oh, that's Herman, then that's it?"

"Are you trying to identify somebody, Randall?"

"I'm beginning to wonder if this somebody is really dead."

"Who might that be?"

"George McMillan. He ran off to Florida with his employer's money. Folly Harper at BeautiQueen asked me to find him, but he was found dead in his hotel room."

"Didn't the police down there decide it was a suicide?"

"I'm wondering about that."

"To answer your question, usually a relative identifies the body, and if there's no good reason to suspect foul play, case closed. Did McMillan commit any other crimes?"

"No, he wrote a letter saying he was sorry he took the money."

"Where's the money now?"

"Mrs. Harper got it back."

"Let's see. Dead body, shotgun wound to the head, no one else hurt, money returned, letter of apology. Sounds like suicide to me. I don't see that a crime was committed here, Randall."

I thanked Jordan and hung up. Next call: Lucy Warner.

"Mrs. Warner, this might sound odd to you, but how did you know the body you saw was George?"

She took a couple of deep sniffs. "Once when we were children, we went exploring in the woods, and George fell out of a tree. He had a distinctive scar on his leg. I knew it the minute I saw it." Muted animal noises in the background made her turn her head and say, "Quiet, dearies." Then she said to me, "What are you saying, Mr. Randall? Are you saying George might be alive? That's impossible."

"I'm trying to cover all bases, thanks."

I hung up and watched the kittens roll on the floor. Speaking of scars, I checked my finger. It wouldn't be any great chore to make a scar on someone's leg, shoot off their face, and make the world think George McMillan had gone to the great beauty parlor in the sky. But who would want to? I needed to have another talk with Folly Harper.

Chapter Twenty

"Now and then there's one with slight defects."

Folly Harper greeted me at the door of her elegant brick mansion on Tudor Club Drive. "I hope you have some good news for me, David."

I followed her through the vast foyer to a parlor decorated in—you guessed it—peach. Peach velvet draperies pulled back from beveled windows, letting sunlight in on a peach-colored sofa and chairs and large arrangements of silk flowers, also peach. Bright aqua cushions on the sofa gave a welcome stab of blue amid all the peachiness. Piles of paper lay on the floor beside a corner desk.

Folly pushed in an open drawer. "I'm cleaning out George's things."

I picked up the nearest stack. "He kept more plans here?"

"These are his recent ideas. He liked for me to go over them."

I scanned George's notes: lipstick mousse, eyeliner strips, complexion changing goo. "Any of these work?"

"Unfortunately, no, but he kept trying. He was certain he could revolutionize the cosmetics industry."

Not with these ideas he couldn't. "I have some news for you," I took a seat. Folly perched on the peach sofa. "First, I want you to tell me what these numbers Camden is seeing for you mean."

She shifted position. "I'm not sure I can."

"It would be a good idea." Because, until I get some answers, you are suspect Number One.

"You have to promise not to tell another living soul."

"I promise."

She kept her gaze on the flower arrangement. "I feel so stupid."

Not exactly the words of a hardened killer, but these days, you never knew.

"The formula for BeautiQueen's new anti-aging cream," she said. "George and I were the only ones who knew it. Now he's dead, and I've forgotten it. That's why I came to Cam. I knew he'd give me some lucky numbers, and I'd use them for the formula."

"Use them? How?"

"George and I experimented with different amounts of ingredients. I can't remember which one was right."

She'd been using the numbers to determine the proportions. "Has it worked?"

"Not yet, but I'm very, very close." She began twisting her rings. "But you mustn't say anything to anyone. I can't tell you what it would do to BeautiQueen if this formula got out. And this is my discovery, mine and George's."

"The same formula he was going to sell to Perfecto Face?"

"Yes." She got up, went to a peach colored cabinet, unlocked a drawer, and took out a folder. "Let me show you."

She handed me a photograph. The girl in the picture was pretty, but there were lines around her eyes and mouth that made her look tired and old. Folly handed me a second photo. In this after picture, the girl looked almost as beautiful as Kary. I looked several times to convince myself this was the same girl and not her gorgeous younger sister. No lines, clear glowing skin, an amazing transformation.

Women would kill for this stuff. Maybe one already had.

"Unfortunately, there are some side effects." Folly handed me a third photo. The glow had dimmed, the lines had returned, and the girl's eyebrows had fallen out.

"Eek," I said.

"Oh, they grew back. I only have to get the perfect proportions for the cream, that's all."

"And George knew these proportions? Damn it, Folly, something this important, and you didn't write it down, didn't put it in your computer or your phone?"

She looked down at the peach carpet. "I was afraid someone would steal it. Competition is so fierce. I couldn't trust anyone except George." She looked up anxiously. "But Cam will find it, won't he? He can see into my mind."

"Camden is involved in his own problems right now. You can't rely on his predictions. You have to rely on the facts. No more secrets. Was George the only one who knew the formula?"

"Yes."

"Did he write it down anywhere?"

"Not that I know of."

"Did he discuss it with anyone else?"

"No, we always swore we'd never tell anyone about it."

"No one else? No one who might have killed him to get it? You never said a word about it to anyone?"

She wiped a tear from her eye. "No one. This was going to be the great discovery that put BeautiQueen on top."

I glanced at the eyebrowless girl. Or bury it. "What about all these notes? Could it be somewhere in that?"

"Actually, that's what I was hoping to find."

I got up and started looking through another stack of papers. Folly looked, too. We read more ridiculous ideas like eyelash lengthening cream and wrinkle smoothing paste. George's scribbled notes in the margins included, "Add more texture," and "Needs crystallizing foam." We found diagrams and calculations and graphs, but nothing that resembled a secret formula.

Finally, I sat back. "Nothing."

"I'm afraid not." Folly pulled herself together and gathered another little bag of cosmetics. "This is for that lovely young lady at your house. I understand she's going to be in the Miss Parkland Pageant. Did I tell you BeautiQueen is going to be one of their sponsors, along with the Psychic Service? Ellin took care of all the details."

The set back in wedding plans hadn't kept Ellin from taking advantage of situations. "That'll be good publicity."

"I so wanted our new cream to be ready in time for the pageant," Folly said. "Is Cam at home? Maybe he can see the right combination of numbers today."

I took another look at the after photo of eyebrow girl. "I think you'd better stick to the cream you're using now."

"We'll have something ready, I'm sure."

I helped her pick up all the papers and dump them into a peach trash can. "Did George keep papers anywhere else?"

"I don't think so." She gave a little shudder. "I feel so odd throwing all that away. It's his life's work."

I checked the desk top. "Calendar? Rolodex? Cell phone?"

"He had an address book."

I found it in the top drawer, another startling blue against all the peach. Only a few numbers were written inside, but in the back I found a letter addressed to Amelia Tilley. It had been returned to George unopened. I opened the letter, thinking George might have sent the secret formula to Perfecto Face. I didn't have to read very far to realize George had other things on his mind.

Folly watched me. "Anything important?"

"I believe George had a crush on Amelia Tilley of Perfecto Face." That was the nicest way I could say it. George's letter to Amelia was more than steamy.

"And she never got his letter. That's so sad."

"I'll take it to her."

"Would you? She'll appreciate it."

I wasn't so sure about that.

◇◇◇

Amelia Tilley frowned as I entered her office. "I need to have a word with you, Mr. Randall. I called the newspaper with an update for your article. You are not from the *Herald*."

"And you weren't straight with me about George McMillan."

She held my gaze for a long moment. "Fair enough. Who goes first?"

"I'm a private investigator. Folly Harper hired me to find out what happened to George. We don't think he committed suicide."

She kept a firm grip on the edge of her desk. "You think someone murdered him?"

I put the letter on her desk. "I found this in his things. I'm guessing it's one of many."

She loosened her grip and sat down, still keeping a level gaze. She didn't touch the letter. "George sent me several letters. After reading the first one, I returned any others unopened. I told him I wasn't interested, but he insisted. Then he became angry and said he would start his own company and run everyone else out of business. I said he was welcome to try. I was sorry it came to that."

"Maybe you got angry, too. Maybe you didn't like his threats."

A dark blush spread across her smooth cheeks. "As far as I was concerned, George McMillan was just another man who couldn't take no for an answer. He was extremely annoying, but I certainly didn't want to kill him. He finally stopped calling and sending me letters. It was over."

"Did he ever tell you about a secret anti-aging formula he and Folly were working on?"

"Yes, he thought this would make me fall in love with him." She sighed. "Mr. Randall, everyone in our business is always working on an anti-aging formula. It's nothing new or surprising. George had a mania for discovering it first." A buzzer sounded on her desk, and she answered the intercom. "Yes?"

A man's voice spoke. "Sorry to interrupt, Ms. Tilley, but you wanted to speak with security before their next shift."

"Yes, thank you," she said. "I'll be right there."

"Problems?" I asked.

"We've had some break-ins lately."

"Would you mind telling me what's missing?"

"I guess not. We're missing some shipments of retinoic acid."

"How does that relate to cosmetics?"

"Vitamin A derivatives called retinoids improve your skin, especially skin that's sun-damaged."

"What about aging skin?"

"Retinoic acid can treat aging skin. I don't know if you've heard of Retin-A or Renova? Those products have tretinoin, which helps the skin renew itself. It reduces fine lines and wrinkles. It also clears up acne."

"Do you sell products like that?"

"Tretinoin is found in prescription medicines, but we use forms of retinol, which is very effective in improving skin texture. Where is all this leading, Mr. Randall?"

"What about vitamin C?"

"Another excellent antioxidant. Vitamin C stimulates the fibroblasts to produce more collagen and elastin."

Most of that was lost on me, but I was beginning to think Ms. Tilley's burglar might be the Drug Palace thief. "When did the break-ins start?"

"A week ago."

Exactly when Ted hired me to patrol the store. "Can you think of anyone who'd want to steal from your company? Disgruntled employee? Unsatisfied customer?"

"The only one who's ever had a grudge against Perfecto Face was George McMillan."

Amelia Tilley let me accompany her down to the shipping department of Perfecto Face to examine the new locks the night shift had installed on the doors. She spoke with the day shift security guards to make certain they understood all the new keys and codes. I walked around the large room past conveyor belts loaded with boxes of Perfecto Face. Employees on one end filled the boxes with bottles and tubes of makeup while employees on the other end sealed the packages and put them on wooden pallets to be loaded onto trucks. I didn't see any other way someone could get in.

"Did George ever come down here?" I asked Amelia Tilley as we took the elevator back to her office.

"Yes, the first time he visited, I gave him the tour."

"Is it possible he could've found out your codes?"

"I suppose so, but this is ridiculous, isn't it? George is dead, and even if he were alive, why would he steal products he could easily get at BeautiQueen?"

Good question.

I had lots of good questions, but no answers. After leaving Perfecto Face, I checked my messages. Ted from the Drug Palace reported that the Rexall on Ames Avenue and Eisner Drugstore out by the shopping center had break-ins. I needed to find out if the thieves had stolen vitamins, as well, so I gave them a call. Sure enough, they were missing the same items. I decided to go by the Drug Palace and ask Ted about Retin-A.

Ted was filling several bottles with small yellow pills. "Retin-A was created round about 1969, I think, as an acne treatment. Wasn't till much later someone discovered it reversed skin damage. Retin-A causes keratinocytes to move to the surface of the skin, improving the stratum corneum, or top layer."

I didn't need a complete translation. "So it's the miracle that women have been looking for?"

"It doesn't work for everyone, and a lot of people don't want to put up with the redness and irritation. You have to use it for eight to twelve weeks to see results, plus you have to stay out of the sun. It's like having a bad sunburn with a great tan underneath. You have to wait until the sunburn fades or peels away."

This didn't sound like something I'd want on my face. "Would someone be able to make their own form of Retin-A using the products stolen from the drugstores?"

"Possibly, but who'd want to use it? I can't see anyone making a profit off pseudo Retin-A. Although—" he paused. "It could be a Mixer."

"Who or what are the Mixers?"

"Rogue pharmacists."

I pictured a group of men in white smocks riding through town, tossing drugs left and right to a grateful populace. "Is this something new, Ted?"

He secured the lids on the pill bottles. "They're out there. Mixing their own stuff, trying out new prescriptions."

"Isn't that illegal?"

"Sure, but a Mixer doesn't care about that. It's the thrill of the mix, the smell of chemicals, the possibility of finding a cure for the common cold."

The thrill of the mix? Ted usually didn't get carried away like this. "So you think these Mixers could be responsible for the break-ins?"

"When it was only this store, no, but now that others have been hit, I see a pattern."

"Ted," I said as calmly as possible, "come back to Earth for a moment and talk sense. If you know who's behind the thefts, tell me, and I'll do something. Don't give me this wild tale about pharmacists gone bad."

Ted leaned on the counter and spoke in a low voice. "I know the Mixers because I used to be one. It was in college, and it was only for fun. Nobody got hurt, and we blew up the lab only once. Nowadays, I can't afford to be careless, or spend time and money goofing off. But I imagine a few of my old buddies still like to mix it up when they can."

"The names of these buddies?"

"I don't know if I should tell you."

"I won't tell them you ratted on them. I can be investigating another break-in. Besides, if it's your old pals, they've stolen your stuff, remember? Or did you leave the back door open?"

"Okay, okay," Ted said. "Lagenfield. Armand Lagenfield."

A rogue pharmacist name if I ever heard one.

"And where might I find Mr. Lagenfield's secret laboratory?"

"He lives on Viewmont Street, past the bakery."

"No wonder those doughnuts won't stay in the box."

"He'll probably talk to you. I don't know about the others."

"How many others?"

"I'm not at liberty to say."

"You want the thief caught or not?" He hesitated. "Ted, did

you take a blood oath? Are you going to violate the pharmacists' code of honor?"

"Nothing like that." He made a decision. "Yes, I want the thief caught. There are six guys I used to mix with. I don't know a lot of the newer members. Lagenfield might. If he doesn't have the answers, I'll get the other names for you."

Lagenfield and O'Neal, Pharmacists At Large. "Okay," I said. "I'll let you know if your pal's been playing Doctor Frankenstein."

Chapter Twenty-one

"I've grown accustomed to her face."

Armand Lagenfield lived in one of the shabbier neighborhoods near the university in a rusty-looking house with flaking paint and a weed-filled yard. I could see the faint outline of Greek symbols over the door and figured the building had been a fraternity house before becoming even too run down for careless frat boys. I expected a shriveled guy with a domed head and bloodshot eyes. Lagenfield looked more like a well-worn surfer dude. He had long stringy bleached blond hair, tanned leathery skin, and sharp blue eyes magnified by a pair of horn-rimmed glasses. He was wearing cut-off jeans and a faded tee shirt that read, "Visualize Whirled Peas."

"Ted sent me," I said, and he nodded.

"Come on up and have a beer." We sat down in two worn green rocking chairs on his sagging porch. He handed me a brown glass bottle and took another bottle from a small cooler by his chair. "Brew it myself."

The beer wasn't bad, but had an odd minty taste. I didn't ask what was in it, but I did ask about the Mixers.

"Yeah, we mix it up every now and then," he said, as if he and the boys went down to the pool hall every Saturday night and took on a pack of astronomers. "It's harmless. Keeps our minds working."

"Where do you get your stuff?"

"Everybody's got a little storehouse of goodies. We borrow from each other."

"So you didn't go borrowing from the Rexall, Eisner, and the Drug Palace the other evening?"

"Naw, man. We may be crazy, but we're not thieves. Hell, I got enough stuff downstairs to last me forever. What's missing?"

"Vitamin A, Vitamin C, mineral oil, products with retinoic acid."

He considered this a moment. "Sounds like the thief has problem skin."

"Could he or she be creating their own wonder cream?"

Lagenfield took another chug of his homemade beer. "Now that's interesting. Cosmetics use vitamins as antioxidants to disarm free radicals."

I got a mental picture of a hefty Vitamin A wresting a machine gun from someone who looked like Lagenfield. "And that means?"

"Free radicals are by-products of something in the environment that would irritate your skin, like the sun, or pollution, or cigarette smoke. But let's say you make a product that has fewer antioxidants, or you mess with the formula. You might get some neat results."

"Neat, as in—?"

"Like you said, a wonder cream, something that stops the aging process, or you could get something that burns your face off. Let me see what the others say."

He got his laptop and chatted briefly online with a fellow Mixer. This one agreed the missing ingredients could have something to do with makeup.

Lagenfield typed a thank you. "I'll check with the rest of them. Have another beer." He clicked away for a while and then closed the laptop. "Looks like nobody knows anything useful."

"You spoke with all the Mixers?"

"All except George McMillan. He passed away recently."

Whoa. Hold on. "George McMillan was a Mixer?"

"Not a very good one. Grand Mess, I called him. All this about cosmetics, you'd think he was involved somehow, but he's dead. Even if he were alive, he wouldn't be able to create a decent formula. The man had trouble making Kool-Aid."

But even Kool-Aid can be deadly if you put the wrong things in it. If George was a Mixer, he'd know where to find the things he needed and how to put them together. Or maybe he wasn't the culprit. Maybe someone was forcing him to create a perfect formula.

Assuming George was still alive.

"Among the Mixers, were there any who might have held a grudge against George?"

"Not likely. As I said, he was sort of the goof of our group."

The goof of the group. I wasn't so sure George was the goof. And why hadn't Ted mentioned George?

On my way home, I called Ted to thank him for the tip. "Lagenfield says George McMillan was a Mixer. Did you know him?"

"George McMillan. No, he must have joined later. I told you it had been a while since I mixed it up. What did Armand have to say about the break-ins?"

"He checked with the rest of the gang, but no one had any information."

"I've heard that name before. Did I read something in the paper? Wasn't he the guy who killed himself in Florida?"

"Apparently. Folly Harper hired me to find out what really happened."

"What do you think really happened?"

"I wish I knew." Although I was beginning to believe George the Mixer was alive and well and mixing up some trouble.

◇◇◇

When I got back to the house, Caroline and Sandra were sitting on the porch playing with the kittens. Several packages wrapped in silver and white paper were stacked in one of the rocking chairs.

"Hello, Dave!" Sandra called. "Where's the happy couple? Ellin's not answering her cell phone."

Trying for a few minutes of peace. "I don't know where Ellin is, but Camden's got two shows today."

"Can we leave these boxes with you?"

"Sure. What's all this?"

"Wedding presents." Caroline picked up one box. "These are ear plugs for all the other tenants, so when Ellin gets wound up, your hearing will be protected."

"We could've used those months ago."

"We bought a cookbook for Ellin, but don't get your hopes up. She can make great biscuits, but that's it." She pointed to another box. "And this is a super new lens for Cam's telescope. We figured he'd be giving the heavens a lot of longing glances."

Sandra set the kitten down and hunted in her pocketbook for her car keys. "Why is Ellin so excited, David? She said Cam could do a new trick. That sounded so kinky we're dying for details."

So Ellin had immediately gone into overdrive. This didn't surprise me. "It would be better if he showed you."

"Oooo, can't wait. Come on, Caroline, let's go. See you later, David."

After the sisters left, I got a snack and went to my office. I heard a car door slam and glanced out my front window to see what looked like a giant peach rolling across the lawn. Angie waddled into my office.

"I'm here to report that everything at the party was just peachy."

"Did you have enough money?"

"No, but I won a couple prizes playing BeautiQueen Bingo."

Angie doesn't fit in my office chair, so we went to the island. She plopped on the sofa. She had an unnaturally orange glow.

"You look gorgeous," I said.

Her little eyes narrowed until they disappeared. "You wanna hear my report or not?"

"Sorry. Go ahead."

"The woman who started the company years ago got the recipe from her frontier grandma. Something to do with scouring powder to clean out the iron cauldrons. She tinkered with the formula and BeautiQueen was born."

I pictured the first brave pioneer woman to put that stuff on her face. "BeautiQueen sounds a lot better than Iron Scouring."

"Some of the gals complained that the rejuvenating cream was not as smooth as usual, and the apricot facial scrub smelled more like melon. Nothing serious."

"Any talk of an anti-aging cream?"

"Oh, all the time. There's this new stuff, Extra Whip Moisturizing Deluxe, supposed to be out this week. We're all champing at the bit for a jar of that." She reached into the folds of her smock and brought out a brochure. She handed it to me. The package for Extra Whip Moisturizing Deluxe had a dramatic black and white geometric design.

"I hope you bought spare eyebrows," I said.

Her regular eyebrows went up. "Huh?"

"Nothing." The brochure had a picture of Folly and a picture of George as "co-creators" of this wondrous product. "This stuff's not out yet?"

Angie reached for the box of tissues on the coffee table. "Not yet. Our sales lady said it would revolutionize the cosmetics industry. Have you heard that before?"

The brochure extolled the wonders of Extra Whip, calling it the latest improvement in retinoic acid-based makeup, safe even in the brightest sunlight. "No more red flaky skin! No more sensitivity to light! Use Extra Whip with confidence. Your face is in our loving hands."

"Sounds too good to be true."

She wiped off the top layer of peach. "Whew, this stuff is thick! I can't stand it anymore."

"I appreciate your sacrifice."

"Did I find out anything useful?"

"Several things." I definitely wanted Camden to see this black and white brochure.

She swiped her cheeks, leaving streaks of different colors. "Cam and Ellin kiss and make up yet?"

"I'm not sure how that's going."

"What about Charlie and his girl?" She'd used three tissues and still looked peachy. "Looks to me like he's getting kinda fond of Kary. What are you doing about that?"

"Plotting his demise."

Angie picked up the tissue box and put it in her lap. "What does Taffy want?"

"Not Charlie, apparently."

"Be serious, Randall. You're always telling me you find what people want. What does she want more than anything?"

I had to think a moment. "A recording deal."

"So get her one. Make it look like Charlie's idea."

"I don't believe I know anyone at Capitol Records."

"Doesn't have to be a big company, does it? Rufus and Buddy and the Frog Hollow Boys make CDs all the time at Visions Studio right here in town."

She continued to calmly clean her face as if she hadn't with one remark solved two of my biggest problems. This was perfect. If Taffy had her own CD, she'd be happy. She could possibly shop it around to bigger companies and have the singing career she'd always dreamed of. If Charlie did this for her, she'd love him more than ever. Then he'd be out of my way.

"That's a great idea," I said.

"I'll get the number for you."

"I've already forgotten Kary, Angie. You're the one I want."

If she hadn't already thrown her wadded tissues in the trash can, I'm sure she would've tossed them at me. "You're too old for me, Randall."

"Did you get all that goop off?"

"I think so."

"Then it's safe to do this." I leaned over and kissed her large soft cheek.

She laughed and pushed me away.

Chapter Twenty-two

"Let a woman in your life."

Kary and Camden got in late after the evening show of *My Fair Lady*, and were wiped out from having two giant performances in one day. Both of them slept late Sunday morning but got up in time for church. Afterwards, Camden fixed lasagna, green beans, and garlic bread for lunch. Underneath the table, the kittens attacked our feet and shredded a fallen napkin.

I explained Angie's idea about Charlie getting a CD for Taffy, and everyone agreed this was the perfect solution.

"As soon as Charlie's sober enough to understand it," I said.

Rufus swallowed a huge bite of lasagna. "How was Taffy's concert?"

"Pretty ghastly. And Charlie almost started a fist fight."

"He's a right spunky little rooster, ain't he?"

"He's going to be a dead rooster if he doesn't slow down."

Camden passed me the bread. "Find anything at Folly's?"

"Love letters George sent to Amelia Tilley of Perfecto Face. Like most women, she was able to resist his charms. Her company's had break-ins, too. Looks like the work of the same thief who's been hitting the Drug Palace."

"So the thief needs makeup?"

I needed two pieces of bread to handle all my lasagna. "I asked Ted, and I learned more about cosmetics than I needed to know. But what I didn't know is Parkland is home to a group of rogue pharmacists who like to play with secret ingredients. I even met one in his lair, and he told me George McMillan used to be one of them."

"A secret ingredient?"

"A Mixer."

"You're scaring me."

"And not a very good one." I passed the bread to Kary. "If George were alive—and I'm beginning to think he is—then he'd have something to prove to his Mixer buddies by creating some kind of special cream."

She took a piece and gave the basket back to Camden. "You think George might be alive?"

"I don't know. I'm missing something. I need to talk to his cousin Lucy again. Why don't you two come along with me? Camden, you might get a helpful vibe."

"I'd like to, but after the show, we have to strike the set, and then I promised Ellie I'd go with her to the caterers and sample reception food."

"I thought that was all settled."

"It will never be settled."

Angie carved out a huge slice of lasagna and plopped it in her plate. "Cam, honey, everything's an issue with Ellin. You'd better tell her about this moving stuff with your mind thing."

He stared at her. "You know about that, too?"

"Saw you playing with the dishes the other day."

"Well, damn, I might as well go on TV and announce it to the world. I did tell her. She reacted as you would imagine."

"A Very Special Episode for the PSN?"

"Oh, yes."

Rufus reached for the basket and tore off another chunk of bread. "Any idea what caused it?"

"Randall and Kary think it's wedding jitters."

"And losing Fred," Kary said. "Too many changes."

Camden looked at Fred's empty chair. "You may be right.

What I don't understand is why all of you can take it so calmly, and Ellie freaks out."

Rufus used his bread to maneuver a wedge of lasagna onto his fork. "She still wants to marry you, don't she?"

"She has ordered me to marry her."

"Sounds like business as usual. Just go ahead and do it."

"There's a little matter of children."

Angie wiped her mouth on her napkin. "How many you going to have?"

"Three. Two girls and a boy. And I'm afraid they'll inherit all this ridiculous talent."

"So?"

"'So'? I don't want them to go through what I had to go through."

"Can't do much about that, can you? They'll be who they are, no matter what. You can help them through the rough spots."

"That's what I told him," I said.

Angie reached down to pry a kitten off her leg. "Ow. I am not a tree, you little pest. Does this mean you don't want to marry Ellin?"

"Of course I do. But it's a lot to think about."

"Then you need to think about something else. How many children are Rufus and I going to have?"

Camden sat still for a long minute, his eyes gazing off into God knows what. "I can't tell for sure. Looks like maybe one."

"One's enough."

"One's too many," Rufus said. "Cam, how come your sweetie and her sisters didn't join us for lunch? Thought they was going to."

"They may come over later. They're still getting their dresses fixed. Please pass the tea, Angie."

She handed him the pitcher of tea. "I would've altered those dresses for free."

"I know, but Jean has to have everything done at a certain shop. And Ellie has a lot to do at the studio this weekend. They're having some kind of Psychics Around the World special."

I pushed the sugar bowl over to him. "Wasn't that one of Reg's ideas? I'm surprised she agreed to it."

"I think with the wedding coming up, she was momentarily distracted."

Kary handed a piece of bread down to Cindy, who waited patiently by her chair. "The PSN is one of the pageant sponsors, and so is BeautiQueen."

The kitten had decided it was his life's ambition to climb Angie. She pried him off again. "Yeah, they talked about that at the party. Folly was encouraging everyone to go." She held up the kitten. "Can we not find homes for these little critters? Kary, how 'bout a free kitten with each piano lesson?"

"I have a friend who works at the animal shelter. I'll give her a call."

"Don't want 'em put down, now."

"Oh, no. We'll find good homes for them, or we'll keep them, right, Cam?"

"I think Ellie would be delighted."

After lunch, Rufus rounded up the kittens and took them outside. I gave Camden and Kary a ride to the theater, and on the way, I showed him the brochure Angie had brought from the BeautiQueen party.

"Those black and white patterns you're seeing. Do they look like this?"

He gave it a long look. "Not exactly. There's one pattern I can't quite focus on."

"This is the new must-have face cream for women of all ages. Folly must have finally gotten those numbers right."

"Oh, did she say what she needed them for?"

"The secret formula."

"I don't think so. I get more of a winning feeling."

"The winning formula."

"The winning numbers."

"I thought you said she wasn't playing the lottery. Hang on. Angie said she won a couple of prizes playing Bingo at the BeautiQueen party."

"I'm seeing Bingo numbers?"

"Let's assume that Folly plays Bingo at her parties. Wouldn't she be thinking about Bingo numbers?"

"But if she's trying to find numbers for a formula, wouldn't she be thinking in that direction?"

"Have you had a conversation with her? I'll bet her brain waves trip over each other." Then something else occurred to me. "Or worse, you're giving her Bingo numbers, and she's using them to make her face creams."

I pulled up in front of the theater to let them out.

"Come back around six and bring your power tools," Kary said. "We need everyone we can find to strike this set."

"Will there be food?"

"Free pizza and chips. Why don't you come watch the show?"

I didn't want to sit through the show again, and fortunately, I had a good excuse. "Ted needs me to watch the store this afternoon. See you at six."

◇◇◇

After an uneventful afternoon at the store, I went back to the theater. The auditorium echoed with the sound of hammers and drills. The cast had changed their fancy costumes for tee shirts and jeans and swarmed over the set, dismantling the flats and hauling away the furniture.

Kary was in the pit with her fellow musicians. Several were furiously erasing all the pencil marks from their scores while others wound up all the cords that connected music stand lights and amplifiers.

The stage manager was glad for my help and said I could assist the other men carrying the flats backstage to their storage space. After that, I helped a young woman take props to the prop room downstairs. She had two lamps that had been in Henry Higgins' parlor, and I took the large xylophone he'd used to teach Eliza the tones of proper speech. The huge prop room was filled with every sort of object, wicker birdcages, swords and spears, old-fashioned telephones and radios, clocks, cameras, a piñata, bicycles, umbrellas, and all kinds of dishes and glassware, including bottles.

Wine bottles.

"Do you know if any these were used in *Arsenic and Old Lace*?" I asked the woman.

"I believe they were."

She rearranged the shelves to make room for the lamps while I had a closer look at the bottles. Most of them were clear glass, but three were tall and dark green. Two of these green bottles were dusty, but the third was wiped clean.

Wiped clean of fingerprints?

"Who has access to this room?"

She gave the lamps a final shove. "During a show, I guess anyone can come down here. Sometimes it's locked, but usually it's open. The only people who would be around would be theater people, and honestly, would you want any of this old stuff?"

I wouldn't, but a clever murderer might.

I helped carry the rest of the props to the room and then found Camden removing a set of steps from another flat. "I think I've found the murder weapon."

He tugged a stubborn nail loose and put it in a metal coffee can beside him. "Here?"

"In the prop room. There are several wine bottles that were used in *Arsenic and Old Lace*. All of them are dusty except one. I think Viola's murderer borrowed the bottle, filled it with poisoned wine, and sent it as a present. When he was sure she was dead, he buried her, retrieved the bottle, wiped it clean of any fingerprints, and put it back in a place where no one would think to look for it. Come see if you get anything off of it."

Camden came down to the prop room and held the bottle. "Nothing. It's like you said. Wiped clean."

◇◇◇

When the set had been dismantled, all loose nails gathered up, and the floor swept, the cast and crew had a pizza party and regaled each other with backstage mishaps and inside jokes. A few of the chorus members had written parody songs, which

Camden helped them sing. I talked to more people, but no one had any information that shed new light on Viola's murder. As for George, the only one who had worked with him was Millicent Crotty.

Millicent was sitting with one of the young women who played a chambermaid. When the young woman excused herself to join another group, I went up to Millicent.

"Mrs. Crotty, I'm David Randall. We spoke on the phone about *Arsenic and Old Lace* and George McMillan."

I could tell by her expression she didn't remember, but she gave a nod. "That's right."

"I really appreciated your information. Do you mind if I ask you a few more questions?"

"Not at all."

She was a lot more mellow than before. Maybe there was something other than soda in her plastic cup. "You told my friend Kary that George tried to make amends with the cast. Was there anyone who didn't accept his apology or his gifts?"

"No, everyone took that BeautiQueen stuff. I didn't like it, but I thought at least he was making an effort to act like a decent human being. Don't know why he thought it was such remarkable foundation. I didn't find anything special about it. It didn't agree with me." A burst of laughter from the group distracted her for a moment. When she looked back at me, her little watery eyes were distant. "You know, I got some very nice gifts for this play, nothing like a little jar of cream. Flowers, candy, even a bottle of wine. Now that's more like it."

I came to attention. "A bottle of wine? For opening night?"

"No, it came days ago. Viola got one, too. I had to remind her to take it home and not leave it in the dressing room. If you leave anything in this theater, someone takes it. I lost a perfectly good blouse here and one of my best hand mirrors. The nerve of some people! No respect whatsoever."

"Who sent you the wine?"

"It wasn't from anyone in particular. There was a card that said congratulations and…" her voice trailed off as she realized what she was saying. "Young man, you don't think that was the bottle of wine that killed Viola."

"Did you drink yours?"

"No, I was saving it for my birthday."

Or you'd be pushing up dirt in your basement. "Do you know where it is right now?"

"In my kitchen cabinet." Millicent looked stricken. "But we're always getting presents from secret admirers. I didn't think anything of it."

"Did the wine arrive on Wednesday, the day you took Viola home?"

"I don't remember. But I made sure she had hers. If you leave anything in the dressing room, someone will steal it. Did you know I lost a perfectly good blouse one time, and my very best hand mirror?"

"Yes," I said. "You told me."

"Did I?" She put a shaking hand to her mouth. "Are you sure?"

"Mrs. Crotty, do you have a way home? The police can meet us there and check on that wine."

She had regained her normal crankiness. "I don't need any help driving, if that's what you mean."

I signaled to Kary and filled her in. "We're going to have a look at that bottle first."

When we arrived at Millicent's house, she told us we couldn't come in. We were to wait, and she'd bring the bottle to us. She was gone so long, I thought she might have forgotten why she was in there, but then she returned carrying a bottle exactly like the ones I'd seen in the prop room.

Camden took the bottle and held it for a long moment. "Nothing on this one, either. It's also been wiped clean."

Millicent was offended. "Well, of course. I keep everything clean in my house."

Camden wiped his own fingerprints off and handed it back to her. She went inside. I called Jordan and explained about Millicent's memory lapses and her possibly close call with a bottle of poisoned wine. He said he'd send a team to her house.

"You're already there, aren't you, Randall? Don't touch anything."

"I won't." And I didn't.

A few minutes later, the police arrived. Millicent grudgingly let them in. After a short while, a member of the crime scene team came out carrying the wine bottle.

We stood well out of the way by our cars. "I'll bet Millicent's faulty memory saved her," Kary said.

"And if there's poison in that bottle, we'll know the killer was after her, too," I said. "But we haven't found a murderer. We've added a potential victim."

◇◇◇

It was late when we got home. J.J. called to say Charlie was up and playing at the Twilight bar, so I decided now was the time to tell him what he could do to win Taffy back.

I hadn't been to the Twilight bar. It had a reputation as a hangout for Goths and everyone who had a secret desire to be a vampire. Sure enough, it was a dark, mysterious-looking place with lots of black wrought-iron furnishings and red velvet curtains. I expected the bartender to look like Count Dracula, but he was an average sized black man dressed all in black with a red tie. Charlie was at a large shiny black baby grand set on a slightly raised stage area. He was playing, appropriately, "I Got It Bad And That Ain't Good."

I greeted the bartender with a nod and went up to the piano. Charlie finished the song and looked up.

"Randall."

"I've got an idea if you want to listen."

There were several cigarettes in an ashtray beside him on the piano bench. He took one, gave it a long pull, and blew out the smoke. "Okay."

"Surprise Taffy with a recording session at Visions Studios. She can make a CD of her songs to take around to producers. She'll be amazed by your support of her career. What do you think?"

He took another puff. "It's great—if Senor Slick hasn't thought of it first."

"Fine," I said. "You deal with it."

I turned to go, and he said, "Wait. Sorry." I faced him. He put the cigarette out in the ashtray. "It is a great idea, Randall, thanks. You know I get a little crazy when I see her with another man."

I know all about that, pal. "Have you talked to her?"

"Not since that night."

"Have you tried to talk to her, I should say."

"I called a couple of times, but she hung up on me." He grinned sheepishly. "I got so mad, I smashed my phone."

I took out my cell phone. "Try again." He hesitated. "I mean it, Charlie. How serious are you about getting back together with Taffy?"

I thought he wasn't going to answer me. "Randall, do you know what it's like to be absolutely petrified of losing a woman?"

"Yes, I do."

"Thought you'd been married a couple of times."

"Twice. All mistakes." No, no, I took that back. If I hadn't married Barbara, I wouldn't have had Lindsey. I would never call Lindsey a mistake. The only mistake was mine, the mistake I made when I lost her.

"You asked me if I was serious," Charlie said. "I'm damn serious. I love her. I won't ever be happy unless she loves me."

That's what I wanted to hear. I handed him my phone. "Call her."

As Charlie punched in the number, I went over to bar and ordered a beer. The bartender handed me the glass.

"You get Charlie to cheer up?"

"We'll see. He's calling his girlfriend right now."

"Got plenty of women interested if she's not."

As long as Kary wasn't interested. That's all I cared about. Charlie was doing a fine job of groveling, and apparently, Taffy was listening this time.

"What do you think, Taffy? I'll set it up. Yes, you can record all your songs. Then you'll have a demo to take around. You might get a record deal. I want to make up for my behavior the other night. Yes, I want you to have a career. No, sing what you want, baby, I don't care."

Taffy must have said something encouraging before she hung up. Charlie closed my phone and brought it to me.

"She likes the idea." He took a deep breath. "I think this is going to work, Randall. At least she listened to me."

"Good."

"I'll call the recording studio first thing tomorrow morning."

"I'll call and remind you."

"I'm not getting drunk again, if that's what you mean."

"Of course you'll get drunk again, Charlie. You're an alcoholic. If you want to keep Taffy, admit you have a problem and do something about it."

For a moment, I thought he was going to punch me. Then he sat down at the bar. "You're right. What's the point of having a future with her if I'm not around to enjoy it?" He offered me his hand. "Thanks, Randall."

I shook his hand. "No problem." I hoped he wouldn't ask me about the woman I was petrified of losing, and he didn't. He went back to the piano. No more "I Got It Bad And That Ain't Good." As I left the Twilight bar, I heard the much more optimistic strains of "I Got A Woman Crazy For Me."

Chapter Twenty-three

"A better companion you never will find."

Monday morning, I called Charlie to remind him about the recording studio. He sounded reasonably alert and promised he'd follow up on my suggestion. Next, I called Jordan to ask about the wine. Kary was right. If Millicent had remembered to take a drink, she'd be just as dead as Viola.

"So that means three people who were in the cast of *Arsenic and Old Lace* were targeted," Jordan said. "I think we can handle it from here."

I didn't tell him I'd already checked with the other actors. I also didn't tell him about my growing suspicions about George McMillan's fake suicide.

Then Camden and I went to get our tuxes. We would have been happy to get bargain tuxedos at Suit City, but Ellin insisted we get the best, and Camden had put it off long enough, so I drove to Reynaldo's, an upscale shop in Friendly Shopping Center.

All the tuxes in this shop were too large for Camden. A serious looking salesman pulled on the jacket, measured, and did some pinning to the back. I grinned. "Wouldn't you have better luck in the junior department?"

Camden could move his head enough to give me a dark look. "Wouldn't you like to leave this shop alive?"

The salesman took pins out of his mouth. "I assure you we can tailor this perfectly. You may have to come in for a few more fittings, that's all."

"Great," he said.

To cheer him up, I tried on three different tuxes that fit me exactly. "Which one does Ellin want me to wear?"

"Whatever goes with what I can wear."

"Excuse me," the salesman said. "I'm out of pins. I'll be right back."

"Not enough pins in the world," I said.

Camden carefully moved one arm. "I still say we could've found a tux at Suit City. I'm only going to wear the thing for twenty minutes, and everyone should be looking at the bride."

"You'll notice we're all in black and white. Is this the mysterious pattern you've been seeing?"

"No."

"How about seeing who killed Viola? And almost killed Millicent? And maybe killed George?"

"I believe that's what I hired you to do. The first part, I mean."

"Jordan thinks it's someone from the cast of *Arsenic and Old Lace*, but I can't figure a motive." I couldn't figure a motive for either murder. An elderly actress and an eccentric employee of a cosmetics company. Even if George managed to come up with a dynamite idea, where did Viola and Millicent fit in? They wouldn't steal it or sell it to another company. They didn't want to have anything to do with George.

"Here we are." The salesman hurried back with more pins. After pinning, measuring, and marking, the tux fit Camden. With the salesman's help, I chose a tux that matched. The salesman took our wedding finery off to the alterations department. While Camden was in the dressing room putting his jeans and shirt back on, I had a call from Wesley Lennox, the director who'd cast George in *Arsenic and Old Lace*.

"I was cleaning out my office and found some things of George's you might like to see. I don't know how helpful they'd be, but you never know."

Right now, anything about George was going to be helpful.

◇◇◇

I didn't recognize Lennox's office. Everything had been cleaned off the desk and the floor. No more stacks of play books, no more piles of paper—even the framed posters were hanging straight.

"There comes a time when you have to shovel out." Lennox grinned.

"It looks great," I said. "This is my friend, Camden."

Lennox shook hands with Camden. "Wesley Lennox. Have a seat, guys. You can actually find the chairs." We sat down, and Lennox handed me a small photo album. "I found this in one of my file cabinets when I was filing all the papers. There are a few pictures in it."

There was a picture of Lennox and George McMillan standing in front of the UNC-P sign. College-age Lennox looked the same as he did now: big and husky. Young George had the same scowl and the beginnings of his trademark moustache. The second picture showed them in front of a fraternity house. Lennox was holding a toilet seat, and George held a six-pack of beer. The third picture was also in front of the frat house, a group shot of eight guys in stupid hats. Standing next to George was a man who could've been his twin.

"Who's this fellow? George's brother?"

"No, that's Edwin Bailey, a friend of ours."

Edwin Bailey was the same height and build as George. Like George, he had dark hair and dark eyes and was attempting to grow a major moustache. "They look very much alike." I recalled what the woman at the Green Palms Hotel had said about the man George met in the lobby. *They acted like they were old friends. I thought they might even be brothers.*

"Yeah, everybody said so. You know, Ed might be the one to talk to. He and George were pretty good friends there for a while."

"Any idea where to find Ed?"

"The college alumni office should have an address."

"Mind if I take this album with me?"

"Keep it as long as you like."

"Thanks. Oh, one more thing about Ed. Did he have any luck with women?"

"Oddly enough, I remember he had plenty of dates. I even borrowed one of them to go to a dance. Kinda funny, now that I think of it, he looked so much like George, but George couldn't get a dog to play with him even with a pork chop round his neck, if you know what I mean."

I'd been living in the same house with Rufus long enough to know exactly what that meant.

I wanted Camden to hold the album, but we waited until we were back in the car. He turned the little book around in his hands. Then he opened it and carefully touched each picture.

"They were good friends, as Lennox said. Ed was not as bright as George. A follower."

"Yeah, I could tell that by the matching moustaches. He was someone George could manipulate?"

"I'm getting that kind of feeling. On George's end, it wasn't so much here's a friend, but how can I use this person? So it's strange that Ed was a babe magnet, and George wasn't."

"Even though they looked alike. Even the hotel reception-ist thought they were related." I started the car. "Once I find him, maybe Ed can give me more insight into the wonder that is George."

◇◇◇

I gave Folly a call and asked if we could stop by her house. She met us at the door, anxiously twisting her rings.

"Any news about George?"

"Not yet," I said. "Would you happen to know a friend of his named Edwin Bailey?"

"I don't believe so. Come on into the parlor and sit down."

Camden and I sat down in the peach-colored parlor. Folly hovered.

"Do you want some tea? Cookies?"

"No, thanks. I want to know if women always play Bingo at BeautiQueen parties."

"Oh, yes, it's my latest fun thing, a special BeautiQueen Bingo. You can win all sorts of wonderful prizes, like Floral Fantasy Bath Spray or Rejuvenating Facial Splash."

"Camden would like to see a Bingo card."

She hunted around in her desk until she found a stack of cards. She handed him one. "Here you go. I tried using a peach color, but you can't see the numbers as well, so I had to settle for a peach decoration."

The Bingo card was a standard black and white card on the front. The back had a design of peaches and flowers. Camden held the card for a few minutes.

"This is it."

Folly looked puzzled. "This is what, dear?"

"The numbers I've been seeing for you." He handed her the card. "Bingo numbers, not numbers for your formula."

"Oh, my goodness." She clutched the card to her chest. "Are you sure?"

"I hope you haven't used those numbers for anything important."

"So that's why none of them worked."

"I'm sorry, Folly."

"It's not your fault! I've been thinking about this new game for the parties, and what with George's death and everything, I must be all mixed up. Have you found out anything else, David?"

Well, let's see. George was a braggart and a lousy actor who struck out repeatedly with the ladies.

"I'm still gathering information."

"I need to write you another check."

She went into another room to search for her checkbook. Camden put the Bingo card on the coffee table. "There's still another pattern."

"I'll ask if she plays checkers."

"It doesn't have anything to do with BeautiQueen, but it definitely has to do with George."

"You can't tell if George is still alive?"

"No."

This could mean several things. Either his brain was too scrambled with his new talent, or he was involved with this case in ways that weren't clear. Since he never saw his own future, we wouldn't know until something happened—usually something drastic.

Folly came back with another peach-colored check. We stayed a few minutes more, listening politely as she told us all of George's sterling qualities and then headed for home.

◇◇◇

In my office, I accessed my Internet search program and found sixty-four Edwin Baileys in North Carolina, most of them too young or too old to have been in college the same time as George. For the next hour and a half, I called the ones who were the right age, but none of them had been to UNC-P with George McMillan. Next, I found the college alumni website, but graduates were listed only by name and class. You had to have a special alumni password to access any more information, and the alumni office line was busy.

I needed a break and food. I came back to the island. Camden was sitting on the green corduroy sofa. He had a two liter bottle of Coke and a large package of Cheetos.

"'Outer Limits' marathon on channel forty-two," he said.

The episode playing was one of our favorites, the one where six blocks of a small town had been transported to another planet, and the people were getting ready to thwart the aliens' plans and sacrifice themselves by turning into rocks when Ellin came in. She surprised both of us by taking a seat on the sofa beside Camden and not making a snide remark regarding our viewing choice.

"Well, hello." Camden put his arm around her, and she further surprised us by snuggling in.

"And me without a camera," I said.

She gave me a mild glare. "Mother and my sisters are driving me crazy. I want to sit quietly for a moment."

"Sit as long as you like," Camden said.

The next "Outer Limits" episode was about those creepy ants with human faces. Camden said he'd pass on that one. I had the remote, so I clicked away, trying to find something else to watch. On the country music station, a sad-looking cowboy warbled about his woman leaving him in the dust. On MTV, angry teenagers pelted each other with mud.

"Geez, life is hard."

The shopping channel featured porcelain baskets. I moved on. The History Channel, in a daring move, was featuring Great Battles of World War II. On the Fishing Channel, two grinning overweight guys in a tiny rowboat hauled in a striped bass. The fishermen were celebrating as if they'd caught the Loch Ness Monster.

Camden glanced down at Ellin. "She's asleep." He eased her from his shoulder to his lap.

Ellin always looks so perfect and serene when she's asleep. I turned the volume down. "I'll check the yard and see if there's a pod lying around."

"She tries to do too much. I wish she'd relax."

"She looks pretty relaxed right now." The emerald and diamond engagement ring sparkled on her finger. "Does she know about the ring?"

"That it belonged to Fred's wife? Yes. She was really touched."

"Did it meet with Jean's approval?"

"Ellie likes it. That's all I care about. But yes, Jean thinks it's tasteful."

"And damn expensive. You know she likes that." I flipped through more channels. Unless there's a game on, Sunday afternoon is not the best time to watch TV.

I hoped Kary might come in, but Camden said she and Angie had gone shopping. There was no telling when they'd be home. We watched ESPN until the ant episode was over, and then I turned back to the marathon. Halfway through the next episode, Ellin woke up from her nap. She yawned and ran her hand through her blond curls.

"Cam, you're still going to marry me, right?"

"You know I will."

"I'm telling you right now I'm not going to have three children."

"Well, not all at once."

Ellin's nap must have done her a lot of good because she laughed. "Come on." She pulled him off the sofa. "I'm hungry. Let's go to Pokey's."

She actually wanted pizza? Good lord, was this the same woman? Camden gave me a wave as they went out, and I gave him a thumbs-up sign. Enjoy it while you can, pal.

Chapter Twenty-four

"With a little bit of luck…"

I finally got through to someone in the alumni office to ask about Edwin Bailey. I used George McMillan's name and the year he graduated, and fortunately, the young woman hadn't heard about George's suicide.

"Sir, I don't have a recent address for Mr. Bailey, but I can give you his last known address."

"That would be fine, thank you."

"Okay. Got a pencil? It's 222 West Tidal Avenue."

"That's 222 West Tidal Avenue. Go ahead."

"Clearwater, Florida."

What? "Clearwater, did you say?"

"Yes, sir. There isn't a phone number, sorry."

"That's all right," I said. "That's more than enough information."

I closed my cell phone and sat staring at my office wall. Edwin Bailey lived in Clearwater. What if George McMillan knew this, met his old college buddy, and then—it sounded insane, but what if he killed Ed to fake his own suicide? He and Ed looked enough alike that it was possible to fool Cousin Lucy, who said she and George rarely saw each other. Lucy claims what she thinks is George's body, and George is free to what? Roam like the Mixer he is, creating miracle face creams?

I had to go back to Clearwater and find out if Edwin Bailey was still alive.

◇◇◇

The only flight I could get left that night and involved driving two hours to Charlotte. The trip from Charlotte to Tampa was a little less than two hours, so I got to Clearwater around eleven. I checked into a motel and got up early Tuesday morning to hunt for Ed's house. West Tidal Avenue was a hot dusty little street. The houses were all cream-colored with palm trees in the yards. I parked my rental car in front of 222. The tiny lawn needed mowing, and newspapers lay scattered in the drive behind a white Camry. I went up to the front door and knocked. After standing for ten minutes, I tried to peer into the windows, but the blinds were closed.

"No use looking for him," a voice behind me said.

I turned. A stubby little woman stood in the driveway with her arms folded. She had on shorts and a halter top in a flaming shade of pink.

"Been by here every morning," she said. "He's done a bunk."

It took me a moment to process her slang. "He's run off?"

"Owes me rent money."

"You're talking about Edwin Bailey?" She nodded. "How long has he been gone?"

She looked me up and down. "What's it to you?"

"He owes me money, too."

This satisfied her. "Haven't seen him for almost a week now."

"When did you last speak to him?"

"Like I said, about a week ago."

"Did he say where he was going, what he was going to do?"

"No. He was rolling his garbage can out to the curb and said hello."

"Has he had any visitors lately? Anyone come by the house?"

"Not that I know of."

I pointed to the Camry. "Is this his car?"

"Yeah."

"Have you called the police? He might be hurt or dead in the house."

"He ain't in there. I got a key. I looked."

"Let me have a look," I said. "He's got something that belongs to me."

She shook her head. "I don't know you. You could be a burglar."

"Is there anything valuable to steal?"

She thought it over. "Guess not. Come on."

She pulled a key on a chain from the depths of the halter top and unlocked the door. The house was furnished in light wood furniture and paintings of the beach. There was a stack of mail on the floor under the mail slot and some moldy food in the refrigerator.

"See?" the woman said, as if she'd proved her point. "Gone to ground, he has."

A prophetic statement if ever I'd heard one.

She let me look around for a while. The only thing I found useful was a phone number scribbled on the back of an envelope. I had called this number before. It was the number for the Green Palms Hotel.

"Get what you were looking for?" the woman asked.

"Yes, thanks."

Back outside, she grumbled her way across the street to her house and slammed the door. I was standing in the shade of the palm tree wondering what to do next when another neighbor came over. This young woman was also wearing pink, but unlike Ed Bailey's landlady, this woman filled out her shorts and top in a very appealing way. Her long dark hair was tied back in a ponytail. Her blue eyes were anxious.

"Excuse me," she said. "Are you another of Ed's college friends?"

"Yes," I said.

"Do you know where he is?"

"No, I'm sorry, I don't."

She put her hands on her hips. "I can't believe he went off and didn't tell anybody where he was going. I could wring his neck."

"How long has he been gone?"

"About a week."

"Have you called the police?"

"I don't know what to do," she said. "It's not unusual for him to go off on fishing trips, but ever since I read about his friend's suicide, I've been awfully worried about him."

"A suicide?"

"George McMillan. You probably know him from school."

"Yes, I do," I said. "What happened?"

"I only know what I read in the paper. George McMillan shot himself." She held out her hand. "I'm Monica, by the way."

I shook her hand. "David Randall."

"Nice to meet you, David. Ed and I have been dating for almost a year now. Ed's a wonderful man."

And, unlike George, a man who has no problem getting beautiful women.

"About a week ago, Ed got a call from a fellow named George McMillan. Ed was so excited. He told me he and George had gone to college together in North Carolina, and they hadn't seen each other in years. Ed was supposed to meet George at George's hotel. The only thing I can guess is he found poor George dead in the hotel room, and he was so upset, he's run off somewhere. Or maybe he thought the police would think he killed George."

"But Ed would call you if he called anyone, right?"

"I'd like to think so."

"And he's not off on a fishing trip?"

"All his fishing equipment is still here. I'm afraid something's happened to him."

Me, too, I wanted to say. "Monica, I remember Ed and George were known for their big moustaches. Does Ed still have his moustache?"

She managed to smile. "I keep asking him to shave it off, but he's so proud of it. He said George had one, too, which is why he liked to keep his. It was some sort of fraternity thing."

Monica brushed tears from her cheek. "Were you in the same fraternity?"

"Yes, I was hoping to see Ed, but I'm going to have to go back to North Carolina."

"He'll be so sorry he missed you."

I was beginning to believe Ed had made the ultimate sacrifice for a fraternity brother. "I'm sorry I missed him, too."

◇◇◇

I told Monica I would file a missing persons report on Ed. This also gave me a good excuse to talk to the local police and see if there was anything new on George McMillan.

A trim young policewoman who had handled George's case agreed to speak with me. We sat down in her office, and she opened a file on her computer. I gave her Ed Bailey's name and description and all the information I had learned from Monica. I told her that Ed's landlady had let me in the house.

"Missing for a week, you said?"

"From the stack of mail in his house, yes."

"And his landlady was the last one to see him?"

"She said he owed her money, so she'd been over every day looking for him."

The policewoman clicked a few keys. "George McMillan's death was ruled a suicide."

"I know he didn't have any teeth left to check. Did anyone check his fingerprints?"

"According to this report, the victim's fingers were badly scarred and fingerprint ID was inconclusive. But a relative, a Mrs. Lucy Warner, positively identified the body. There was no evidence of foul play, and the personnel at the hotel did not hear anything other than the gunshot."

"So it's possible the man found dead in the hotel was Edwin Bailey."

"What motive would someone have for killing Mr. Bailey?"

"I think it's possible George McMillan wanted to fake his own death, and Bailey looked enough like him to make that work."

"For what reason?"

She had me there. "Somehow it ties in with a case I'm working in North Carolina."

"Well, you can keep us posted, Mr. Randall, but unless you have more evidence, this case is closed."

◇◇◇

I thanked the policewoman for her time and got some lunch. Then I went to the Green Palms Hotel. The same perky little redhead was at the desk and glad to see me. She and her bosom stood at attention.

"Oh, hello! I remember you."

"I remember you, too," I said. "I need to ask you a few more questions about George McMillan."

"You can ask me anything."

"You said that he met another man here, a man that looked like him. You mentioned you thought they might be brothers. Both of them would've had thick moustaches."

"Yes, they did. I don't really like that on a man. I like your look. I like it a lot."

I tried to keep the conversation on track. "You said George was glad to see him and they shook hands."

"Yeah, come to think of it, it was a funky handshake, like a secret society or something."

Or a fraternity.

The redhead leaned forward on the desk. "Now why did you really come back?"

"I'm tying up loose ends today. Do you remember which room George rented?"

"He always stayed in 130. He liked the ground floor so he could get his dog in and out easily."

"Anybody in there now?"

She checked her computer. "No. You want to see it?"

"If it's not too much trouble."

She gave me a look that said nothing would be too much trouble for me.

Of course, after a week, there was no trace of George, but I wanted to cover everything. The room was painted a shade of peach that Folly would've admired. The king sized bed had a tropical print bedspread that matched the curtains. Pictures of parrots and huge flowers hung over the bed and mirror.

The woman sat down on the bed and patted the place beside her. "The bed's really comfy. Come try it out."

"I'll take your word for it."

"Oh, relax, why don't you? I know you didn't come back just to ask questions about George."

Fortunately, a maid passed by with her rolling cart and gave the woman a look that made the redhead hop up. "I'd better get back to the desk."

Alone in room 130, I tried to imagine the scene. George meets Ed and they come back to the room. George kills Ed and flees—but how? He left his SUV because Lucy claimed it when she came to ID the body and pick up Danger.

Room 130 was on the corner with easy access to the outside. I walked out and looked around. The Green Palms lived up to its name. There were plenty of palm trees and bushes, all kinds of places someone could hide. George could've had a suitcase packed and a cab waiting up the street, but he had only moments to get away, because hotel employees heard the sound of the shotgun.

I tried out my theory. I could walk from the hotel to the nearest street using the palm trees as a cover in two minutes. The street was lined with coffee shops and restaurants. George could've ducked into any one of these and even had a leisurely meal while all the excitement went on at the hotel. If he had blood on his clothes, he could've changed in any restroom. And if he had some sort of fake ID, he could've rented a car and driven back to North Carolina.

I realized I was giving George a lot of credit and imagination, but he supposedly killed himself on May 10th. According to Monica, Ed had been missing since the 9th.

I wasn't going to take any chances with the redhead at the Green Palms, so I returned to the motel where I'd stayed the first night. I called home to let Kary know I'd be back later and promised to tell her all the details. Then I had three calls. The first was from Charlie.

"Randall, I'm calling to let you know everything went great at Visions. Taffy's thrilled with her CD. She can't stop talking about it. Catch you later."

One crisis averted.

The second call was from Ted at the Drug Palace. "Randall, Ted here. When you get a chance, come by the store. I'm getting rid of those bracelets and thought Kary might like to have one."

The third call was from Folly Harper. "David, are you there? This is Folly Harper. I have wonderful news. We've finally got the right formula for our Extra Whip Moisturizing Deluxe cream! We're launching it at the preliminary competition of the Miss Parkland Pageant Thursday night. This is so exciting! Is Cam there? Tell him all about it. I'm sure he'll want to know, even though the numbers he saw were Bingo numbers. That's certainly not his fault if that's what he saw in my head."

Well, hooray for BeautiQueen. No more eyebrowless women.

Now I had to make a call. I wanted Lucy Warner to know that George was possibly alive. I imagined the news was going to be shock.

When she answered the phone, I could hear cheeps and growls in the background.

"Yes, Mr. Randall. What's this all about?"

"Mrs. Warner, I don't think the body you identified in Florida was George. I think someone else was murdered, a man that was supposed to be George."

"But I'm certain that was George."

"I'm sorry to mention this, but wasn't most of George's face gone?"

"I would've known that moustache anywhere."

What was left of it. "I believe the person you identified was Edwin Bailey, a classmate of George's with very similar features."

"But why would someone kill him? That sounds crazy."

"I think it has to do with a valuable formula for a skin cream."

"So you think George is alive?"

"It's entirely possible."

"But then, why wouldn't he contact someone, Mrs. Harper, or the police?"

Because for one thing, I believe he murdered Edwin Bailey. "I don't know. Maybe he's afraid the killer will come after him."

"Surely he would try to contact me, if only to find out if Danger is all right."

"I think that's exactly what he'll do. You've got to let me know the minute you hear anything. Tell him I know someone has stolen ingredients in an attempt to duplicate the anti-aging formula. Once we find these thieves, I bet we find the person responsible for the murder."

She sniffed as if trying to hold back tears. "This is so bizarre, Mr. Randall. First I think George is dead, and now you say he may be alive, but hiding somewhere, all because of some stupid face cream?"

"That's what it looks like. Is there anyone else he might turn to?"

"I have no idea."

Unfortunately, neither did I.

Chapter Twenty-five

"Without you…"

Wednesday, I spent going around to the taxi companies in the area and asking if they'd had a fare matching George's description on May tenth. No one had. Next I tried the rental car companies. No luck there, either. One woman remembered a man with a large moustache, but she was certain it had been red. Maybe George dyed his moustache. More than likely, he would've shaved it off. Maybe he had a getaway car stashed somewhere in the bushes near the Green Palms Hotel. Would he have gone to such elaborate lengths?

I had a flight out early Thursday morning, but thanks to mechanical problems and a couple of thunderstorms, I didn't get back to Parkland until after five. When I got to 302 Grace, no one was home. I figured Rufus and Angie were checking out the house on River Street, and Kary was at pageant rehearsal. Camden had probably been dragged away on wedding business.

I went into the kitchen to fix some peanut butter crackers. I was searching in the cabinets for the crackers when Kary came in, carrying the black and white kitten.

"Hi, David. We weren't sure when you'd be home."

"Got in a little while ago. Where is everybody?"

"Rufus and Angie went to a friend's birthday party, and Ellin wanted Cam to help her figure out the seating arrangement for the wedding reception. You can imagine how excited he was about that."

"I'm sure he was thrilled. Are we out of crackers?"

"There should be some above the fridge."

I found a pack of saltines and brought them to the counter. "Here's the latest on George. You know I went to Clearwater to track down his old college buddy, Ed Bailey. Ed hasn't been seen in a week, and his girlfriend's worried about him. She said he went to meet George at George's hotel and never came home. She thinks George's suicide upset him. I think Ed is more than upset. I think it's entirely possible George killed him and took his place."

"Why?"

"Maybe this skin cream formula is more valuable than anyone thought."

Kary sat down across from me and put the kitten in her lap. I'd noticed how often she cuddled one of the little fur balls. Connecting with a baby. Any baby. "I had a talk with Amelia Tilley at pageant practice last night. I didn't have any trouble getting her to talk about George. She told me all about him. I'm sure it's the same thing she told you, only this was the full version, live and in color. The interesting thing was, she said they got along at first. She felt sympathy for him because he told her she was the first woman who listened to him and his grand plans for the cosmetics industry. It was only when he started talking about how they could be partners in this adventure that she got concerned."

"Wait a minute. She went out with him? She didn't tell me that."

Kary gave me a long meaningful look. "Women don't tell you everything, David."

Ouch. "Point well taken. But this could be important. How long did they date?"

"She went out with him only a few times before she realized he was getting way too serious."

"Serious as in wanting to marry her?"

"She was afraid things were headed in that direction. She said she tried to let him down easy."

"He was bound to think, I finally found the right woman, and she won't have me."

"So when she refused him, he went nuts? Does that sound reasonable?"

"I'm not sure anything about George is reasonable. Did he propose to Amelia?"

"He did."

"And she said no." Knowing how strongly I felt about Kary and how devastated I'd be if she completely refused me, I had a second of empathy with George. Only a second. "Does Amelia seem like the kind of woman who'd find a way to get rid of a pest like George?"

"I don't think so. She said this happens to her all the time, but George was one of the most persistent."

"She doesn't live alone, does she?"

"She mentioned her sister was in town for the pageant and staying with her. Do I need to warn her?"

"No, don't frighten her. I'm still not certain."

"But you believe George McMillan still walks among us?"

"I told Lucy Warner to call if he contacts her. If he's alive, I figure he'll want to know how his dog is getting along."

Kary picked up the knife and spread peanut butter on a cracker. "Now here's my big news. I found someone else at the theater who remembers George. Our set designer has a niece in the pageant, so he came to the theater last night. He also did the set for *Arsenic and Old Lace*. He remembers George and told me he didn't think George would commit suicide because he thought way too much of himself. He thinks his one reason for being in a show was to meet women. He heard George in the wings all the time, bragging about how important he was to BeautiQueen, how they couldn't run the place without him. I asked him if he ever heard George mention Folly Harper or Amelia Tilley, and he said when George wasn't talking about himself, he was in a corner going over his lines or getting into character. Like Nathan, fellow who played Colonel Pickering in *My Fair Lady*. 'Don't speak to me. I'm centering.' He never wanted anyone to talk to him before he went on stage. There's a big difference between Nathan and George, though. Nathan could act. And he got the women, too."

From what I remembered, the fellow playing Pickering was an older man, old and bald. George must have been boiling with frustration.

"Did you ask the set designer if George had made any enemies in the *Arsenic* cast?"

She licked a stray dab of peanut butter off her thumb. "Yes, and he said he didn't think so, even though George was stand-offish. He tried talking to him, but he wasn't very friendly. He didn't understand why George wasn't having a good time playing Teddy, because it's almost impossible to mess up that role. You yell, 'Charge!' and run up the stairs. But he did remember one thing that might be the clue we're looking for. He was backstage painting some scenery when he overheard George and Viola having an argument."

"Please tell me he remembered what it was about."

"Oh, he did. Viola told George he was a crass little man and she could not believe he'd given her such a shoddy product. George said what are you talking about, and Viola said his cream was horrible and had irritated her skin. He started spluttering apologies and begging her not to tell anyone, and she interrupted him, which must be the worst thing you can do to George. He got angry and called Viola a bitch and an interfering old biddy, and that's when the designer stepped in and told George where to stick it. He said he couldn't stand by and hear Viola called such names, and that George stalked out, furious. He remembers because Viola didn't thank him for coming to her defense. She said she could take care of herself and for him to mind his own business. He said that was the last time he would try to do anything nice for her."

"'His cream was horrible and had irritated her skin.' That doesn't sound like BeautiQueen."

Kary rearranged the kitten, who was trying to reach the counter. "Viola must have had an allergic reaction to the cream."

"And George pleads with her not to tell anyone, or his career would be jeopardized."

"But she threatens to tell, so he has to kill her, and he figured he'd better kill Millicent, too, because the two women were friends, and Viola might have told Millicent."

"Millicent might have threatened to tell on him, too. Camden said he sensed something odd in Millicent's face and hands, and at the cast party she told me the cream didn't agree with her. What's George doing going around giving out bad cream?"

"It must have been a mistake, or something in the cream didn't agree with those two women. Isn't Folly always tinkering with the formula?"

"But if it's an allergic reaction, all George had to do was apologize and report the problem to Folly. It wouldn't ruin his career, would it, unless it's indicative of a bigger problem." I reached for the peanut butter. "Of course, all this hinges on the somewhat sketchy idea that George is alive. I'm not sure how I'm going to prove that."

"Be on the lookout for more sub-standard face cream and bottles of poisoned wine."

"That's entirely possible. Excellent work, partner."

"Thank you."

I fixed another cracker. "On the lighter side of the news, Charlie took Taffy to Visions Studio so she could make a CD of her songs, and now all is well."

Kary chuckled. "You thought Charlie was after me, didn't you?" As I stammered for a reply, she said, "That's why you went to such lengths to get him and Taffy back together."

Why did I think I could hide anything from her? "Okay, you got me."

"David, Charlie is charming and talented, but I've done enough baby-sitting in my time. He drinks and smokes too much and is totally unreliable. If she wants to, and if she's got the patience, Taffy's the one who can straighten him out."

I'm sure I looked pathetically relieved. "I'll admit I was a little worried."

"No need to worry. We're working on a relationship, aren't we?"

"Well, I am, definitely."

I hoped she'd reply with something even more encouraging, but she changed the subject. "Do you know if Cam sent his mother a wedding invitation?"

Camden's foster parents had passed away, and despite his reluctance, I'd found his birth mother, but she didn't want to make contact. At least, that's what she told me.

"I doubt she'd come."

"But she might want to know. You have her address and phone number, don't you?"

I'd kept that information just in case Camden ever changed his mind. "Yes, but you'd better wait and see what Camden says about that."

"And Daisy? Didn't you find her, too? She might like to come."

Camden had reconnected with his foster parents' daughter, but she was much older and hadn't been able to travel. "I don't know. Camden's the one who should call her."

"Is Sophia going to be able to come?"

My mother was on a round-the-world cruise. "She sends her love, but she'll be frolicking in the Mediterranean on May 31st."

"I want to make sure his side of the church is full."

"Are you kidding? You know how many friends he has. Ellin will have Reg, Bonnie, and Teresa from the PSN, a few more family members, and that's it."

"You're forgetting her mother's society friends."

Country club on one side, circus on the other. "Then it ought to be an interesting ceremony."

◇◇◇

As I lay in bed that night, I thought of my own weddings. I didn't remember a lot about my first wedding. I did remember how beautiful Barbara looked. My second wedding, a disastrous attempt to reorganize my life and start another family, was also a blur, filled with anxiety and guilt. The marriage hadn't lasted very long. And now here I was, contemplating another marriage. But this one would be different, wouldn't it? I loved Kary and I hoped she loved me, and if we could find some common ground regarding children—which I was afraid we couldn't manage—then all would be well.

I couldn't sleep. I turned on my CD player and listened to the New Black Eagle Jazz Band long into the night. It didn't matter what they played. I wanted the lively music to keep me from thinking about anything else.

◇◇◇

I hardly ever oversleep, but all my soul searching made me sleep later than usual. It was almost ten thirty in the morning when I came down to the kitchen. Camden must have had a sleepless night, as well. He was fixing his usual nutritious breakfast of brown sugar Pop-Tarts and Coke.

"You get shanghaied last night?" I asked.

"Twice. Once to choose the type of cake, and then again to go over the list of people who've said they're coming to the wedding and where they will sit."

"And the cake of choice is?"

"It's down to yellow cake with strawberry cream frosting versus chocolate cake with buttercream frosting. I ate as much as possible while they were deciding."

"You and the entire Belton women clan?"

His Pop-Tarts popped up, and he put them on a plate. "Sandra and Caroline are having a big old time, but if Ellie and her mother get any more tense, they're going to snap in two." He took his plate and large plastic cup of Coke and sat down on one of the stools at the counter. "What did you find out in Florida?"

I got a bowl out of the cabinet and brought the cornflakes and milk to the counter and sat down across from him. "Edwin Bailey's missing. His landlady thinks he's run off to avoid paying the rent, but his girlfriend's really worried about him." I shook cornflakes into the bowl and added milk. "She told me Ed was excited to meet his old college friend George at the Green Palms

Hotel, but Ed never made it home. She thinks he found George's body and it freaked him out. I think George figured his buddy Ed's body would make a good substitute for his own."

"Why would he kill Ed?"

"Yeah, why fake his death, at all?" I crunched a few spoonfuls of cornflakes. "For some reason, George wanted his cousin Lucy to be the one to identify the body. I guess he wanted someone reliable to come get his dog and his car, someone who hadn't seen him since last Christmas." I ate a few more bites of cereal. "How's your new talent coming along? Levitate some toast over here."

"You can levitate your own toast. Everything's under control this morning."

"You'll also be happy to know Folly has the right numbers now, and the deluxe face cream will premiere at the Miss Parkland Pageant."

"Kary said something about that."

"Kary also said you might like to invite your mother to the wedding."

He gave the Pop-Tarts his full attention. "She wouldn't come."

"She might. Send her an invitation and see what happens. And did you invite Daisy?"

"I did. She's not sure she can make it."

"I can go get her."

"She knows that's an option. She's not feeling well."

I could tell that was the end of this discussion. "Kary found out some interesting things about George and Viola that may be the connection I've been looking for. The set designer for *Arsenic and Old Lace* overheard a conversation in which Viola accused George of giving her a defective cream. When she threatened to tell, he begged her not to."

"Begged her? That doesn't sound like George."

"Didn't you tell me you felt pain in Millicent's face and hands? I think George gave both women some BeautiQueen that didn't agree with them."

"An earlier version of the secret formula?"

"He probably thought he was doing them a huge favor by letting them preview the wonder cream. We know Viola was concerned about getting older. She may have been excited to try it and really disappointed when it reacted on her skin."

"*Arsenic and Old Lace* was in February. Wouldn't Viola have told Folly by now?"

"Viola was a crafty gal. I think she agreed not to say anything so she'd have something to hold over George to make him leave her alone."

"What about Millicent? The same thing happened to her."

"She either went along with Viola, or she forgot. If Viola changed her mind and was planning to expose George, he'd have to get rid of her. His wonder cream was going to win over Amelia—whom he proposed to, by the way—and make enough money for him to create his own company. A bad review from a powerful woman in the community would ruin his chances. He's got all the motives for murder, greed, revenge, jealousy, and love."

"Okay, so how did he do it?"

"Let's suppose Viola calls him. She's decided to expose him, maybe even go to the *Herald*. He says can we talk about this. Maybe offers her money. He comes by her house with a peace offering, a bottle of wine. No, wait. Millicent made sure Viola got the bottle of wine."

"George could've stopped by to make certain she drank it."

"All right, we'll say he does. He stops by. He's on his very best behavior. They come to an agreement. They drink on it, only George doesn't drink. Viola is poisoned, dies, and he buries her. He has plenty of time to dig a grave. He's a muscular guy, so he can haul her body down to the basement. Problem solved."

"Except he may be dead."

"That's the kink in my theory. Are you getting any sort of feeling one way or the other?"

He refilled his soda. "I'm having a little trouble concentrating these days. If you want some black and white patterns that aren't making sense, I've got plenty of those for you." He finished his

Pop-Tarts. "I do know Ellie and her sisters are on their way. Let's get out of the house before they carry me off again."

◇◇◇

Our first stop was the Drug Palace where Ted handed me the last of the yin yang bracelets. "Might as well get rid of these things. Maybe Kary would like it."

"She will, thanks."

"Sorry I don't have but one left, Cam. If you think Ellin would like one, I could order another."

"Let me see that." Camden took the bracelet in his hand. He stared at it for such a long time I thought it had turned him to stone.

"Camden?"

"This is it," he said. "The dominant pattern. I could never get it to stand still."

"This is the pattern you've been seeing?"

"Yes."

Ted looked at me and shrugged. "It's a long story," I said.

Camden kept staring at the bracelet. "I wonder what it means."

"It's one of those yin yang things," Ted said. "It's supposed to stand for negative and positive, male and female. It's Asian."

"I know what the design is. I'm trying to figure out why I've been seeing it."

Ted shrugged again. "You knew I had them in the store, and I was going to give Randall one, how about that? These visions of yours don't always make much sense, do they?"

"No, and especially not lately." He gave me the bracelet, and I put it in my pocket.

"Anything else missing?" I asked Ted.

"Nope. Guess I won't need you for a while."

"Thanks for thinking of Kary."

"Got to keep at least one of your women happy," he said. "Did she go to the BeautiQueen party?"

"No, our friend Angie did. Again, thanks for the tip."

"I guess the gals have to stick together and keep their stratum corneums as perfect as possible."

"I'm afraid to ask."

"The outside layer of the skin," Ted said. "All those old cells get pushed to the surface where they die, flatten, and form the outside layer, the stratum corneum."

"You are a fount of knowledge, Ted."

"Well, I always found it ironic that all these skin creams and lotions women put all over their faces are products for cells that are dead."

"And I have learned way more than I need to know about women and their skin care products," I said. "Catch you later."

When we got into the car, Camden stared off into the distance. "Stop by George's house."

"You think George is there?"

"Something's not there that should be."

I put the car in gear. "You know I love it when you go all cryptic on me."

◇◇◇

I still had the key Folly had given me, so we let ourselves in George's house. Camden stood in the middle of the living room. He slowly looked around.

"I keep seeing a pattern of black and white."

"There isn't anything black and white here unless—wait a second." There was something missing. "There should be a big stack of BeautiQueen boxes. I remember them from last time."

"Were they black and white?"

"I don't know. They were flat, and now they're not here." I checked the other rooms. No boxes. No sign of forced entry. "I wonder if someone from BeautiQueen came by and got them." I took out my phone and called Folly. "Folly, I'm here in George's house. He had a big stack of unassembled BeautiQueen boxes. Did someone from the company come get them?"

"I'll have to ask and see," she said, "but we wouldn't need them. We have new boxes for the new cream."

"Were the old boxes black and white?"

"Yes, and so are the new ones, but we've changed the design a little."

"Camden and I would like to see the new design."

"Of course! Come on over. I'll meet you in the lobby."

Chapter Twenty-six

"You did it."

At the BeautiQueen company, Folly took us to the show room where samples of all the products were displayed. The boxes for the Age-Defying Extra Whip Moisturizing Deluxe Face Cream were white with a black and white design like a modified yin yang symbol. Camden was relieved, but he couldn't stop staring at the box in his hand.

"Folly, I don't know how to explain this, but I feel there's something very wrong."

"About the design? But it's very much like the old box, only we're calling this Age-Defying Extra Whip Moisturizing Deluxe Face Cream instead of plain Extra Whip because of our new formula. We didn't want to stray too far from our original BeautiQueen logo, and we didn't have a lot of time to create a whole new design before the pageant."

"I'm not sure this feeling is about the design."

"The formula, then? But we've tested it rigorously!"

He handed her the box. "I'm sorry. Sometimes these feelings don't make sense at first."

"Have you had time to test this formula?" I asked.

Folly turned to me. "We gave it top priority in the lab. Our facilities aren't very big, but they're state of the art, I assure you. We've been working on this for weeks. I only needed the proper proportions. You say the older boxes were missing from George's house? That doesn't make sense, either."

Unless George was still alive and had some use for them. I didn't want to trouble Folly with this theory. "We'll figure it out. Congratulations on the new formula."

"Thank you," she said. "I simply can't wait until pageant night! Think how gorgeous all those girls are going to look! Will you two be there? I hope you can come. I plan to have a short tribute to George. After all, this was his life's work."

"We'll be there," I said.

◇◇◇

"Is something wrong with the formula?" I asked Camden when we got back into the car. "I don't want anyone's eyebrows falling off."

"I'm seeing two sets of boxes, and there's something wrong with one of them." He pushed his hair out of his eyes and rubbed his forehead. "That's all I'm getting right now."

"Maybe some leftover telekinesis is getting in the way of the true vibes."

My cell phone rang. This time it was Ellin.

"Is Cam with you?"

"Yes, he is."

"Tell him to turn on his cell phone."

I turned to Camden. "Is your cell phone off?"

"For this very reason."

"Randall, he needs to have his final fitting. Would you take him there, please?"

"Since you asked so nicely, sure." I hung up. "Your sweetie has the rest of the day scheduled for you. How about a couple of hot dogs to fortify you for the tasks ahead?"

◇◇◇

We stopped by Janice Chan's hot dog place for chili cheese dogs, fries, and Cokes. It was two o'clock, way past the lunch rush, but all of the tables inside and out were full, so we ate in the car. Even fortified, Camden wasn't ready to get back into his tux. I suggested we take a detour by the theater and check out Kary's pageant practice.

The stage had been transformed into a series of glittery staircases with sparkly hologram stars dangling from the ceiling. The pageant contestants were rehearsing the opening number. Kary gave us a wave as she twirled by.

We found seats near the back of the auditorium. Camden still looked preoccupied.

"Everything's good and fuzzy right now, although I'm picking up something that's not quite right here."

"All those scheming queens. Their vibes are bound to be shrieking."

"I don't know what it is."

"Is a sandbag going to fall on someone?"

"No sandbag."

"We have got to get you married and back on track." I had a chilling thought. "You don't see anything happening to Kary, do you?"

He didn't answer my question. "Something's not right. If this stupid pattern would just stand still."

"Is it one pattern or a whole bunch of patterns?"

"It's the same pattern on those bracelets at Ted's and on the BeautiQueen boxes. But it means something else."

"Use your scary new power to make it stand still."

A serious-looking woman with a clipboard came up the aisle and told us we had to leave. "The pageant starts at eight," she said. "Buy a ticket."

We gave Kary a good-bye wave and left the theater. Back to Reynaldo's. It took an hour to get the suit exactly right, and I'd exhausted my supply of snide remarks. I told Camden I'd wait for him in the car.

As I got into the Fury, I noticed the BeautiQueen brochure on the floor of the passenger's seat. I picked it up for a better look. Sometime during our lunch, either Camden or I had dropped a big glob of mustard on the brochure, right on George

McMillan's picture. The mustard covered George's moustache. Random thoughts suddenly jumped into my mind.

I remembered Camden wiping off his makeup and saying, "I don't know how women stand this stuff. It's like wearing a mask." I remembered Millicent Crotty telling me she taught George how to use stage makeup. I thought about the girl with no eyebrows, how Danger the doberman seemed completely at ease with a woman who said she rarely saw his owner, and how the pattern Camden finally recognized depicted male and female together in one symbol.

I looked at the picture of George with mustard where his moustache should be. I'd had earlier thoughts about this being a good way for George to disguise himself. He was a medium-sized man with the compact build not uncommon in some women. What if George shaved off his distinctive moustache, plucked his eyebrows, slathered on a ton of peach makeup, and put on a wig? Presto! He becomes bereaved Cousin Lucy, who claims Edwin Bailey's body as George's and no one's the wiser. Would he start stealing ingredients in the hopes of making his own skin cream? Why go to such incredible lengths to duplicate a formula that might not work?

I needed to have a talk with Cousin Lucy.

"And I'm going with you." Camden hopped into the car, still in his tux.

I must have been broadcasting louder than I realized. "Did you get all that?"

"The possibility Lucy might be George? In wide screen and Technicolor."

"You want to change clothes first?"

"No time," he said. "That something very wrong about the BeautiQueen boxes I mentioned? It has to do with Lucy, or George, or whoever he is."

If Camden was seeing something very wrong, I wasn't going to argue, but one thing puzzled me. "Why didn't you sense he might be hiding his identity behind BeautiQueen goo?"

"Are you kidding? With everything I've had to deal with? You're lucky I'm getting anything at all that has to do with you."

As I drove out to Lucy's house, he examined the brochure.

"It's a good thing one of us is a sloppy eater," I said.

"His hatred for women is growing stronger. He's planning something."

"I thought he wanted to create the ultimate skin cream."

"I need to see inside the house."

◇◇◇

The van and George's SUV were parked in the driveway of Lucy's house. I knocked, and Lucy Warner peered out. Seeing the stout square figure in the doorway, the wide shoulders and thick legs I'd thought were the result of a somewhat butch P.E. teacher's days as a tennis coach took on a whole new meaning.

"Oh, it's you, Mr. Randall. Have you found out anything more about George?"

"I sure have," I said. "May we come in? This is my friend, Camden. We'll only be a minute."

"I'm really very busy." Now I could hear the masculine overtones in "Lucy's" gruff voice. "You'll have to come back another time."

"But I've found George."

"What?"

"I'm looking at him."

"Looking at him?"

"I think the folks at the theater would be surprised that you're such a good actor."

She took a step back. "You're crazy. Get out of here before I call the police."

"Go ahead. I think the police would like to know what you did with Edwin Bailey's body. Maybe you buried it in the cellar, too."

"Edwin Bailey? What are you talking about?"

"Your fraternity pal, Ed, the one who looks enough like you to be your suicide stand in."

"Lucy" spun and dashed into the house. Camden and I ran after him. George opened the back door and let the doberman in.

Danger rushed for me, teeth barred, looking like every hideous doberman attack I'd ever seen on TV. The dog came straight for my throat. For a horrible second, I thought my last sight on earth would be mad eyes and a foam-flecked mouth filled with fangs. Even if the dog didn't kill me, I could be maimed for life. I braced for the impact and the ripping of flesh. God, there was no way out!

"Danger, stop!" Camden shouted. The dog halted in mid-air, jaws open, muscles bunched, claws outstretched, and stayed firmly in place, quivering, thanks to Camden's latest talent. I caught only a glimpse of this, being occupied with George McMillan trying to rearrange my face. I elbowed him in the jaw, grabbed his arms and forced him back. He twisted out of my grasp, so furious he didn't notice the animals, cushions, and knickknacks drifting up and around to join Danger in suspended animation.

We were surrounded by screaming airborne cats and birds frozen in mid-flight as Camden's power filled the room. At one point in the struggle, I stepped on the poor lizard's tail right before it joined the creatures above us. I didn't know they made noises like that. With a wild cry, George leaped at me. His fingers clawed at my collar, gripped it tight, and smacked my head against the floor. He might have done more damage, but his wig slipped over his eyes, giving me the chance to punch him smack in his peach-colored face. He fell back with a grunt. I scrambled to my feet and hauled him up. He was a wreck, his wig askew, his thick makeup oozing off in sweaty streaks.

I gave him another punch as animals and objects sank slowly to the floor. The cats ran off, tails bristling, and the birds settled onto the back of a chair except for the parrot, which clung to the draperies, squawking. The lizard gave me an offended look and burrowed under a cushion. Camden sat on the floor, Danger affectionately licking and chewing his hair. He kept a firm grip on the dog's collar.

I shook George hard. "What I really want to know is why you killed Viola Mitchell."

He laughed harshly. "That old bag! She was pissed because the cream I gave her didn't work on her! Nothing would work on her ancient skin! She threatened me, held that threat over me, said she'd go to the media. Turns out I have her to thank."

I saw the stack of BeautiQueen boxes in the corner. "Thank for what? Are you working on a BeautiQueen knock-off?"

George's skin flushed red under the streaks of makeup. "Ha! Better than that! You don't know anything! Even if you did, it's too late! I've already put the wrong formula into the cream."

"Using all the stuff you stole?"

He laughed. "All I had to do was increase the ingredient that had irritated wrinkly old Viola. BeautiQueen is finished! Thousands of women will burn their faces! Then they'll come crawling to me for the remedy!"

I held George in a hammerlock with one arm, so I had a hand free to call 911. "I'm sure Folly can stop the shipment of the cream."

George grinned like a shark. "It's already gone out. BeautiQueen is finished, I tell you."

I was half-listening as I gave the police the address. "Yeah, yeah. You ever hear of product recall?"

"Women have it now." He collapsed into laughter. "It's too late for a recall."

"Now?"

"I've already delivered the boxes to the auditorium. The boxes look so much alike, no one will guess that some of them have my special cream, especially Miss Perfecto Face, Amelia Tilley. She was a fool to turn me down. I could've given her everything. I could've made her company number one in the country. We'll see how she likes my version of Age-Defying Extra Whip Moisturizing Deluxe Formula Face Cream."

Realization hit me so hard, I almost dropped my phone. The auditorium. My God. The pageant.

Camden's eyes widened. "Go! I can hold him here."

To make sure George didn't try anything, I gave him another punch that sent him sailing across the room to crash into the wall. Then I ran out of the house and jumped into the car. It took me three tries to fumble the key in the ignition. For once, the Fury sputtered to life without hiccupping. A spray of gravel flew as I jackknifed down the driveway and onto the street. I didn't know the number for the auditorium, so I called 911 again and kept speeding back to town. I'm not sure how many stop signs and stop lights I ran. Everything flew by in a blur of lights and angry faces.

The Fury shrieked to a stop in front of the auditorium. I yanked open the door and dashed around to the stage entrance, pushing past stage hands and bowling over startled chaperones. As concerned as I was for Kary, I didn't even savor one of my childhood fantasies, bursting into a dressing room full of half-naked beauty queens.

"Don't put on any makeup! It's been tampered with! It'll burn you!"

There were screams and shrieks and frantic face scrubbing.

"Kary!" I couldn't see her. Please, God, don't let her have already put that stuff on her face!

Kary sat further down the row of lighted mirrors, motionless, a jar of BeautiQueen Age-Defying Extra Whip Moisturizing Deluxe Formula in her right hand, her left hand poised to scoop out a glob.

I leaped for the jar, batting it out of her hand to smash against the wall. She sat, wide-eyed, her face as white as the splattered cream. I bent over her, anxiously searching her perfect complexion. "Are you okay? You didn't put any of that on your face, did you?"

All around us, the other women shrieked and babbled, tossing cream jars into the trash, crying and trying to cover up exposed skin, but my eyes were solely on Kary's face. It was all right, skin still smooth and fine, color finally returning.

"It would have burned you," I said. "Some bad stuff got in by mistake."

She whirled to see. "Is everyone all right?"

I looked through the long room. Several seats over was Amelia Tilley, her beautiful caramel complexion unmarred. She frowned at the jar of cream on the counter in front of her, not touching it, before turning to study my face, then Kary's.

"I think so."

I wanted to stay, to check for myself that everything was all right, that the jars were being gathered up, but the chaperones hauled me off into the hallway where I was met by a scowling Ellin Belton.

"You must stay up nights planning your raids, Randall."

"You'd rather the girls lose their faces?"

"What are you talking about?"

"George McMillan sabotaged the new face cream. After a few minutes on the skin, it would have started to burn holes." There were several jars in the hallway where the girls had thrown them. I picked one up and held it out to her. "Here, try some if you don't believe me. Be my guest, Ellin."

"Don't do it, Ms. Belton." One of the chaperones unwrapped her hand from a towel filled with ice cubes to show us her blistered fingers. "I didn't believe him, either, until a few minutes ago."

Ellin winced at the jar as if she expected it to start frothing acid bubbles. "My God. What sort of sick bastard would do something like that?"

"A sick jealous bastard." I punched Camden's number on my speed dial. "And one I have to get back to right away."

Camden answered. "No problem. Jordan's here. Danger's calm, the birds are back in their cage, the cats said to tell you thanks, and I can't find the lizard. One of the patrolmen will give me a ride to the auditorium."

When Camden arrived, he looked like he'd gone ten rounds with a pack of wolves. The tuxedo was a total loss, ripped and covered with animal hair, scales and little bits of debris clinging to the sleeves.

He brushed parakeet feathers from his hair. "Had to calm everyone."

"You look like the survivor of a zoo explosion," I said. "By the way, thanks for the diversion."

Ellin took one look at Camden and shrieked.

"I know, I know," he said. "It gave its life for a good cause."

She walked around him to better assess the damage. "What in the hell are we going to do? It took them forever to get this right! Can you possibly find another tuxedo in time for the wedding?"

"Guess I'll have to wear my tee shirt."

"You most certainly will not!"

"It's okay," he said. "We'll think of something."

She looked at him for a moment and then performed one of those bizarre about-face attitude shifts that were going to make his life a living hell. "Cam." She threw her arms around him, feathers and all, and delivered a passionate kiss. "I don't care what you wear. I'm just so happy we're getting married."

Kary beamed at her as if she knew Ellin was going to say something sweet. "I got it."

We all turned to her expectantly.

Kary pointed to the costume room at the other end of the hallway. "I'll bet they'd let you use your Freddy suit."

Camden blinked, impressed, and Ellin smiled so brightly, I could almost see why he was in love with her.

"Kary, that's perfect," she said.

"The one you wear when you sing 'On the Street Where You Live,'" Kary said.

"Yes!" Heedless of feathers, scales, and her perfect plans, Ellin hugged Camden close. "That's the one."

Chapter Twenty-seven

"On the street where you live…"

I have to say this: It takes more than a deadly face cream to stop a pride of beauty queens. The pageant went on as scheduled, with only a slight delay as the women substituted Perfecto Face products for BeautiQueen.

Kary didn't win, but so what? She was safe and unblemished and I had rescued her. BeautiQueen recovered from the Miss Parkland fiasco, due in part to their generous payments to all the contestants for their emotional damage and to full-page ads in the *Herald*. The paper explained that the sabotage was the work of one unstable criminal, who now faced charges for the murders of Viola Mitchell and Edwin Bailey, as well as the attempted murder of Millicent Crotty. Thanks to yours truly, he wouldn't be a threat to anyone for a long time. I got good publicity out of this case, new clients, and more than one beauty queen slipped me her number or left extremely thankful calls on my machine.

So the next major event was the wedding. Actually, the next major event was Camden's bachelor party, planned and hosted by Rufus, which was held at the Crow Bar headlining Buddy and his band partner, Eveline, on banjo and hammered dulcimer ripping through the classics. Rufus and Buddy, dressed as Bonnie and Teresa in a send up of the PSN, gave Camden psychic advice on how to handle Ellin. A large plastic kiddie pool filled with Jello encouraged those who wished to go skinny dipping, the requisite strippers and goats danced around, and something Rufus called "Redneck champagne" flowed freely—Mountain Dew mixed with moonshine. Camden wisely avoided the drink, but uptight PSN emcee Reg, to everyone's surprise, got completely plastered and passed out in the Jello, a photo op that immediately lit up the rounds of social media.

The morning of the wedding was calm, but Camden reported that folks in the Belton household were running around frantically taking care of last minute details. Charlie phoned to say that he and Taffy were heading over to Visions Studio for another recording session but would be finished in time for the ceremony.

"That's great," I said. "Congratulations."

"Taffy is one happy gal."

"So it was worth it?"

"Oh, yes."

"Did you kiss and make up?"

"Many times. We'll see you at the wedding."

◇◇◇

Around one o'clock, we all dressed up and went to Parkland Methodist Church. Kary looked amazing in a light pink dress with fancy lace. Camden appeared as neat as possible in the borrowed Edwardian gray suit and striped tie. He wasn't at all nervous, and no objects went flying in all directions. When we got to the church, mother of the bride Jean had Caroline and Sandra rearranging the candelabra and redoing all the bows on the pews because they didn't suit her. Ellin's sisters were on their best behavior and elegant in their bridesmaid dresses. No puffy sleeves or strange designs. The short, light-green dresses flattered them.

"Hope you have the ring, David," Caroline winked.

I patted my suit pocket. "Right here."

"Ready to go, Cam? Where's your tux?"

He adjusted his boutonniere. "It's a long story."

"Well, you look great. Very distinctive and dashing."

Jean motioned to her daughters. "Girls, quickly get in place."

"See you later." Sandra waved. "David, don't forget to walk us out."

"Looking forward to it." Because Camden had so many friends and didn't want to leave anyone out, he'd decided to have just a best man, so it was my duty to escort the sisters down the aisle when the ceremony was over.

Camden and I met the pastor back in his study for a few more encouraging words before coming out for the ceremony to start. Ellin's side of church did look properly polished and bejeweled. Camden's side had come to party. Kary, Rufus, and Angie shared a pew with Buddy and Eveline. Rufus and Buddy were sober and grinning like goats eating briars. They had slicked their hair down with God knows what and squeezed uncomfortably into suits. Lily, Camden's spacey little neighbor who believed she was an alien abductee, sat behind them in spangly purple and a huge hat decorated with peacock feathers. There was a whole row of people next to her I didn't recognize at first until I realized it was the entire Super Hero Society in their Sunday clothes instead of their costumes. In the next pew were Janice and Steve from the hot dog restaurant, Jordan and his wife Marie, our cab driver friend Toad with his niece Evangeline, Charlie and Taffy and the rest of the Hot Six. Members of the Parkland Chorale, the Little Theater, the Magic Club, and Bonnie, Teresa, and Reg from the PSN filled the rest of the church. Reg had pulled himself together, but was still glassy-eyed.

Ellin had chosen yellow roses, green and white lilies, and a blue flower I didn't recognize. The sweet smells of the lilies mingled with the faint vanilla aroma of the candles. Parkland Methodist is a huge church with massive stained glass windows reaching from floor to ceiling. Rather than scenes from the Bible, the windows are swirls of patterns meant to represent the heavens. These whorls of yellow suns and silver stars in radiant blue skies spilled across the pews and aisle. Easy to imagine we were floating in space, an appropriate setting for Camden.

The string quartet had finished their opening selections, and the musicians turned pages in their books to begin the processional. Right before the music started, one of the ushers escorted a woman to the back pew. I couldn't see over Lily's hat, but Camden took a strange little breath and whispered, "It's Daisy."

Camden's foster sister had helped me in my search for his birth mother. Since his foster parents were dead, she was the last connection he had with the family that had taken him in. "Good."

"She needs to be up front."

He walked down the aisle and escorted Daisy, moving slowly to match her steps. She looked the same as I remembered, a large round woman, her gray hair in an untidy bun. She'd done her best to dress up in a flowered dress with a wide lace collar and a small straw hat with faded flowers. She carried a white purse and wore lace gloves. Camden placed her in the front pew and gave her a kiss.

"I'm so glad you came."

"I couldn't miss it." She patted his hand.

He'd gotten back beside me when he said, "And there's Sophia."

"What?"

My mother came in, waved, and sat down.

"She needs to be up here, too."

Now I went down the aisle. I still wasn't used to seeing my mother in her new stylish clothes and red hair. She wore a bright red suit with leopard print buttons. The skirt had a not so-modest-slit, and her high heels were decorated with sparkly feathers. "Mom, I thought you were in Greece or something."

"I decided this was more important."

I escorted her down the aisle and sat her next to Daisy. "Daisy, this is my mother, Sophia. Mom, this is Daisy, Camden's sister."

I'm not sure what the rest of the guests thought of this last minute seating, but Camden looked happier than I'd ever seen him.

Jean entered, wearing a jeweled dress that probably cost as much as the entire wedding. She was escorted by one of her relatives. Then Caroline walked down the aisle, looking deceptively demure, followed by Sandra, who gave me a wink. A fanfare announced the entrance of the bride, and the congregation stood. I have to admit Ellin looked like a princess. Not just any princess. A fairy princess, which I did not expect. Her gown was flowing and strapless, soft layers of filmy white fabric and shiny white ribbons gathered the top and streaming down as she walked, revealing a formfitting skirt below. She carried a bouquet of yellow roses and green lilies. Instead of a veil, she wore a white ribbon braided through her gold curls and held in place with a jeweled clip in the shape of a star. Her father looked relieved to give her away, but that might have been my imagination.

As far as I could tell, Camden and Ellin might as well have been on the planet Camden believes is his real home. They spoke their vows and exchanged rings, all the while gazing at each other and smiling as if no one else existed. When the pastor announced they were husband and wife and Camden could kiss his bride, he and Ellin gave a little start and came back to the real world. They shared a perfectly respectful church kiss, and everyone applauded as they walked down the aisle.

With Caroline on one arm and Sandra on the other, I followed. Then I went back for Daisy and my mother.

Mom scooped up her little leopard patterned purse and gave my arm a squeeze. "What a lovely wedding."

"Such a beautiful girl," Daisy said. "Looks like a real sweetheart. Will she make him happy, David?"

"She already has."

All problems regarding the reception hall had been solved, so the wedding party enjoyed a huge room glittering with crystal chandeliers and ornamental trees covered in little white lights and strung with fancy paper lanterns in yellow and green. I knew Jean had made certain all the white tablecloths were immaculate and all the candles and flower arrangements perfect and extremely expensive. More flowers surrounded the wedding cake on its own table, a towering culinary structure covered with spun sugar stars. Waiters served glasses of champagne. In the corner, the string quartet played soft classical melodies.

Mom and I watched Camden give Daisy a big hug and introduced her to everyone. "I'm really glad she was able to come," I said.

"Did you go get her?"

"No, she came on her own."

"Even better."

I gave her a hug, too. "I'm really glad you came on your own. With Daisy and you here, Camden can say he has two mothers."

Kary tapped my shoulder. "Make that three."

I turned. There stood a trim woman with dark curly hair and dark eyes, in a light blue dress and flowered jacket. Denise Baker Rice, Camden's birth mother, was the woman I'd found who told me that part of her life was over and she'd rather not see him. I couldn't interpret her expression, which was hesitant, fearful, and glad all at once.

"Mrs. Rice. This is a surprise." I hadn't contacted her, and I was certain Camden hadn't.

"I gave Denise a call," Kary murmured.

Denise Rice's eyes were on Camden. "Ever since your visit, Mr. Randall, I couldn't stop thinking about what you said. I don't even know if I should be here, if it might be too much of a shock, or if I should leave…" her voice trailed off.

Camden stopped and turned toward her as if she'd called his name. He stood still for so long I'm sure Ellin thought he was having a strong vision, and she touched his arm. He smiled, patted her hand and whispered. Ellin's eyes went wide, and she responded, probably along the lines of, "Are you kidding?" They crossed the room to Denise, who tensed, not knowing what to expect. Maybe she thought Camden and his new wife would ask angry demanding questions or throw her out. But Camden would never do that, and Denise had to be able to tell by the light in his eyes that she made the right decision to come.

For once, Ellin stayed quiet while Camden and Denise looked at each other. It was odd to see them together. They didn't share a single feature. Denise Rice could've been any woman off the street who happened to wander into the reception.

"Camden," I said, "this is Denise Baker Rice, your birth mother. Denise, meet John Michael Camden."

"Michael," she said faintly.

"I told him that was the name you'd chosen for him."

"So I took it," Camden said. "Thank you."

Her voice wobbled as if she was holding back tears "You really shouldn't thank me for anything. I couldn't keep you. You have every right to resent me."

"I don't." He reached for her hand. "You did what you had to do. I always wondered about you, that's all, you and my father."

"His name is Martin, and you look exactly like him. I wish I could tell you more, but it was a long time ago, just a fling, I'm afraid."

Since Camden was holding her hand, no doubt he could see this was the truth. "Did you ever wonder what happened to me?"

"I have to admit I tried to forget. It wasn't until Mr. Randall found me that I began to get a little stirred up."

"That's what Randall does best, stir things up."

This made her smile. "I'm glad he did."

"Me, too."

A group of people had gathered around us, curious about the woman who was the focus of Camden's attention.

"Denise, this is my wife, Ellin. This is my sister, Daisy Camden, and my sister by choice, Kary Ingram. This is Rufus Jackson and his wife, Angie, and Randall's mother, Sophia. I want you to meet all my friends and the rest of my family. Can you stay?"

Can you stay? Camden must have asked that question a thousand times as he tried to figure out why his mother left him. Stay, if only for a little while. Stay, so I can find out who you are and how we are connected.

Denise hadn't let go of his hand. "Yes."

◇◇◇

There was dancing and feasting and presents and wedding cake. Denise watched with unmistakable pride as Camden and Ellin danced. With her flowing gown and his old-fashioned suit, they looked as if they'd drifted in from another era, a couple of graceful ghosts. Then Camden escorted his mother to the dance floor while Ellin danced with her father. I gave Mom a few spins before claiming Kary's hand for the next round. As we passed by my mother, I saw her give us a long considering look that had more than a tinge of anxiety.

Don't worry, Mom. I'm taking this slowly. I want Kary to love me as much as I love her. I want us to find a way through our grief. I want a family.

I surprised myself with this last thought. A family. Until I met Kary, I never wanted another family.

"What are you thinking about so hard?" Kary asked.

This wasn't the time to get too serious. "Weddings, of course. Doesn't this inspire you?"

"It was a beautiful ceremony. Strange, isn't it? We've had a funeral and a wedding in the space of a few days."

"Think Fred would've liked all this?"

"He'd be over by the buffet tables, complaining about the tiny rolls and eating as many as he could."

Rufus and Angie sailed by, surprisingly light on their feet. Rufus winked. "Ya'll look finer than frog hair. Better catch that bouquet, Kary."

They twirled back into the crowd of dancers. The song ended, and Kary said she'd promised Buddy a dance. "But we'll have another, David."

We could go dancing through life, I wanted to say. But that was up to Kary.

Camden and Denise sat and talked until she had to leave. I overheard her promise to visit again soon, and she told him he was welcome to come see her any time. We threw birdseed and blew bubbles at the happy couple as they hopped into Ellin's car, Ellin driving, of course, heading to the coast for their honeymoon.

Daisy had a way back to Virginia, and Mom, as independent as ever, waved off my offer of a ride and took a taxi back to the airport to rejoin her tour in Greece. Rufus and Angie went for a ride. That left me and Kary at home. We changed out of our wedding finery and sat down in the rocking chairs on the porch. Kary cuddled one of the kittens in her lap. We'd found homes for the others, but decided to keep the black and white one. I'm sure there was some deep abiding significance to this, but, at the moment, I didn't care. Camden had not only gotten the girl of his dreams to marry him, he'd had major closure, thanks to me. And Kary.

"That was an excellent thing you did, calling Camden's mother."

"I had to give it a try."

"What did you say to make her change her mind?"

"I said, your son is getting married on May 31st, and it would mean the world to him if you were there."

"That's it?"

"I may have mentioned something about being estranged from my own family and how much it hurt."

I couldn't believe she'd brought up such a painful subject. "Kary."

"I might as well use all that angst for Good. A negative into a positive. It worked."

"Fantastic."

She rubbed the kitten's ears. "There's no way my father will ever walk me down the aisle. He's already given me away. And I can't imagine my mother showing up at my wedding. But at least I could make part of that happen for Cam."

"Speaking of your wedding."

"Way in the future."

We rocked for a long time with only the purring of the kitten and a few blue jays calling from the trees. Black and white, right and wrong, male and female. Absolutes. There were no absolutes in this world, only thousands of shades of gray.

No, I could think of one absolute. I love you, Kary. I started to say it when Kary got up.

"I'll go start dinner." She plopped the kitten in my lap. "Tuna casserole sound okay?"

"Sounds fine." The kitten yawned and curled up in a fuzzy ball. "I hope you're comfortable," I told it, "because you won't be there for long."

But I let him stay. With the kitten purring softly and a warm spring breeze blowing, it wasn't hard to visualize two little girls out on the front lawn, one blonde and one dark. Beth and Lindsey, dancing in a circle, hands together, twirling around, singing a childhood chant, not "Mother, May I," not "Red Rover," but "London Bridge is falling down, falling down. London Bridge is falling down, my fair lady."

When Kary called me in for supper, the children were still singing.

To receive a free catalog of Poisoned Pen Press titles, please provide your name and address through one of the following ways:

Phone: 1-800-421-3976
Facsimile: 1-480-949-1707
Email: info@poisonedpenpress.com
Website: www.poisonedpenpress.com

Poisoned Pen Press
6962 E. First Ave. Ste 103
Scottsdale, AZ 85251